Published by Foxtrot Publishing

ISBN-13 978-1-49964-595-8

Also available as a Kindle ebook
ISBN-13 978-1-84396-218-2

Pre-press production
www.ebookversions.com

SPICE

Richard Page

FOXTROT PUBLISHING

Chapter 1

Dr Winston Roy sat at the bar in the hotel courtyard nursing a glass of Bourbon, an expensive taste he had acquired while studying medicine in the United States. He examined the now near empty glass and sighed. He seemed to be able to afford more Bourbon when he was a student than he could today. He nodded to the barman for a refill so as not to dwell on why the bottom had fallen out of his financial world.

After what had clearly been a good alcoholic meal in the dining room, tourists were starting to thread their way to the pool area at the back of the courtyard. Chattering and laughing, their shadows danced by the light of flaming torches thrust into metal holders in the stone walls. English, he guessed. They seemed too purposeful to be Americans. A few looked towards him. He lifted his glass slightly in response.

He turned to the barman.

"Who's playing La-Jab-Less tonight, Al?"

The barman merely shrugged and continued polishing glasses.

A black youth struggled past the bar carrying a wooden crate. His job was to set up the stage for the cabaret. He squeezed through the tourists now settling on pool loungers and wooden chairs. He tried to place the backdrop to the stage, now unfolded as butterfly wings, down carefully in front of the audience but dropped it with a mighty clatter. He looked up and grinned a gauche apology then pulling into position, scooted a retreat.

Al the barman picked up his notepad and moved around the tourists taking their orders for drinks. He gave a little nod and bow before moving on to the next customer. Dr Roy thought him much too subservient.

Four members of the cabaret troupe – two young men, a woman and a girl in her late teens – slipped unnoticed into the courtyard through a side door. One, carrying bongo-drums and wearing a colourful shirt that was as loud as you could get, pulled up an empty chair to the side of the stage. He, too, grinned at the audience, now quietening, as he sat down.

The torches flickered in the light, warm breeze. The tourists sat in silence as the drummer began to beat out a rasping, insistent roll. He now had their total attention.

Only Dr Roy did not look up. He was casually examining a mark on his new white suede shoes when La-Jab-Less, summoned by the drums, came on stage. But he knew she had arrived. He could sense, rather than hear, the audience`s sharp intake of breath. She looked astounding: her body was covered from head to foot in a tight black skin. Onto it was painted (in more or less correct anatomical detail, Dr Roy noted idly) a human skull and its skeleton.

La-Jab-Less shimmied to the beat, the illusion of a skeleton dancing made unearthly by the deep Caribbean night.

The drummer bent his head low over the skins of the drums as he played on. The bony beauty slinked sinuously around in time with the music. Suddenly, the drumbeat came to a sudden stop. La-Jab-Less had jumped off the stage and folded herself motionless on the courtyard flagstones.

The two remaining performers now leapt centre stage. The man's trousers were shiny white and tight over his crotch. He wore a flashy red bow tie that glowed against the white of his immaculate shirt. His partner wore a thick gash of lipstick and a short red dress with plunging cleavage. Both were a little too scarlet to be innocent.

The barman was back behind the bar, swiftly and quietly dispensing drinks.

"Hey, Al!" said Dr Roy. "How many times you heard this?"

"Hush up!"

Al was concentrating on his work. A long line of rum punches were stacking up on a large tray. Joe briskly peppered the glasses with powdered nutmeg.

With a single loud bang to startle the audience, the drummer began a primitive rhythm. The dancer in the red dress began to sway slowly and provocatively, trying to tempt the man with the movement of her hips and the thrust of her breasts.

The drummer started to sing and the tension in the audience relaxed.

"If you are married, you must beware,
Be careful, man, of the siren's stare….."

The male dancer mimed resistance to the woman's seduction. She writhed even more enticingly, her movements more impassioned. She moved faster, her short skirt rising. As her partner faltered and hesitated, La-Jab-Less began to move menacingly around the dias, unseen by the dancers.

"If you are caught in adultery
"La-Jab-Less the demon you will see…"

With the merest flick of his lips with the tip of his pink tongue, the male dancer signalled the end of his resistance. First his shoulders, then his feet started to move to the rhythm. He grabbed his partner and they swayed together, their bodies moulded together moving in time to the music.

"La-Jab-Less!
"She knows when a man do stray
La-Jab-Less!
The spirit who'll make you pay.."

The finger of La-Jab-Less stabbed accusingly as the dancers, locked in a lustful stare, slowly began to stroke their hands up and down their bodies.

All eyes were now on the off-stage figure of La-Jab-Less, writhing between the audience and waving a warning finger at the men around her.

"La-Jab-Less!
"She comes as a glimpse of hell..."

Dr Roy watched a couple of men shift uncomfortably on their hard seats and smiled knowingly. On the stage, the couple, locked in a final fatal embrace, kissed.

Suddenly, La-Jab-Less jumped onto the stage and pointed a finger dramatically at the male dancer. He gasped in horror and slumped to the floor lifeless as his partner stepped back in shock.

"La-Jab-Less!
"One look from her and you don't feel well."

The calypso finished to laughs, whistles and claps as the performers took a bow. The singer rose from his drums and leapt onto the stage. The audience again fell silent.

"Ladies and gentlemen, welcome to Grenada – a jewel set in the Caribbean. You will find that we are a happy people. Who would not be happy on a beautiful sun-kissed island that has been likened to Eden? There is much here to tempt you." (The dancer in the red dress bowed low, displaying her breasts.) "The soft white sand that caresses you... the blue sea that beckons you in... the hot sun that plays on your body. The rum punches that will make you feel sooooo good....." (The dancer shook her breasts again.) "Here we have tropical forests, but with no fierce animals to threaten you. In our Eden there are no poisonous snakes to bite you. So throughout time, our folklore has served to remind us to behave. Remember La-Jab-Less!" (The skeletal figure leaped forward and ran around the tourists, stopping to shake her bones in front of the men.) The audience laughed a lot.

"Enjoy your holiday. Thank you and goodnight."

Al the barman was back pouring more drinks.

"Hey!" said Dr Roy. "Do you believe all this folklore stuff?"

The barman turned and shrugged.

"You tell me. You's the psychiatrist round here. Who cares anyway? It's good for business."

Dr Roy raised his glass to his lips and sipped as the final round of applause died away.

"Cheers! To La-Jab-Less. Vengeful spirit of fornicators. Ha! Fairy tales for gullible tourists!"

The barman deftly picked up a new tray of rum punches to deliver to his customers.

Chapter 2

Lou was given the news one morning while she was in her final year at university in Florida. The economics lecturer was wrapping up a particularly dull session when a secretary came in with a written note. He read it, looked up and said that the principal wanted to see Lou Hope in his office.

The principal was in his early sixties and after 20 years in the job he still hadn`t found a way to manage these occasions. He smiled wanly from his chair behind the desk.

"Miss Hope. Lou. Please."

He pointed to the chair in front of his desk. To Lou`s surprise, he stood up and walked to the window. Just looking across the campus, at life going on, gave him the spur to speak the unspeakable.

"Bad news I`m afraid, Lou. From your home. Your father is dead." He turned to look at her: "Is there a friend on the campus we can get for you?"

She shook her head, took the news inside and kept it there. He felt strong enough now to get behind his desk again as she asked the obvious question.

"How?"

He shook his head.

"I don`t know. There`s trouble out there. You know that?"

She nodded. News of the coup in Grenada had been on the television and radio. But why her father?

Lou never found out why. He was gunned down as he sat at his desk working, as usual, in the Government building. The replacement military government under Prime Minister Maurice Bishop had no wish to find out why, either.

She flew home for the funeral. Maisy, her step mother, expected Lou to weep a lot but there were no tears. Nor did Lou cry much when she was on her own. Not in the room at the top of the old plantation house on the island where she had slept since she could first remember. Nor back in her bleakly utilitarian room at college.

Instead, Lou kept all her feelings to herself. Just as she had when the principal broke the news.

Immediately, the once confident and sassy young woman withdrew into herself. She shunned the bright and pastel colours she had worn and opted for greys, browns and blacks. She single-mindedly threw herself back into her college studies and stopped dating.

Tall, slender, with long black hair and sizzling looks that had no need of artificial aid, she was probably the most sought after girl in her year. Now she kept men away by dressing as a drab sophisticate and smoking cigarettes in a long holder.

Asked for a date, she would stare at the young man`s fly, flick ash from her cigarette holder and drawl: "I think not." She was soon known by students and lecturers alike as Little Miss Firewall. That suited her fine.

Maisy recognised Lou`s brittle and hard new personna as a defensive front. It troubled Maisy mightily. The lively, loving, well-balanced girl had changed. In her place was a morose, detached and prickly young woman.

The advertisement in the island`s newspaper caught Maisy`s eye.

DR WINSTON ROY
PSYCHIATRIST
QUALIFIED IN THE USA
NOW AVAILABLE FOR
PRIVATE CONSULTATIONS.

A fan of everything American, Maisy pointed out the advertisement and the Grenadan telephone number to her step-daughter.

Lou responded by putting her hands on her hips and shouting defiantly.

"You think I need a psychiatrist?"

"He might be able to help."

"Help with what? Are you saying I`m mad?"

"No, Lou, but since your father`s death…"

"So I`m not unbalanced then? Or plain loopy?"

"Well, no – but…"

"Then I don`t need to see a psychiatrist."

"But you`re not happy!"

Lou threw herself down on the sofa.

"How can you expect me to be happy? I`ll be the best judge of whether I`m happy or not. And I`m happy with me as I am."

Maisy made a secret and hurried phone call to Dr Roy anyway. She felt reassured. He sounded well-educated and cultured with a confident voice that was strong but relaxed. He lectured at the island`s medical university as well as seeing patients three sessions a week at the mental institution.

Dr Roy said he would drive out to the old plantation house.

"Your step-daughter can only say No but it`s worth a try. I`m sure I can help. If she will let me."

In the small dusty room in St George`s that served as his office, Dr Roy replaced the receiver carefully and considered his investment in the newspaper advertisement money well spent.

The Hope family was well-known on Grenada. As well as being a high level civil servant, Lou`s father had owned a small banana plantation on the west side of the island. It was a relic of British colonialism to which the Hopes, one of Grenada's mixed race families, had been inextricably linked for generations. An endorsement from the Hope family would help Dr Roy build his private practice.

That was why, before setting off for the plantation house, Dr Roy gave especial attention to what he wore. Off came the casual shirt and pants. On went a white linen suit and white shirt open at the neck.

In the open porch, covered with trailing bougainvillaea, he checked his appearance before knocking on the door. He heard a woman's heels click-clacking down the hall then the door was flung wide open. Maisy appeared flustered as she greeted him. She was clearly uncomfortable. Had she had second thoughts about asking him to make a house call? Dr Roy smiled, bowed very slightly and stuck out his hand confidently and decisively. "Mrs Hope. Glad to meet you." One moment was enough for him to take in the atmosphere of the house`s colonial history. Maisy Hope led him through the echoing hall and into the drawing room with faded drapes and old but good furniture. He felt the evocative and unmistakeable whiff of genteel seventeenth-century England. Slave owners, of course.

Dr Roy put on his most charming smile.

"Well Mrs Hope, all that we can do is find out if Lou will see me. If not, then nothing is lost."

Lou was swinging gently in a hammock strung between two coconut trees at the back of the house. Her head was deep in a heavy book and she was singularly uninquisitive about the car she had heard stopping at the front of the house. Increasingly, she found economics, where all human behaviour is calculated in numbers and theorems, preferable to contact with people.

Dr Roy walked to the French windows where he could just catch sight of Maisy remonstrating with her step-daughter in the garden. Finally Lou threw her book to the ground, rolled from the hammock and stomped out of sight.

Dr Lou whistled quietly through his teeth. That was some tantrum. And that was some beauty.

When he heard Lou enter the room, he turned and smiled. She stood sullenly, her feet bare and her hands folded across her chest. She was wearing a drab brown linen top and a grey skirt that skimmed her ankles.

She ignored his greeting, flounced across the carpet and flopped onto a long sofa. Dr Roy pointedly turned back to the window.

"What were you reading when I disturbed you?"

She paused, as if considering whether it was worth replying.

"Keynes. John Maynard Keynes."

He kept his back to her.

"The General Theory of Employment, Interest and Money?"

Lou was surprised.

"Yes."

"I`ve read it but could not properly understand some of it. Do you think you could help me?"

The conversation was not taking the course Lou expected.

She felt that the quesiton was not whether she could help this tall, black Grenadan with the trace of an American drawl in his voice. It was why she should even be bothered to try to help him. So she said just that. Dr Roy turned and gave her an unperturbed smile that was as easy as his manner.

"I stand corrected," he drawled. "Personally, I am more modest. I do not know whether I can help you. But if I can..." He reached into the inside pocket of his jacket and pulled out a card. "That is my number." He gave a slight bow. "I`ve enjoyed our meeting." Lou did not stand when he walked to the door. She felt like a silly child but could not work out why. She brushed her skirt down and heard his voice from the doorway, where he had stood soundlessly observing her. "As it happens, I would very much like to meet you again." He shut the door quietly behind him.

Chapter 3

Dr Roy generally focused his attention on the island`s prettier nurses. For Lou Hope, he felt that he might just make an exception.

She did not call. In his office, where business was so quiet that he wasn`t even making enough to cover the rent, he considered what to do. On impulse, he punched out the number of the Hope plantation house. Lou picked up the phone.

"Hi Lou. This is Winston. Dr Winston Roy. Y`know I set up this private practice? Well, business is so slow that I`m soon going to need professional help for my depression. So why not come on out here and cheer me up?"

Lou was momentarily at a loss for a reply. She found herself laughing at his boldness.

"As it happens, I`ve still got your card."

"Well, you know where I am. C`mon over. I'll be very glad to see you"

His effrontery astounded her. She put down her book, went upstairs to change and wondered why she had reached for her favourite perfume. She drove to St George`s in Maisy`s car.

He welcomed her with a slight bow and gestured to her to sit down. She had a choice. There was a hard backed wooden chair at the head of the psychiatrist`s couch, where she assumed Dr Roy sat during his consultations. Or there was the couch itself, its old leather cracked and faded. Dr Roy stood by a leather chair behind his desk, waiting for her to make her choice.

She perched on the edge of the couch.

"A drink? No refrigerator, I`m afraid. I can only offer you a glass of warm wine. I was saving it to celebrate my first patient… but you`ll have to do."

He grinned and she saw his perfect white teeth. She nodded for the wine.

"I`m sorry business is so bad."

"You, Miss Hope, were my best hope – no pun intended. Your patronage would have helped business wonderfully."

He saw the surprise in her stare.

"I assumed that information on your clients would be kept strictly confidential."

He grinned again.

"I am entirely shameless in the pursuit of money." He handed her the full wineglass and took one for himself to the desk. He sat down and leaned back until the chair touched the wall, put his feet on the desk and raised his glass. "To your good health and excellent results in your finals!"

Lou was at a loss.

"Have you really read Keynes` General Theory of Employment, Interest and Money?"

"Phooey! I have always found it sufficient merely to collect the names of authors and titles. Thus Dostoevsky and The House of the Dead, Crime and Punishment and The Brothers Karamazov. Or, more in your line of economics, Adam Smith and Wealth of Nations. Or Ralph Waldo Emerson`s Self-Reliance and Compensation. Or Edward Gibbon`s The History of the Decline and Fall…"

He seemed capable of going on endlessly and she cut him off, not knowing whether he was serious.

"You`re making fun of me."

He took his feet off the desk.

"Lou, I would never do that. What I am doing is letting you in on the secrets of my trade. " He topped up her glass. "Take conversation. I have always found that a quotation impresses. One from each subject is usually enough. Thus for Ability `They are able because they think they are able` - Virgil. For Bribery `Though authority be a stubborn bear, yet he is oft led by the nose with gold` – Shakespeare. For Character `Most people are other people. Their thoughts are someone else`s opinions, their lives a mimicry, their passions a quotation` - Oscar Wilde..."

Lou raised a hand.

"You sound like a fraud."

He stood up with a pen from his desk and walked round the room, pointing to diplomas on the walls.

"I am as honest as any man. But I ask you – why bother to read a book when you can read a book review?"

She laughed. The man was totally outrageous.

"I don`t know whether to believe you."

He settled back in his chair and lazily lifted his feet back on the desk.

"That doesn`t matter. Just repeat what you just said and do it the same way."

She spoke slowly.

"I don`t know whether to believe you."

He shook his head from side to side in long, slow motions.

"No. Do it with the laugh in your voice."

She smiled.

"Will that do?"

"It`s a start. You see, I reckon we owe it to other people to be happy."

She frowned.

"Easier said than done."

And so their consultations began.

Dr Roy certainly intrigued her. Perhaps he also helped her, because he could make her laugh. After their third session together, she suggested that he submit an invoice to her step-mother. Dr Roy nodded solemnly.

"I think that would be wise, Miss Hope. It will ensure that our relationship remains entirely professional. Moreover, I need the money real bad."

On the drive home, Lou wondered whether she wanted her relationship with Dr Roy to be entirely professional.

At their next consultation, Lou prodded the old leather couch on which she sat and asked whether anyone had ever lain on it.

"Not while I`ve owned it," said Dr Roy. "But be my guest."

She lay back and found it comfortable. When she looked round, Dr Roy was no longer behind his desk. His voice came from behind her head.

"If we`re going to play this game properly, we might as well be in the right places."

Lying rigid with her eyes fixed to the ceiling, she slowly started to talk. He gently led her to the events surrounding the death of her father. Dr Roy was not greatly surprised to discover just how greatly she blamed Prime Minister Maurice Bishop for her father's murder.

"I feel such anger. Rage. Bitterness and hate. I need to focus all my feelings on one person," she explained.

"I know exactly how you feel," said the psychiatrist. "I have much the same feelings for Maurice Bishop."

Lou sat up and turned round on the couch.

"Really? Why?"

"Well, I am bitter and vengeful because Maurice Bishop has cost me a lot of money. And he costs me a lot more every month that he continues to be Prime Minister. "But that's enough of my problems. Let`s try to help you first, Lou. If I manage that, I`ll let you in on my secret. Is that a deal?"

She nodded.

Next morning, Dr Roy found a message from Maisy Hope on his telephone answering machine. She prattled on until the tape ran out – how she thought Lou was becoming much more like her old self; how she had also noticed that Lou was beginning to wear brighter colours again. Dr Roy had made that observation, too. He had also noted (but kept his opinion to himself) that she was no longer wearing shapeless T-shirt and slacks but a short skirt or dress when she lay on his couch.

With only a few weeks to go before Lou returned to college in Florida, she was studying hard and enjoying the relief from work that her consultations with Dr Roy represented. She also enjoyed being with him. He spoke directly and gently:

"I expect you`ll feel able to get out and about a bit more socially when you`ve finished your finals. If not in the States, then maybe when you return back here to the island."

Lou looked at him quizzically, then tossed her head to flick from her face tendrils of hair that had fallen over her cheek.

"What sort of places do you go to, socially?"

Dr Roy laughed and stood up.

"Well, I do a mean dance some nights at a hotel disco but it`s no fun dancing alone. Of course, if you were not my patient, I`d ask you along. That`s why you are safe with me. I am, so to speak, untouchable."

He held open the door for her. Perhaps it was his imagination but as she walked past him on her way out, she brushed her body lightly against him.

He smiled to himself. Dr Roy had thrown down a challenge. The more he seemed to be beyond her reach, the more she would want him, and he knew it.

At their end of their next meeting, Lou sat on the edge of the couch and crossed her legs. The hem of her pink dress shot up to expose a silky thigh the colour of milky coffee. Dr Roy affected not to notice. He merely scribbled on his clipboard notepad before speaking very softly and moving to the door.

"Well, time`s getting on, Lou."

She spoke softly, too.

"When I go back to the States I`m going to miss you."

He gave what he hoped was a neutral professional smile.

"Well, if you need me when you return…"

She was just a little shorter than Dr Roy and her lips were just below his. She moved her head slightly and kissed him. He briefly held her gently to him.

Then he became very professional again.

"Lou, this is most irregular. You may feel entirely differently about me next time you visit. Just think about it over the next week. At your next appointment I`m sure you will want me to regard you strictly as my patient and not as a very attractive woman."

Lou said nothing but left with that tiny pout that he found so irresistible. In her bed the following nights, she had no doubt of her answer. She arrived early for her next appointment, dressed in a way that would tempt a monk. Dr Roy merely bit his lip, put on a solemn expression and stepped neatly round the hard wooden chair at the head of the couch where she lay. He walked to the venetian blinds with his clipboard in his hand and peered through a gap to the street below. Moments passed as began to frame the questions he needed to ask to draw out her inner conflict.

When he turned back to face her, he sighed heavily. He realised, with great reluctance, that the moment had arrived when he would have to stop sending his invoices to Maisy.

Chapter 4

Sir Geoffrey Waltonbury leaned back on the leather upholstery of the Government limousine and stared glumly out of the window at the stationary traffic all around him. He was returning to the Foreign Office from a pleasant lunch. He belched delicately, recalling the Dover Sole and a rather fine Chablis. Not to mention the crepes. He wiped his small, greying moustache with the side of his hand as if to remove any lingering grains of sugar. Outside he could see the Houses of Parliament under a cloudless sky. It was an unusually warm day, heralding the start of spring. He looked across at the rhododendrons in Parliament Square, their buds fat and promising. To pass the time, he picked up the briefing papers at his side. He was due to chair a meeting at 3pm. The chimes of Big Ben told him that he had 15 minutes to get to his office. He glanced at the papers and threw them down with the irritation of a man who had already made up his mind. Sir Geoffrey was renowned in Whitehall for not chairing a meeting unless he had already decided its conclusion.

The traffic began to move again. The car inched forward and turned into a narrow entrance flanked by pillars and railings. A uniformed policeman stepped forward, peered in the back of the car and ostentatiously inspected the austere, greying figure in his mid-fifties. Satisfied that this was indeed Her Majesty`s Under

Secretary of State for Foreign and Commonwealth Affairs, the policeman waved the car into the courtyard. Under his helmet, he reflected once more what an arrogant, self-satisfied and charmless git Sir Geoffrey appeared to be.

The car pulled up neatly in line with the entrance. Sir Geoffrey waited until the driver had jumped out and opened the door for him and then, without a smile, a thank you or a glance about him, strode into the Foreign Office.

Two floors above this unremarkable scene, a tall man in a black pinstriped suit stood at the window of an obsessively tidy office. It was devoid of any personal items or general clutter. On the desk, behind the blotter and pencil, stood a squawk box and two wire trays, both empty. Henry Turville did not believe in sitting on paper work. He believed that once it came IN it should almost instantly go OUT.

His hands were gripped so tightly behind his back that the knuckles whitened, Henry Turville remained tense and motionless at the window save for the slightest twitching of his lips. He was a little more than middle-aged, slim, six feet tall and fit for his years.

Through the window, he could see the roof of an office building on which pigeons perched. He was counting them, his voice no more than the merest mutter.

"One, two, three, five, seven, nine..." More pigeons landed on the roof, others flew away and he began again. "Three, six, eight, ten, twelve…" A pigeon flew off from the far end of the roof and, infuriatingly, his counting couldn`t keep track of the new ones which had landed at the other end. He began again. "Three, six, nine, twelve…"

A car backfired in Parliament Square and the birds soared upwards.

"Damnation!"

He swung round and looked at the clock on the wall, the second hand taking it to almost 3 o`clock. With three steps, he was at the huge map of the world pinned to the wall. He peered at the Caribbean and focused on a tiny dot in it – the island of Grenada.

Behind him, the squawk box blasted a shrill, disembodied voice.

"The Minister is ready, Mr Turville."

He leant over the box, his face lean, intelligent and emotionless.

"Thank you." He squared the blotter on his desk, ensuring that the pencil was exactly parallel with its top edge and spoke quietly to himself. "Excellent. Excellent."

With four strides, he was at the door. He knew it was four because he always counted them. His polished black Oxford shoes marched towards a distant door at the far end of the corridor.

A door to his side opened and a similar pair of polished black shoes stepped out and marched in step with his. Henry did not need to turn his head to know who had fallen in beside him. Each of the doors he passed was marked with a small white card announcing its occupant.

Henry raised his arm to examine his wrist watch. Neither his gaze nor his step faltered.

"It would appear that the meeting will start on time, for once. Waste of effort. Just another opportunity for more CIA nonsense. Spotting reds under beds."

The man beside him was similarly dressed but younger.

"Quite so, old boy, but the difference is that Grenada is within pissing distance of dear old Uncle Sam."

Without the benefit of a handkerchief, Henry made a loud, disrespectful trumpeting noise that sounded as if he were blowing his nose.

"We`re talking about a speck in the ocean!"

"Careful, Henry. Your obsession is showing…."

Henry`s head shot round at the impudence but he bit back the planned retort. He would not demean himself. Instead, he popped an extra strong mint in his mouth. The pervasive smell of peppermint habitually enveloped Henry Turville.

Ahead of them, more doors opened and other dark-suited figures joined the long march to the office of Sir Geoffrey Waltonbury. The diplomat immediately ahead of Henry and his colleague stepped into Sir Geofrey`s room, leaving the door open for all who followed. Henry`s companion slowed in deference to his seniority and noted in wry amusement as Henry`s left foot performed a military-style quick half step, so allowing his right foot to cross the threshold first.

With a sweep of his head, Henry took in the conference room, superior in decoration and furniture to his own. That did not interest him. He was looking for the best place to sit at the long table set with blotters, pads of lined paper and pencils. At the head of the table sat Sir Geoffrey, frowning and oozing irritability. At the other end of the table stood a projector displaying a blank screen onto the wall.

Henry`s gaze absorbed the figures round the table, all dark suited except for a man in his mid-forties seated close to the top of the table. The man was unmistakably an American. His face was plump but rugged, as if it had been knocked around in its owner`s youth. He wore a loud check suit, a red shirt and green tie on which rippled the pattern of a banana. Henry smirked and headed for the chair opposite the American. An elderly diplomat ambling for the same chair shuffled away in response to Henry`s vicious dig in the ribs with his elbow. Without a smile, Henry sat down opposite Marcus Mariowitz and addressed him in a stage whisper.

"More pictures of Commies for us today, Mark?"

"It`s Marcus."

The two men glowered across the table as Sir Geoffrey cleared his throat noisily.

"Gentlemen. If you are all ready. Mr Mariowitz? I believe you have an update on the situation in Grenada."

Mariowitz drawled back at Sir Geoffrey.

“Minister, may I use your overhead?”

“Of course. Feel free.”

The young private secretary seated beside Sir Geoffrey opened her notebook and prepared to take notes.

Mariowitz picked up a package of slides from the table and sauntered up the room to the projector. Henry felt his blood pressure rising. Only Mariowitz could turn a saunter into a statement of arrogance.

The first slide flashed onto the screen, then another and another. All were faces of Cubans.

“Since taking power six months ago, Grenada`s Marxist-Leninist regime under Prime Minister Maurice Bishop has received 50 Cuban military advisers.”

Mariowitz flashed onto the screen a picture of a small merchant ship.

“A Cuban ship has unloaded trucks, arms and ammunition.”

The screen blurred with pictures of trucks and Soviet rifles. Henry leaned back and huffed at the implication that the Foreign Office didn`t know what a Soviet truck or a Kalashnikov rifle looked like.

“Our intelligence from the island is that the Marxist-Leninist Government is being set up as a staging post for the Soviets and the Cubans in their long march for wider global control. This island has become a potential threat to the United States of America. Gentlemen, the island of Grenada is in the United States` back yard. And we question, again, whether your Government should be aiding a Communist regime. Financially aiding a Communist regime.”

In readiness for battle, Henry shifted slightly in his seat and lined up his pencil on the top edge of the pad of fullscap paper in front of him. He swallowed his peppermint and cleared his throat. Sir Geoffrey smiled on Mariowitz and spoke with a voice redolent of good cigars and the special relationship that links Britain to her American cousins.

"Thank you Mr Mariowitz. I found that most helpful. I don`t think there are any questions..." He looked around the room. His private secretary, a plain, bespectacled woman in her late-twenties had already shut her notebook and stowed her pen in her handbag. Henry felt compelled to speak.

"Minister..."

Sir Geoffrey saw Henry and looked straight through him. His private secretary sniffed and put her handbag on the table ready for a quick getaway.

"Yes, I was right. There are no questions." Sir Geoffrey glanced at his watch and with the other hand smoothed his hair as if in preparation for his next, important destination. "Now...I have a meeting with the Prime Minister..." As he stood up, he finally allowed Henry to catch his gaze. "...about cutting British Government aid to Grenada."

That evening, Henry worked out in his local gym in South London. He strode on the walking machine and counted the 1,832 steps that he took. He lifted the weights 30 times. And he left to last his workout on the rowing machine because that was his favourite. He pulled on the oars 200 times and in time with each pull he gasped.

"One. Bastard! Two. Bastard! Three. Bastard!"

The bastard he had in mind was Sir Geoffrey Waltonbury.

Skilled as they were in the art of diplomacy, none of Henry`s colleagues actually mentioned his defeat at the hands of Mariowitz and Sir Geoffrey. Yet as he stood for greater periods of each day at his window counting the pigeons, his colleagues knew that his career was drawing to an early close. Henry had joined the Foreign Office from university, a fast-track diplomat headed for the top. Somewhere in his thirties, the early promise had failed to materialise.

He refused to think of any of this as he worked out with increasing vigour in the gym, jogged the streets round his home and began both counting the paving slabs to and from the railway station while simultaneously avoiding the cracks.

Almost imperceptibly, the flow of papers throughout the Foreign Office diverted and fewer arrived in his IN tray. His attendance was required at fewer and fewer meetings. It was as if his Foreign Office colleagues had formed their chairs into a large circle and edged them forward until one day Henry realised that he was alone on the outside looking in.

Eventually, he found that he was spending most of each day tracking and counting pigeons.

Chapter 5

It was early evening and still light as Henry jogged towards his home. The neighbours in the affluent suburb were becoming increasingly used to the figure in shorts and singlet. He set out to pound the streets within moments of arriving home early from the Foreign Office.

By day, Henry was now lecturing at the Civil Service College, but not a lot.

As his gabled detached house came into view on his first circuit of the estate, he slowed. Emerging from the front door was a smartly-dressed man in his early thirties. He had the cocky confidence of someone keenly ambitious. Pausing outside the new saloon parked on the drive, the man put his briefcase down on the gravel while he fumbled for his car keys.

Henry slowed and returned Jack Reardon`s wave.

"Good evening Mr Turville!"

Henry began jogging on the spot.

"Ah, Mr Reardon. The year-end accounts for Jean`s shop coming on OK?"

"Yes, we`re on the last lap now, Mr Turville…"

"Excellent. Excellent." He glanced at his wrist watch and gave another brief wave. "Can`t stop. One more circuit to finish."

The next evening Henry walked back home from the railway station at what was, by recent standards, late. For much of the day he had kicked his heels in his office counting pigeons and waiting for the Foreign Office to tell him what his future was to be.

As he approached his home, sweating in his pinstriped suit, he gripped his briefcase, swung his umbrella viciously and trod heavily on the gravelled drive. Built in the 1950s, its unimaginative first owner had called the house "The Gables". A more imaginative subsequent owner had reduced the number of bedrooms from five to four so as to equip two of the remaining rooms with en-suite bathrooms. A double garage had been added later.

The rear garden was large by modern-day standards and was sheltered from prying eyes by established shrubs and trees. The front garden was big enough to accommodate two fully established horse chestnuts that infuriated Henry each autumn by dropping conkers all over the gravel on the drive.

As he inserted his key into the wide, oak front door Henry muttered to himself.

"Seven hundred and ninety eight steps from the station. Five more than yesterday. As if I hadn`t enough to worry about."

He entered the half-panelled hall with his right foot first over the threshold and slammed the door behind him. He carefully rested his briefcase against the telephone table and dropped the umbrella in its stand. The umbrella fell sideways. The tension and anger of the day exploded as he grabbed the umbrella and thrust it again into the stand.

"Stay upright, you bastard!"

The umbrella obeyed and Henry advanced down the hall, through the open living room door and on towards the french windows. As he strode, he called.

"Jean! Jean! Jean!"

On the threshold of the terrace, he stopped in mid step. Beyond lay a picture of verdant beauty and tranquility. The sun was setting behind the flowering azaleas. The viburnum cast shadows over the neatly cropped lawn cut in lines that were exactly parallel . Over stone walls around the terrace, blue aubretia tumbled. Perfectly tended flowerbeds promised riotous summer colours. Winter pansies flowered on into the first days of spring. Amid the glory of this garden, reclining on a sun bed under a cherry tree about to burst into blossom, snoozed a plump woman whose blue cardigan indicated that she had reached that point in middle age when fashion gives way to comfort.

Henry advanced onto the terrace and called again.

"Jean!"

The figure snoring gently on the sun bed was surrounded by business papers, an empty glass and half empty bottle of wine. Against the trunk of the cherry tree rested a half closed sunshade.

Henry stood motionless in front of his wife. His forehead still speckled with tiny beads of sweat from his vigorous walk, his voice rose from its usual, educated mellowness to a rude bellow.

"Oh great! My future is in the past. My career has disappeared up my backside. And my wife lies there drunk and snoring!"

Jean woke with a start and sat upright, awake but agitated.

"Henry? Henry! What is it? What`s wrong?"

Her husband pulled himself upright and his voice became quiet, measured but with an underlying menace.

"End of year accounts for Kiddies Swear OK? Yes?"

Jean sank back on the sun bed, relieved.

"It`s Kiddies` *Wear*, Henry, not Kiddies *swear*. As you well know."

She reached down to begin to tidy her papers. Henry took a great gulp of breath.

"I have news from the Foreign Office. I am told I am taking early retirement. I did not ask for it. But the Foreign Office has spoken. After my current round of lectures, I go. Finished. Kaput."

He idly grabbed the sunshade handle and with one

swift swipe removed the flowering head of a winter pansy.

"Gone."

Another pansy died.

"Dead."

And another.

"Finished."

Jean reached out anxiously to try to grab the sunshade but sat back helplessly as he raised it beyond her grasp.

"Henry, no. Please! Not the pansies!"

She sat back and began to absorb Henry`s news.

"You mean you`re going to retire early?"

He stretched out to reach another pansy sheltering in the lee of the sun bed.

"That`s what I said."

For Jean, Henry`s sudden retirement was overwhelmingly worrying and depressing. Yet she felt she could disclose no trace of her true anxiety. So she lied.

"But surely, isn`t that wonderful news? There`s so much…we can…"

She was cut short by her husband jabbing the pointed end of the sunshade at her.

"I was once tipped to become Head of the Foreign Office."

He jabbed at his wife.

"Permanent Secretary."

He jabbed again.

"I could have been Sir Henry Turville."

And again.

"And you could have been Lady Turville."

And again. He became momentarily reflective.

"I might even have become Lord Turville."

Jean abandoned the pretence of wifely kindness and grabbed the end of the sunshade, yanking it from his grasp. He looked down in surprise, as if unaware of what he had been doing, as she put it at her side and out of his reach.

"I never wanted to be..."

She stopped in mid-sentence. It was clear that Henry was not listening. Instead, he was looking down and pacing in a small but perfect square on the grass, oblivious to his wife.

"They`re mad. All of them. Quite bloody mad. They seem to think that one tiny island in the Caribbean can threaten the mightiest empire the world has ever known!"

At that moment, Jean realised what horrors lay ahead with Henry retired, at home. Her head was swimming. Perhaps she had woken too quickly. She spoke more to herself than to him.

"Oh dear. Dear, dear."

He became aware of her again and stopped pacing his square. Straightening his shoulders, he addressed her as if she were a public meeting.

"The bloody Yanks don`t understand! They`re obsessed by Grenada. The Soviet Union is just handing out a few sweeties to the poor islanders to wind up the Yanks. If Her Majesty`s Government cuts aid it will only make the inhabitants poorer, Bolshier and more inclined to listen to Communist claptrap." Jean was about to try to explain that none of this mattered any more if he was retiring but before she could speak, he spun on his heel. "I`m going inside to change."

In the bedroom, he performed the ritual that he had developed over the last ten years. He took off his jacket, laid it carefully on his single bed and removed the wallet, pen and comb from his inside pocket. He placed these items on the white bedside cabinet that matched the entire bedroom suite, carefully ensuring that all items were parallel with each other – first the wallet, then the pen and finally the comb.

Next he reached into his trouser pockets and removed his two packets of extra strong mints - he always kept one as a spare – and laid them parallel with his wallet. Pulling the loose change from his pocket, he put the coins in piles in a line, descending in size of coin, each with the

Queen`s head up. As he did this, he muttered to himself.

"A total of 13 coins. Thirteen. One plus three equals four. The fourth letter of the alphabet is D. D is for 'despair'."

Chapter 6

Henry had learned the trick many years earlier. It always made each member of the audience feel that he was addressing them alone. The trick was to choose a face somewhere in the middle of the audience and speak to it as if it were an interested friend.

Yet today the trick didn`t work. His problem was that he just couldn`t stop his eyes wandering.

The 50 pairs of foreign eyes in the audience gave him their full attention as he stood on the dais. Most of the audience were black or brown skinned, all from Commonwealth countries.

He slipped another slide into the overhead projector and displayed onto the screen a new line of civil service management control. With a conscious effort, he made himself look into the rows of young men and women seated on chairs in the low-ceilinged lecture room.

"So ladies and gentlemen, we all know the formal relationship between the Minister and his civil servants. We can - and most of us have - written pages on the intricate formality of that relationship. Yet there is another, almost indefinable aspect of that relationship which can have a powerful impact on a Minister."

And then it happened again. He felt his gaze slip inexorably and uncontrollably to the right, to about five seats away from where he should be looking.

To the beautiful young woman with skin the delicious colour of milky coffee.

On the dais, he made himself turn against his will towards the flow chart on the screen and pointed with his pencil.

"Just there is the juncture at which the civil servant can pause, raise an eyebrow and pause again. A quizzical or surprised look can sometimes do more to make a Minister think again than five pages of closely written argument."

He ignored the rather pushy and obvious young woman in the back row in a tight baby-blue sweater. She made a point, he noted, of repeatedly crossing her legs if his gaze alighted upon her. His eyes swept easily over the vision of Eastern tranquillity in a Sari. Always he came back to the woman in her early twenties who had poise and an inner calm – an indefinable stillness that intrigued and attracted him.

Henry was nearing the completion of the lecture, one of the last of the series before his early retirement. He smiled condescendingly as he reached his finale, into which he always liked to drop a piece of culture.

"The art of the civil servant can sometimes be likened to a Chekhov play."

The stunning young woman in her cream suit with the large lapels and hem that finished just above the knee shifted forward slightly in her chair. She turned a little to one side so that her neat court shoes pushed more comfortably under the chair. With a hand she brushed back long strands of wavy black hair and looked a little more intently at Henry. Again he forgot to address the middle of the audience and spoke as if only to her.

"As with Chekhov, sometimes most meaning is conveyed by silence. A civil servant`s moment of studied silence accompanied by a look of disbelief bordering on contempt may at least make the Minister think again."

Most of the audience appeared mildly shocked at the prospect of treating a Minister with contempt. Henry realised that his subtlety was wasted on this audience. Then he saw the beautiful woman`s eyes narrow slightly and her full lips twitch at the corners in a tiny smile.

He felt relief that she, at least, had understood him.

"And so ladies and gentlemen, I hope my thoughts and experience will be of help to you in your studies before you return home. Civil servants like you steer the destiny of your countries. It is what has made our Commonwealth strong."

He flicked off the overhead projector and snatched another glance at the beautiful face. Popping a peppermint in his mouth, he looked at the watch on his wrist and stepped down from the dais.

Some of the students gathered around him. A young woman from Malawi told him she was worried about treating her Minister with contempt. Henry tried to explain the importance of body language in inter-personal relations. The woman became more confused and he looked around hoping that the beautiful woman would join the group. He caught sight of her bending to pick up her handbag from the floor and talking briefly to the Indian woman in the Sari. Then a civil servant from Pakistan blocked his view and began to question him on his career.

"Has your entire career been spent in the Foreign Office?"

Henry pursed his lips and thought back to the happiest years of his working life.

"Well, no. I spent three years in the Ministry of Defence."

"Doing what?"

"I was the link man between the Foreign Office and our Special Forces – SAS, Special Boat Squadron and so on. But all that is very hush hush."

He caught a glimpse of the vision in the cream suit making her way past the group. Close up he could see that her skin was flawless. He rudely ignored the

Pakistani and caught her eye and smiled. She gave him the tiny smile he had seen before and walked past.

An earnest young man from Jamaica pushed forward to challenge Henry on the Government`s policy towards Third World aid. After abusing the British Government, the Jamaican stood back in triumph. Henry delighted in wiping the triumphalism off his face.

"I couldn`t agree more with you."

The Jamaican was aghast.

"But it`s your Government!"

"Not for long. I think I mentioned at the start of my lecture that I am retiring."

As the group began to disperse, thanking him for his lecture and wishing him a happy retirement, he touched the Pakistani`s sleeve with his hand and took him aside.

"Tell me, who is that woman in the cream suit?"

The Pakistani looked puzzled.

"You mean Lou? Lou Hope?"

Henry repeated her name.

"Where is she from?"

"Grenada."

"Ah, Grenada."

A week later and with the days ticking by to his retirement, Henry extended his exercise regime to jogging early in the morning as well as the evening. He also told Joe, the muscle-bound manager at his gym, that he would soon be working out there more regularly.

As he heaved the weights up and down, he enjoyed the way that the sweated pain blotted out all thought of his imminent farewell drinks party at the Foreign Office. He loathed the inevitable false affability of colleagues and the distant sneers of his contemporaries still sailing up the promotion ladder. Worst of all, he feared that Sir Geoffrey would make an appearance and present him with a going-away gift. That would mean shaking his hand. Henry heaved the weights more vigorously, trying to blot out the prospect of Sir Geoffrey`s flesh pressing his. He knew that Sir Geoffrey disliked him and the feeling was mutual. But he also knew that Sir Geoffrey would feel he had a responsibility – for the good of the Foreign Office and morale – to make the gesture. He could imagine Sir Geoffrey`s weary sigh to his private secretary as she reminded him of the catalogue of important things he had to do that evening and how he (and thus she) would not be finished until 11pm if he insisted on seeing Henry off..

"Noblesse oblige, my dear. Noblesse oblige."

Henry put down the weights and moved to the rowing machine. He regarded it as his fitness finale. His mother had urged him to eat up his greens first and save the nicer bits on his plate until last.

Sweat poured down his face and neck and onto his already sodden singlet and shorts as he pulled on the oars.

"Thirty six. Bastard! Thirty seven. Bastard! Thirty eight. Bastard!"

The bastard he had in mind this evening was Marcus Mariowitz.

It was as he pulled for the thirty ninth time that a long pair of slender legs, so fine that they could have been chiselled, came into his line of view. The colour of the legs as much as their sheer, long elegance grabbed his attention. They were the colour of milky coffee. Or golden honey. As soon as he saw her feet and calves, his head rose as his eyes travelled over her knees and up her thighs until they disappeared tantalisingly into a white leotard. Upwards and onwards his eyes travelled, pausing to admire the tautness of her waist, her full breasts and long, slim neck until they rested on the face of Lou Hope, staring straight ahead as if on a catwalk.

Lou would not have noticed him, not deigned to have looked down, had Henry`s surprise led him to forget to pull on the oars. As a result, the spring load in the machine threw him forward. He slumped at her feet as if in silent adoration.

It was the noise of Henry`s lungs collapsing that drew Lou`s attention. As Henry looked up at her, she looked down briefly at him as if trying to locate him in her memory. She tightened her lips as if she half recognised the face but was unable to place it in its red, puffed and sweaty state.

With a final wrinkle of her brow as she again pummelled her memory, Lou flicked back the strands of black hair that had fallen over her face and continued without faltering her pace.

Chapter 7

Jean reached for a bottle of white wine from the kitchen rack. She filled a glass and put the bottle into the refrigerator, then changed her mind and retrieved it to take it out with her onto the terrace. Settling on the sun bed, she tucked her legs up under her and adjusted the grey cotton smock that she had put on that morning. It did not flatter her but at least it covered a lot. She had put on too much weight – probably two stone too much - but could not even face the thought of doing anything to reduce it just now. She pulled at her dark hair that was too long over her ears and shoulders to be fashionable, then fluffed it up a bit with her hands. It felt comfortable – that was the main thing.

She had gone into the garden to think quietly about the implications of Henry`s retirement. It was not something she really wanted to contemplate. At the back of the garden she watched a blackbird pecking a grub out of a small pile of last year`s leaves. From the top of the house, a thrush sang with such joy that she felt pain as she listened. Such happiness as the thrush`s she could scarcely remember in her own heart. Certainly not for a good ten or fifteen years.

Finally, she could put it off no longer. What would Henry do when he was retired? What he needed was another job. But he wouldn`t even talk about it. She had tried.

"Henry dear, with your experience you could get a job – perhaps part time – maybe as a consultant to a company."

He had merely snubbed her with a studied look of contempt. He was becoming increasingly silent and sullen. She picked up the bottle from the grass and topped up her glass. She sighed wearily. The husband she lived with now was very different from the Henry she had married more than twenty five years earlier. It might all have been different if they`d had children.

She shivered as the sun began to slide behind the shrubs.

She could see now how much he had changed. She could see that over the last five years – since they had set up Kiddies` Wear – she had increasingly hidden herself in the business so as not to recognise what was happening inside her marriage. Holidays had become a formality to be endured rather than enjoyed. Social life had wilted. Henry`s insularity had shown itself by more jogging, longer hours at the gym and more unbroken silences of an evening as he kept his head in a book.

It was the exercising that irritated her most – probably, she admitted to herself – because it underlined her helpless failure to discipline herself to get her waist down. She looked down guiltily at the bulge of her stomach under the smock.

Henry`s excessive exercising had begun when he was working in the Ministry of Defence. Initially, she had dismissed it as his response to visiting super-fit special forces soldiers. Instead of fading away as she had expected, Henry`s fitness regime had not just continued but was now accelerating to the point of obsession. There was certainly no-one else in the neighbourhood who was out jogging as much as her husband. She knew that exercise could become a drug. So could white wine, she admitted, as she poured the remainder of the bottle into her glass. In her case, drinking helped numb the main problem with her marriage: loneliness and boredom.

Henry was clearly bored with her, too, and had taken to reading obscure biographies of European statesmen. He refused to sit with her companionably to watch television. Instead, he sat with his head in a book until bedtime. He was a self-contained circle of silence and gloom.

She pulled the cardigan tighter around her shoulders and wondered about a long holiday for them both as soon as he retired. She had always fancied a cruise but there might not be enough exercise or challenge in that for Henry. Henry was a big boy at heart who liked playing at being in the SAS. Except, of course, he wasn`t a boy. And she was no longer sure he had a heart.

She rejected the idea of a holiday. Rose, her new assistant at the shop, was too young and inexperienced to be left in charge of the shop for two or three weeks. A strange girl was Rose, with the studs in her nose and ears and weird clothes. But she was a good worker. And the shop's sales figures were not showing up too well at the moment. As Jack Reardon had pointed out, the monthly takings showed a gentle slide downwards.

She gave the empty bottle a tiny kick and watched it roll on the grass. She tried to feel positive and optimistic as she folded the sun bed, picked up the bottle and walked indoors. Perhaps Henry would surprise her when he retired and do something new and exciting that would bring a buzz back to their lives.

In the kitchen, she looked at the clock. Henry should soon be back from the gym or jogging or wherever else he was doing to exhaust himself. She wondered for a moment whether on his return to suggest that he took her out for a meal. She decided it was easier to put on spaghetti bolognese than risk Henry`s irritation.

Later that evening, after Henry shut his biography of Robespierre and put behind him the terrors of the French Revolution, he lay in bed listening to Jean`s gentle snoring. He experienced the sort of hatred that would not have been out of place in revolutionary France.

He put his hands behind his head on the pillow and realised that it was not so much that he loathed Sir Geoffrey Waltonbury and Marcus Mariowitz as people. What he truly hated was what they stood for. Mariowitz`s swagger represented America`s high-handed conviction that it could stroll into any part of the world with the unshakeable conviction that what was good for the USA must therefore be right for everyone else. Sir Geoffrey was just an upper-class berk.

As he heard the long case clock downstairs chime twice, he put aside Sir Geoffrey and Mariowitz and his thoughts turned to Lou Hope. He recalled her tiny smile at his cynical comment about contempt for politicians. He liked her all the more for that. It showed that there was a smart brain in that exquisite head. Slowly, as the night wore on and the clock struck four times, Lou Hope, Sir Geoffrey and Mariowitz merged into a single thought in his mind – beauty and beasts who had one thing in common. Grenada.

Next evening he went to the gym hoping that she would be there. She wasn`t and he found himself thinking of her as he pounded, lifted and pulled. That night he again did not sleep well. He blamed his insomnia on his lack of brisk mental stimulation. Lou Hope again fuelled his night-time thoughts.

"Bewitched," he said quietly to himself in the early hours. "Bewitching and bewitched."

The next evening he did not go to the gym. It was his farewell drinks party. He toyed with the idea of simply walking out of the Foreign Office early and leaving his colleagues to get on with drinking inferior French wine without him. But he knew that to do so would lead his colleagues to laugh at him behind his back. Better to stay to 6pm and take it like a man. He walked down the corridor to a small conference room, doing his best to look brisk and happy but knowing that the next three quarters of an hour would be a precise replica of all the excruciatingly awkward farewell parties that he had ever attended. Except that this time he would be holding the box wrapped in shiny vulgar paper. He would not need to unwrap it to know the contents. Cut glass wine goblets. It was always wine goblets. There was lots of hand shaking, earnest back-slapping from ex-colleagues and assertions that what businesses out there needed was the help and experience of someone like Henry Turville. The only indeterminate that evening was whether Sir Geoffrey would show his face to hand over the gift box. Five minutes before the end, Sir Geoffrey did indeed enter, bluff and tired in the dark blue suit that still displayed a smudge of cigar ash on one lapel. A murmur of appreciation, neither felt nor expressed by Henry, rippled round the room.

"I`ll say a few words," said Sir Geoffrey as the steely grip of the Deputy Secretary steered Henry unwillingly to the Minister`s side.

"Distinguished career...spanned administrations...United States...special relationship...European Union, tireless protagonist of British interests...immensely liked...greatly respected by colleagues... expert on Caribbean affairs...great asset... and sadly missed."

Sir Henry handed over the box. Henry gritted his teeth as he shook the Minister`s soft, fleshy hand, smiled and switched to auto pilot to control his brain and mouth.

"Great privilege really...enormous fun... truly wonderful colleagues...great sadness... thinking of you all...golf course."

As Henry wound up, he saw by the door the stern, unsmiling face of Sir Geoffrey`s singularly plain secretary positioned to hurry her Minister to his next appointment. Sir Geoffrey was on his way out of the room even before the polite applause for Henry's speech had quite finished. Sir Geoffrey strode down the corridor, the secretary at his side.

"The man was a bloody danger. Good riddance."

Henry left the Foreign Office as he had countless

times before but on this occasion did not make his way directly to the railway station. He walked down to the Embankment, just along by Westminster Bridge. The daily throng of the capital's office workers had mostly gone home. Few tourists strolled there at that time of the evening.

Over the parapet, he noted with satisfaction that the river was up. With not a moment's hesitation, Henry raised his arm and hurled the box in his hand over the side . A second later he heard the pleasant plop in the water. The wine goblets disappeared into the brownish murk of the river Thames within moments.

An elderly man in a dinner suit out for a stroll before dinner stopped to watch Henry. Henry walked swiftly past him

"Hey old man, you shouldn`t do that sort of thing. Use the litter bins provided."

Without looking back, Henry muttered in reply "Piss off, you silly old bugger."

He felt better for that and walked briskly to the station, sucking heavily on a mint while avoiding the cracks and counting the paving stones.

That night in bed, he thought again of Lou Hope. Lou so demure and tantalising in her cream suit. Lou`s long legs disappearing into her white leotard. How Lou might look emerging from her leotard. Perhaps because his work was finally over he enjoyed a sense of freedom that he had not known since his twenties. Perhaps that new freedom fuelled the wave of desire he then felt coursing through his veins. It was a feeling of such intensity that he could not recall anything like it for many years. Measured on an emotional Richter scale, his desire for Lou was equally as strong as his hatred for Sir Geoffrey and Mariowitz. As the wakeful hours ticked through the night, the feelings in his head and his loins became enmeshed. Towards dawn, what started to emerge was too indistinct to be described as a plan. All he knew for certain was that he desperately needed to see Lou again. That was the starting point.

Chapter 8

Outside the gym Henry loitered on the pavement by the grafitti-strafed wall. Gone was his pin-striped suit and his jogging kit. Instead he wore an immaculate black blazer, white open-necked shirt with a perfectly tied cravat, slacks and polished leather shoes.

As he stood there, among the empty soft drink cans and discarded fast food packaging, he realised that it was not a good place to hang about. Neither did he blend inconspicuously into the surroundings. The gym was a converted warehouse in a street where parts of South London begin to turn from expensive suburbia into downtrodden inner-city decay.

Henry looked both ridiculous and suspicious and he knew it. His fear was confirmed when a police car trawled past slowly and the officer in the observation seat gave him a long and hard look.

Keep fit enthusiasts came and others left. Henry nodded to some he knew and looked the other way when those he didn`t know stared at him. He didn`t know whether Lou was in the gym. He kept looking at his watch. Sometimes to tell the time. Sometimes because it was a particular habit of his to do so.

He wondered whether to have a word with Joe to ask if Lou Hope was training today. But Joe could be coarse and leery and so Henry decided to linger outside a little longer.

The air was warm as he strolled to and fro close enough to the steps to watch through the glass doors. The early spring that everyone said could not last was going on and on.

The streets were greasy and dusty through lack of rain. A plastic bag wafted across the street in the light breeze. A mongrel paused by Henry and lifted its leg on the wall.

Henry was about to turn and stroll away when he saw her through the glass doors. She was unmistakeable. Tonight her hair was pulled back and held in check with a pink ribbon so that it flowed like a dark river down her back. Henry liked that but couldn`t decide whether it was better than when her long hair was left loose so that she had to flick it back from her face. Either way she was sensational, sexy and altogether much too good to be wasted on a tiny island in the Caribbean.

She was at the doors now and Henry stepped briskly up the steps as if he had just arrived and was on his way inside. He stopped and pulled one of the doors open for her to step through. She had with her a small, grey canvas bag in which – he guessed – she kept her leotard.

Lou gave a smile of thanks that was brief but so dazzling that Henry thought it could break any man`s heart.

"Hello," he said quickly. I believe we`ve met." She stopped and took a wary half step back so as not to be too close to him. She looked puzzled and Henry felt his pulse thudding in his temples. This was the woman who filled his thoughts each night and she didn`t even recognise him. "At my lecture on civil service management."

She relaxed and smiled. His heart leapt like a hare in March.

"Oh yes! Of course! I was trying to place you. I saw you on the rowing machine, didn`t I?"

Henry was smiling now. He felt it might be a bit too broad a smile. Was a silly grin plastered all over his face? He tried to look more serious.

"An incredible coincidence. We must both live in the same area." He paused as if expecting a reply but she said nothing. She just stood, the smile fading on her face in direct proportion to the desire rising in his loins. "You must let me buy you a drink." He knew it was the wrong thing to say as soon as the words leapt from his lips. His brain was screeching "Mistake! Mistake!" It was too late. Lou was now looking serious, weighing him up with a stare that made him feel uncomfortable.

"Thank you," she said with the merest trace of politeness on her lips. "But, no. I must get home."

He could feel himself sweating. His mouth seemed to be gaping. He didn`t know what to say to her but his brain was screeching that he had to DO something.

"Not home to Grenada, surely? Not yet."

Henry felt that he wanted to lean against the wall for support. The responses he had expected from her were not coming. Lou just gave another polite but wary smile.

"No. Not Grenada. Not yet. My flat. Please. You must excuse me. I`ve a letter to write."

With the merest mechanical smile, she walked off quickly. He stood watching her, so straight backed in her white suit and matching kitten-heeled shoes as she disappeared down the street.

For the tiniest moment he wondered whether to abandon all hope of winning her. He stood, watching her swinging hips in the distance, thinking that, for all he knew, she might never return to the gym.

"Information. I must have more information." He might have been muttering. Or gibbering. There was nothing else for it. He would have to pump Joe the Gym for information about her. He went inside and stood at the counter in the foyer where the application forms spilled untidily onto the counter and a slight smell of cat pee greeted the visitor. He shouted.

"Hi Joe! You about?"

From the darkness of his office emerged the sixteen steroid-induced stones of Joe Mason, manager of the

Hytone Gym. He leant on the counter, put a hand under his armpit and scratched furiously.

"Hi. What can I do?"

"Lou Hope. What`s her membership? Occasional or regular?"

Joe studied something under his fingernails that had been dug from the depths of his armpit.

"Regular." Then he leered. It was the leer that Henry had feared. Joe`s big upper lip went up like a donkey`s and exposed huge, white teeth.

Joe leaned forward on the counter and Henry smelled the stale sweat on his black T-shirt.

"Got the hots?"

"I lectured her."

Joe`s head went up and down in great seriousness.

"You LECTURED her? Well! That`s mighty impressive. So what do you want to know all this for man?" Joe gave Henry a playful punch on the shoulder that sent him reeling. "Do you want to LECTURE her some more? Or do you have something MORE in mind?"

Henry inadvertently swallowed his mint and choked. He reminded himself that the knowledge that Lou was a regular rather than an occasional member was surely worth Joe`s jibes.

"I`m also a friend," said Henry, turning for the doors.

If he had looked back, he would have seen Joe making a very rude up-and-down arm gesture with a half closed fist.

Early the next evening, Henry sat in the front seat of his car parked a hundred yards from the gym. Over the top of a newspaper that he wasn`t reading, he looked through the windscreen towards the gym`s exit. The sun cast long shadows from the scattered plane trees that had so far escaped vandalism.

It was Lou`s long legs that he first saw as she came down the steps. She turned onto the pavement and walked away from his parked car. She wore a thin white dress, pulled in at the waist with a wide pink belt that matched her shoes. He noted that her hair lung loose. Yes, he definitely preferred it that way.

He shut the car door as quietly as possible. Hugging the wall of an old brewery next to the gym, he followed her. His eyes repeatedly swivelled from her retreating figure down to the ground. His feet needed to avoid the cracks in the pavement. Pursuing her quietly without being her noticing gave him a new and curious sense of excitement. Lou walked on into the seedier part of the district with Henry following.

Broken windows glowered from the pre-war houses where old mattresses and sofas rotted quietly in the weed-infested front gardens. Youths lounged on street corners, whistling at Lou and staring insolently at Henry.

Down the street rolled two youths, one black and the other white, their hands stuck in the pockets of their jeans. With long but quick steps that still fell only on the centre of the paving slabs, Henry closed smartly on Lou as the youths looked her up and down. One shouted something to her that Henry could not make out. Lou steadily walked on by with head down. The youths cat-called again and laughed at their own cleverness. Henry ground his teeth.

When Henry passed the slouching youths, they spat on the pavement. He ignored them but closed the gap between him and Lou. It was an instinctive reaction. He wanted to protect her. As the danger passed, he fell back a little. She walked on with her faithful, silent shadow behind her. The district changed and a small oasis of residential prosperity appeared around a corner.

Lou stopped by the sliding glass doors of a block of newly-built flats. The doors opened, swallowed her and shut. Henry sidled up and through the glass saw a curved reception desk. Behind it sat a security guard. Entry to the lobby was gained by punching a code into a small black box on the wall by the glass doors.

The guard looked up, saw Henry and narrowed his

eyes. Henry dropped his gaze to the watch on his wrist and turned away.

Back home in bed that night, Henry felt a quiver of excitement. He knew where Lou lived. Again, he lay awake long into the small hours, counting the chimes of the clock in the hall. As Jean`s breathing rose and fell slowly in the single bed beside him, he began to convince himself that he needed to talk to Lou about Grenada. She could help him prove that the British Government was wrong to cut off aid to the island. Quite what he would do then did not occur to him. What mattered was that he had found an excuse to speak again to Lou.

In the morning, after Jean had left for Kiddies` Wear, he stood in the hall, the telephone receiver to his ear arguing with directory inquiries.

"Try Louise Hope. Or she might be listed as L Hope." He wrinkled his brow as he waited for the operator. "Damn it!"

Henry had no intention of trying to phone Lou at her flat to discuss Grenada and British aid. He needed to see her face-to-face to do that. Just having her phone number would have given him another fillip of pleasure, like the comfort he derived from knowing where she lived.

It was early closing day at Kiddies` Wear and Jean arrived home seeking to jolly Henry along in his first days of retirement.

"Shall we go out for lunch, dear?"

He said it was too late.

"What about dinner?"

"Er, I`ve fixed for the gym." That was a lie. All that he planned to do at the gym that night was to wait outside for Lou.

Somewhere inside Henry, a spark of guilt flickered. He told himself that this ceaseless desire to see Lou was a weakness he should perhaps overcome. To prove he was strong and in control of himself, he would go for a very long run – so long that when he had finished there would be no time left to wait outside the gym. Resolved that he could beat his obsession, he made a promise to his wife.

"I thought I`d try a new jogging route later this afternoon. If I`m to go in for the London Marathon next year, I`m going to need to get some really long-distance work under my belt. So when I get back and have showered, perhaps we could go out together for a late supper."

"That sounds very nice." Jean`s voice was flat. She looked at Henry's impassive features and eyes that seemed to look right through her. She knew better than to book a table. She would only be disappointed.

It was early evening when she looked up from her magazine at what sounded like an exhausted, panting Doberman Pincher. It was Henry, re-appearing on the terrace.

"You`re earlier than expected," she shouted cheerily. "I`ll book a table, shall I darling?"

Henry shook his head at his wife as he ran past. He gasped his reply jogging upstairs to shower.

"I`m going to the gym."

The last flicker of guilt died in him. Half way round his long run, he had realised that he must continue his quest for Lou. So he had run the second half of the route like a man demented. That was actually what he was.

Jean opened a tin of salmon and a bottle of wine, made a salad and settled down in front of the television.

"I`ve left yours in the kitchen," she shouted.

Henry didn`t hear her. He was already in the car and reversing out of the drive.

Chapter 9

Marcus Mariowitz stood up from his desk where he had been working on the computer screen for three hours. He reached down to the large check jacket that hung from the back of his chair. From a pocket he removed a large banana. He loved bananas. Strolling happily round the room, he exposed the soft, white flesh with three long pulls of its skin. With three bites, he had consumed it.

He stood, wringing the skin gently in his great paw, looking for his bin. God damn it! He was snarling now. Where was his bin? Clearly, it wasn't at the side of his desk where it should have been, but he looked all the same. He looked in the corners of the room and by the side of the filing cabinets and the glass-fronted bookcase.

In fury, he hurled the skin where the bin should have been and buzzed his secretary on the intercom. He shared with another Agency chief the secretarial services of Marie Hoover, a dowdy, middle-aged lady with nicotine-stained teeth and prematurely grey hair kippered brown at the front from continuous exposure to her own cigarette smoke.

"Yes, Mr Mariowitz?"

"Where's my bin?"

"It's been removed, Mr Mariowitz."

"I can see that. Where the Hell is it?"

"No need for bad language, Mr Mariowitz."

As the pause went on, he realised she was waiting for an apology.

"God damn it – I'm sorry Miss Hoover."

She took it as an apology.

"Security took the bin away."

"Security!" Mariowitz felt a frisson of fear. Why had Security removed his bin? What had he done? More to the point, what did Security think he had done?

Through the communication wire, Miss Hoover sensed his fear.

"Other bins *may* also have been removed."

"Whose?"

"It's just a rumour. It could be that just yours has been taken. I'll check round with other secretaries." She clicked the intercom off and then on again. "Oh, you'll find there's a memo about your bin on your computer screen."

Mariowitz realised that he was sweating with anxiety and anger. For three hours he had been working on his security report on Grenada. How was he supposed to have time to read memos about missing bins? He sat down at his screen and called up the memo.

"Your bin has been removed. Unauthorised security material has been deposited in bins. Use the shredder – Security."

Marcus stood up and kicked at where his bin used to stand. Instead of the usual pleasure of seeing the metal bin winging its way across the room, his foot sailed on through the air and he was forced to grab the edge of his desk or topple over.

He cursed Security again but underneath his anger he felt deep worry. Nothing happened in the CIA without a reason. Even if there was no reason, everybody found a reason. His insecurity over his area of responsibility – Grenada – intensified. He knew that Grenada was the centre of a Commie plot to sneak up on his beloved US of A. But the Agnecy wasn't what it was when he joined in the days of the Cuban missiles crisis. He sighed. Jack

Kennedy and the CIA had known how to deal with the Soviets in those days. How he remembered that three minute countdown to a nuclear world war. He smiled at the memory. But today? He went to kick his bin again but stopped in time. He noted that the banana skin on the carpet was turning brown.

He buzzed Miss Hoover again.

"What am I supposed to do with my banana skin?"

"I really don't know, Mr Mariowitz."

She pushed the switch down and resolved that if she had passed yesterday's interview for a job with a computer company, she would tell Marcus Mariowitz exactly what he could do with his banana skin.

Mariowitz looked at the clock on the wall. He had 15 minutes before his presentation. Time enough and more to feed a banana skin through a shredder. The shredder jammed. He could not pull the half-shredded skin out. The remains remained firmly clenched in the shredder's teeth. He grabbed his file, written report and slides and headed for the door. He wanted to get to the conference room early. To test the projector. He remembered the bin and pressed the button on the intercom.

"Any news from the other secretaries?"

"Er, difficult, Mr Mariowitz." She cleared her throat. "It could be that yours is the only bin to have been removed." He felt the colour draining from his face. "Or it culd be simply that other people are not owning up to having their bins removed."

"Did you tell them my bin was gone?"

"Well, they're going to guess, aren't they, if I go around the building asking everyone if their bin has gone missing?" Miss Hoover put the switch up and shook her head in mute disbelief. And that man was supposed to be in intelligence!

Mariowitz told himself to calm down in an effort to stop the sweating. He could feel it trickling under his armpits. He rushed up the corridor to the conference room, remembered that he had not checked that his door was security locked behind him and ran back. It was locked. He had not remembered doing that.

At the conference room door, he punched the security code into the small black box and pushed the door. It remained closed. He tried again. And again. He turned, fearful of being seen at the door with a security code that did not work. He rushed back to his office and told himself not to panic. It could be that the code had been changed and someone had forgotten to tell him.

What he needed, he told himself, was to get behind some high roller in the CIA who was sure to have the right code. Then he could slip in behind them. Mariowitz opened his door half an inch and waited. Figures began to file past on their way to his presentation. He looked at the clock. A minute to go. Then he saw an important back. It was Richard Hurlingham, his regional director. Mariowitz slipped out and walked on tip-toe behind his director for fear that Hurlingham might stop, slap him on the back and then expect him to do the business with the security code. From behind him came a chortle.

"What ya done, Marcus? Shat in your pants?"

Another voice piped up behind him.

"Naw. He usually does that *after* his presentation."

Hurlingham, tall distinguished and with flecks of silver in his blond hair, turned just as he reached the door.

"Hi, fellahs"

Mariowitz knew that Hurlingham was looking right through him and to his tormentors behind. For one fearful moment, Mariowitz thought that Hurlingham was standing there waiting for him to catch up and punch in the magic numbers. But Hurlingham's fingers darted confidently over the keypad. Six numbers were needed. Mariowitz memorised the first five and then Hurlingham shifted his position and he lost the last one.

The conference room was already half full when Mariowitz stood on the dais and tried the projector. He could not get it focused so he walked round the front and peered at the lens. Earlier that year some funny guy had smeared chewing gum on the lens just before he arrived in the room. He knew it was someone at that meeting because it was still wet and gloopy when he tried to pull it off. The lens looked all right this time. Hurlingham stepped onto the dais.

"Let me to that, Marcus."

Hurlingham instantly got a clear picture on the screen.

A creep in the audience shouted out.

"That's why he's regional director."

Hurlingham smiled and stepped down to the floor. Mariowitz noticed that single step down. So did the audience. If Hurlingham chose not to stand on the dais, it meant that he was not about to give his protection to the poor sucker giving the presentation and operating the projector. Mariowitz swallowed. He knew how the Christians felt before the lions came out.

Mariowitz flicked the first slide onto the screen. It read:

CONCLUSION – SOVIET-BACKED BUILD-UP IN GRENADA THREATENS US NATIONAL SECURITY.

Mariowitz looked at the screen in horror. He had picked up the last slide instead of the first one. He flicked it off and started again. The wiseacre in the audience shouted again.

"We preferred it the other way, Marcus! It cut out the crap!"

Even Hurlingham had to stifle a snigger.

Mariowitz flicked up the slides one by one. Essentially, it was the same series of pictures that had impressed Sir Geoffrey Waltonbury in London. When he flashed up the conclusion – for the second time – there was a long silence. Then a woman's voice called out.

"And that's it, Marcus?"

Mariowitz stared through the lights to where the voice came from. She was about 50, dressed as if she were 20 years younger, with the flesh pulled tight across her face. Her hair was styled to camouflage the evidence around her ears of her face lift. Around her sat five similar women. In the Agency, they were known collectively as The Valkyries.

"Yes." It was all that Mariowitz could think of to say. The Valkyries shrieked.

Hurlingham intervened.

"Well, thank you, Marcus." He paused for effect. "But I have to say that nothing much seems to have moved on. OK, so there are a few Cubans on the island. OK, there are some trucks. Ok, there is the occasional very minor Russian or East European official. In short, OK, OK, OK."

In the audience, all the heads nodded in time with each OK.

Mariowitz made a grave error.

"This data was sufficient to persuade the British Government to withdraw its aid from Grenada."

The Valkyries shrieked in derision again and a bald man in the audience stopped chewing gum long enough to put Mariowitz down.

"The Brits shouldn't have been giving money to a Commie outfit in the first place. But what's good enough for the Brits ain't necessarily good enough for the US."

Hurlingham intervened.

"I have to say, Marcus, that in terms of United States national security this…" He jerked his head towards the projector "…does not justify the conclusion you have reached. I think you need to revise your data."

Mariowitz grimaced. Voices shouted from the floor.

"What the Hell, Marcus?"

Mariowitz refused to back down.

"My first years working for the CIA were spent watching the Cuban missile build-up. Kennedy almost left it too late."

"You're out of your depth, Mariowitz!"

"You're letting Cuba colour your judgement."

Hurlingham had to stand on the dais before the jeering quietened.

"OK. OK. That's enough." He turned to Mariowitz. "Marcus, you're doing a damned fine job. We'll await your next briefing."

He stood down and the shouts resumed.

"Yeah. With deep interest!"

"We can't wait, Marcus!"

On his return journey along the corridor, Hurlingham caught up with one of the Valkyries.

"I thought that went very well. Didn't you?"

Chapter 10

It was dark and the street lights had come on when Henry, close to despair, saw Lou skipping quickly down the steps of the gym. He thrust the newspaper he had been pretending to read onto the passenger seat, popped a mint in his mouth and, as he stood on the road watching her turn for home, didn`t worry about slamming the car door. Tonight he was purposeful. He strode out along the pavement, quickly closing the gap that lay between them.

Lou was in the cream suit that she had worn at his lecture. With each step, her slim body sashayed symmetrically. He drew close with her and then, for a few steps, hung back, savouring the pleasure he had earlier experience just from being close to her.

Tonight, he put on a final burst of speed that took him just steps behind her. He was mesmerised by her legs. He could see red painted toes peeking from her sling-back shoes.

Sensing someone close behind her, Lou pulled over towards the wall. Henry stayed half a pace behind her until she turned her head, her face anxious and a little drawn. He waited until she recognised him before speaking.

"Hello. I…we…We need to talk. About Grenada."

He cursed inwardly. The words hadn`t come out as he had repeatedly rehearsed them as he lay in bed awake into the early hours. She hesitated, then looked straight ahead and walked on quickly. She tried to sound very businesslike.

"I'm afraid ....I'm very busy."

"Lou, Lou – please."

He spoke her name quietly, yet with desperation. She took two more hesitant steps and then reluctantly stopped. She sighed and half turned towards him, waiting for him to explain himself.

"This is important. Please. " He took the few steps to her side and for the first time smelled her perfume, spicy and heady. The perfume seemed to imprint itself on his senses. He knew that he would smell her perfume even when she was nowhere near him. He would forever associate it with her. "I need to talk about Grenada. It`s important – very important to me. Couldn`t we have just a quick drink? I need to discuss the aid question with you." He could see her hesitating and pressed his advantage. "Just a drink?"

She pursed her lips.

"Oh well. OK. But just one drink."

She began walking again, heading to the public house on the other side of the street. Henry had only seen it from the outside, a curious mixture of mauve pebbledash and blue, white and red painted window frames around unwashed glass. He thought the Pharoah and Ferret looked much too rough for Lou.

"I think we should drive somewhere. It looks fairly..."

She shook her head and nodded towards the pub.

"No, this will have to do. I haven`t much time."

She walked on briskly as he sought to explain why Grenada was so important to him.

"You see, I`ve been to Grenada – I have a special interest in the region."

"Oh really."

Lou`s interest was as perfunctory and polite as her smile.

"The decision by the British Government to cut off

aid to Grenada is madness. I found it simply impossible to accept."

She turned and nodded in agreement as they walked through the side entrance of the Pharoah and Ferret. Pop music blared through the half open pub doors but Lou pointed to the back garden, lit by lamps. Henry nodded in agreement. The back garden was more appealing than he had expected. Only a handful of crisp packets fluttered in the breeze and the lawn was freshly cut. Young couples sat at tables in the artificial twilight. Henry steered Lou towards the only free table, next to three teenagers who stared lasciviously at her. He felt anxious about leaving her alone to go to the bar to order an orange juice and a pint of bitter. She would be out of his sight.

She sensed his caution, smiled, took a firm grip of her handbag and told him to hurry up with the drinks or it would be too cold to stay outside.

When he returned with the tray, she took a sip of her orange and then crossed her arms as if against him.

"Mr Turville…"

"Please call me Henry."

She uncrossed her arms and leant forward slightly.

"Mr Turville, I agree that it is madness for Britain to cut off economic aid to my country. When I return to Grenada, I`ll be working for Mr Coard, our Finance Minister, and..."

Henry beamed.

"Oh, Coard. Yes, I know Coard."

"Well, Mr Coard is not exactly a hard line Soviet-style Communist – at least, not in matters of finance." She shrugged and rested her hands on the table. "I mean, Grenada is hardly of much significance in the wider world but it is a fact that Mr Coard is highly thought of by the major Western democratic finance ministers."

Henry slapped his hands on his thighs.

"Bravo! You sound like a loyal, Government supporter."

Lou gave Henry a withering look. Even he realised

that his remarks and laugh were patronising. She knew, too, that she was telling him nothing that he did not already know. She stared thoughtfully at the table and swirled the bottom of her glass in a puddle of spilled beer on the table top.

"In fact, my father was killed in the coup that ushered in the present Government."

Henry shifted in his chair with embarrassment.

"Oh God! I`m sorry. So sorry."

"He was a civil servant. I`d gone to university. In the States. It happened in my final year out there."

Henry`s brow furrowed as he trawled his memory.

"As I remember, only three people were killed in that coup."

Lou nodded.

"Daddy was just unlucky to be one of the three. Not that it has made his death any easier to accept."

Henry thought her voice sounded bitter and that a hardness seemed briefly to grip her features. Then it passed. She had stopped playing with the glass and her hands lay on the edge of the table. Henry noticed that she wore no rings on her fingers or jewellery in her ears. Nor a necklace. Such ornaments, he reflected, would have detracted from, not enhanced, her beauty. He was gratified and reassured by the ringlessness of her fingers. He leaned forward and gently put his hands on hers.

"You`re clearly upset. Perhaps we should have a spot of supper. It`s the least I can do. My car is just up the road and I know a place that we could…"

She looked down at his hands and gently removed hers. She gave him a hard look. He felt uncomfortable as she examined him. He was too old for her, too serious, too starchily dull and too obviously interested in her. Also, there was something creepy about him that made her edgy. And most important of all, she was not available. It was as simple as that. She was not interested in a one-night stand or some sort of fling while she was in Britain.

"Look Mr Tur...Henry...In two weeks I fly back to Grenada. I`m sorry about your early retirement. It is early isn`t it?" Henry nodded quickly. "I thought so. Why don`t you take a long holiday?" She flicked back the hair that had fallen over her face and looked at him with a curiosity wrapped round her smile that he found unsettling. "I suppose there`s a Mrs Turville?" He said nothing and she gave that tiny, hard smile. "I guessed there was. Take Mrs Turville on a long holiday. And then enjoy your retirement. Together."

She pulled her handbag from under her chair, stood up quickly and smiled. She intended to walk off without a backward glance but his eyes were plaintive and his face suddenly drained. He caught her gaze and held it for a moment before quickly consulting his watch. The words came with a rush.

"You can`t go. You mustn`t. I`m...I`m love with you."

She turned her face to him with a look that made him feel like a child. She quickly sat down again with her handbag on her lap. Henry pulled his chair closer to the table as he heard the yobs at the next table snigger, then guffaw. Lou dropped her voice to a whisper. She didn`t want to humiliate or embarrass him.

"Oh no! Oh, come now. Don`t be so silly! People don`t just fall in love after a few glances and a chance meeting. Anyway, I don`t believe in the concept of love. Kindness, yes. Tenderness, yes. Trust, yes. Sex, yes. But love – no. Now, thank you very much for the drink. I really must go. Goodbye, Henry."

Lou smiled again, as if he were a small child who would learn one day to be a man, and walked away. Henry stood up and muttered.

"I`d settle for the sex."

Chapter 11

At Henry`s insistence, breakfast had always been a healthy but somewhat spartan affair in the Turville household. The meal was eaten in the dining room, on the large Victorian gate-leg table that they had bought when they moved in. Each morning they both drank black coffee and ate home made muesli. Henry neither knew nor cared whether Jean liked muesli. He could not see her over his morning newspaper. In fact, each morning on her way to Kiddies` Wear she stopped at the nearby café and picked up a take-away bacon sandwich to fill the yawning gap between a healthy lifestyle and a hearty appetitie.

That morning, Henry seemed particularly stiff and distant.

Since his retirement, he had ordered all the morning newspapers and at the breakfast table worked his way swiftly through them, propping each in turn against the coffee pot before discarding them in an untidy heap on the floor.

He read aloud to her the occasional references to Grenada in the foreign pages and then added his own commentary. Today`s comment was in much the same vein as she had heard many times lately.

"The Foreign Office will come unstuck over Grenada, you mark my words Jean."

She stared at the back page of The Times which was currently obliterating Henry`s face and, as it was a Thursday and early closing day, decided to try to tempt him out that afternoon.

"Perhaps we could go out somewhere together this afternoon. Visit a stately home perhaps?`

"Too busy."

"Oh Henry, can`t we do something this evening. Dinner? Just for a change?"

"Jean, I said I`m too busy."

Jean sighed. Henry had a routine that filled his day: two lots of jogging, two sessions at the gym interspersed by visits to the library and bookshops to secure more biographies of increasingly obscure European statesmen. It scarcely met her definition of what it was to be busy.

"Could you hang the washing out for me this morning, darling?"

He grunted and she didn`t know whether he had heard her. Invariably he forgot or deliberately ignored her requests. On the mornings when the cleaner or gardener came, he spent particularly long spells at the gym or out jogging on the grounds that he would otherwise distract them.

For the rest of the time, he sat in the lounge reading his books in his special chair. It was Edwardian, huge and upholstered in soft, brown leather.

"I think I`ll start an affair with the window cleaner, dear."

He grunted.

"Excellent. Excellent."

She sighed, stood up and began to clear the few pieces of crockery from the table.

Henry scooped up the pile of newspapers from the floor as she headed for the kitchen.

"Perhaps we should take up golf, dear. Lots of couples play golf. And I do need to lose some weight. It would be good exercise for you because…"

"Stupid game for pratts," he said as he went up the stairs two at a time.

`Wasting my breath again,` sighed Jean as she put the bowls and cutlery in the dish washer. She checked her face in the tiny mirror in the hall and at the front door, car keys in her hand, called out again to her husband.

"I`m off now, Henry. I`ll be back just after one."

There was no reply.

In her small, blue runabout – just enough for going to and from Kiddies` Wear – she looked in the rear mirror and saw that her hair was a mess. She knew she had been letting herself go but could not summon the interest or energy to stop her decline. Why hadn`t she fixed a hair appointment for that afternoon? The answer, she told herself, was that she just couldn`t be bothered. She wondered whether she was depressed. Then she returned to the question she had been putting off for weeks. Or was it months? Or even years? Did she love Henry? She found hot tears sliding down her face. At the traffic lights she mopped her eyes and blew her nose loudly.

She put the car in gear and decided that she did still love her husband. She expected the resolution – or was it, she wondered, a revelation? – to lift her spirits. She moved up to second gear and then third. But there was no change to the way she felt. When they had first met, Henry had been quite a catch: lean, handsome, affectionate and ambitious. Clearly, over the years he had grown distant and indifferent to her. She was in top gear now, motoring along the dual carriageway. She came down through the gears, turned into the car park by her shop and self pity welled up in her. Reversing into a tight spot took all her attention and kept the tears back momentarily. Then she took the keys out of the ignition, bent down to pick up her handbag and found herself weeping with great sobbing gulps. She groped for the door handle and stumbled out.

"Sod the shop!"

A young woman wheeling a baby buggy along the

pavement looked up, startled. Jean blushed and hurried by. She was getting like Henry. She had noticed his lips twitching as he muttered to himself.

Get a grip girl, she told herself. What you and Henry need is a good holiday. The shop could go hang. Rose would have to sink or swim with it. What did it matter? Henry now had a good pension, so yes, they`d have a holiday and save their marriage. A positive decision.

She told the girl behind the counter at the café to stick an extra slice of bacon in her regular takeaway sandwich.

Inside Kiddies` Wear, Rose was already awaiting the first customers of the day. She tugged at the tiny metal stud in her nose as she pondered the problem. She had noticed Jean`s red eyes and wondered what to say. Jean noted Rose`s interest and tried to bluster her concern away.

`Hay fever,` said Jean. `It`s come early this year.`

She felt better by the time she turned the CLOSED sign on the door. It was time to head for home.

As she put the key in the front door, she felt a twinge of uncertainty. The open door revealed two large black suitcases in the hall.

Bewildered, she put her handbag down on the oak chest and noticed a folder of papers on the telephone table. She moved to investigate them. As she did so, Henry came quickly down the stairs with a hand lightly on the banister. She reached the telephone table just before he did and picked up what she could now clearly identify as airline tickets.

For a glorious moment, she really had believed that Henry was springing a great surprise on her – that he was taking her off on a surprise holiday. She flicked the tickets with her fingers and then saw that there was only one set and his name was on them. Unsmiling, he tweaked the tickets from her grasp and tucked them into his inside jacket pocket. She just had time to read the destination: Grenada.

"Grenada? You`re going to Grenada alone? But why can`t I come?"

Henry spoke quietly.

"Because I`ll be working. For a couple of weeks. That`s all."

"But you don`t work for the Foreign Office any more!"

Henry took out his wallet and checked the contents.

"That doesn`t make it any less work. I`m going to prove that the CIA is wrong about Grenada."

She threw her arms up and down in agitation.

"But it doesn`t matter if the CIA is wrong or right!" She began to speak deliberately and slowly, as if to a child. "You…don`t…work…for…the…Foreign Office. Not any more. And anyway, I could come with you."

He became charming. She recognised it as Henry`s diplomat mode. It was a side of him she couldn`t recall witnessing for months, possibly years.

"But my dear, what about your shop? How can you possibly leave Kiddies Swear on its own for three weeks? "

"Three weeks! You said you were going to Grenada for two weeks!"

"It`s an open ticket. I might be back in two." He thoughtfully cocked an ear. "That could be the taxi."

During their marriage, she had never had any cause to doubt his fidelity. But this extraordinary behaviour – his indifference, all this obsessive fitness..?

"Henry! Is there another woman?"

He returned his wallet to his inside pocket and adopted the diplomat`s manner again, putting his hands on his wife`s shoulders. She angrily shook them off.

"Jean, dear. I am not having an affair."

"That`s not what I asked, Henry. Is there another woman?"

"No."

He pecked his wife on the cheek, picked up his suitcases and opened the front door.

Outside, Henry walked down the drive to the taxi with his suitcases. He was muttering to himself.

"Another woman? Ridiculous! She's scarcely more than a girl."

The taxi driver got out to help him with his luggage. He gripped the suitcases and staggered under the weight.

"Blimey, guv. What you got in here?"

They were, of course, neatly and tightly packed with Henry`s biographies of European statesmen.

Chapter 12

The aircraft was over the Caribbean at 20,000 feet when Henry glimpsed Grenada. Set in azure waters, the shallows and shoals off the Atlantic coast showed up as a streak of pale yellow. In the centre of the island - only 21 miles long and 12 miles wide – was the black slash of tarmac on which the plane would land.

He turned in his window seat and looked around him. There was just one other passenger in his row, a middle aged woman asleep with a paperback book on her lap. He looked again through the window but now there was nothing to be seen but sea and sky as the plane banked steeply ready for its landing approach. A stewardess leaned over, smiled and reminded him to fasten his seat belt.

Normally, Henry did not like flying. He had always considered it unhealthy. To reduce the risk of dehydration to his body, he always removed his shoes, refused all alcohol, made frequent trips to the toilet so as to exercise his legs and bored the cabin staff with repeated demands for bottles of water. On his travels up and down the central gangway, he silently counted the number of seats and the number of passengers so as to produce an arithmetical ratio.

As he settled back in his seat and fastened his belt ready for landing, he felt that he had, unusually, enjoyed his trip. With the flight had come a sense of release, a freedom that he had not experienced since going to university. Once more, he had relished the exhilaration that came from being his own man. Though thoughts of Jean had occasionally intruded into his consciousness during the flight, he had swiftly and deftly filed them to a part of his brain where they caused no noticeable problems.

Ever since the premature end to his career had been sealed at the Foreign Office, his mind had become a great bubbling stew of thoughts of Sir Geoffrey, Marcus Mariowitz, Lou and Grenada. Somewhere in the stew, too, was a sizeable chunk of disaffection and boredom with Jean. As the stew bubbled under the pressure that Henry felt he constantly endured (or perhaps put himself under), he was pushed in various directions.

Initially, he was impelled towards Lou but he rationalised it by feigning interest in Grenada. Now he convinced himself that he was flying to Grenada not so much to see Lou as to carry out further research. It would, of course, be entirely coincidental that by the time he had completed it, Lou would have returned to her island home.

The landing was faultless and, on his way to the exit steps, Henry paused outside the flight deck to congratulate the captain.

"Excellent. Excellent," he murmured.

As he stood at the open cabin door, the humidity hit him in the face like a wet flannel.

He stood on the runway and looked up. The blue skies had suddenly turned black.

He joined the rush with the other passengers and crew towards the airport`s tiny terminal building. He had read on board that Grenada is deluged by up to twelve feet of rain each year. With the terminal building almost in reach, the skies opened and Henry felt that a good half inch of that year`s rainfall had gone down his neck. Inside the terminal building, he kicked his heels, steaming in the heat and listening to the drumming of the rain – in Grenada it falls so heavily that it is listened to as much as felt or watched – and waited for his suitcases to arrive in the terminal. When the rain stopped, the cases arrived. Soaked.

He stood outside the terminal looking for a taxi. As if instantly cleansed by the downpour, the skies were again blue. In the air, the smell of spice was rich. He was suddenly reminded of Lou`s heady perfume and it seemed that it had never left him. He could smell it as if she were standing by him in the street by the gym.

Henry joined the short queue for taxis and wondered if it was possible to tire of the smell of spice which pervaded Grenada.

A battered black Ford taxi pulled up and the driver waved to him. Henry gave the name of his hotel. He had chosen one to the east of St George`s, the island`s tiny capital, within easy reach of the Grand Anse beach. The guide books described it as a gleaming, two-mile semi circle of sand lapped by clear, gentle Caribbean surf. Useful for his exercising.

With his cases in the boot of the taxi, he stopped before climbing in and watched a brilliant rainbow form over the island, spilling a spectrum of colour over the green mountains.

It seemed to be a good omen.

The driver was middle-aged, fat and laid back to the point of near-coma. Henry wondered idly how he could fit himself behind the steering wheel. From the moment the car drew away the taxi driver started talking in a slow, mechanical drawl. The pitch he was intent on selling to Henry centred on batik, the island`s skill in painting fabric with hot wax. Henry suspected that this was a regular speech given to all gullible tourists..

"So," said Henry interrupting the driver in full batik flow, "tell me about your Government. Is it true what we hear in London that it is stuffed full of Communists?"

The driver fell sullenly silent and Henry settled back to enjoy the drive from the airport to St George`s. The route bisected Grenada.

The mountain that from the air had looked squat now rose up majestically, its flanks swathed in tropical forest. The winding road ran through tree ferns and plantations of nutmegs, cacao and bananas. Tiny, pretty villages sat alongside the Great River valley before the scenery gave way to the Grand Etang, a lake in an old volcanic crater. Then the road struck through the Grand Etang forest. By the roadside, cocoa trees grew. In flat places, sugar cane leapt, tall, thick and green like a lawn but with razor sharp fronds that could cut deep into flesh.

At the hotel, Henry looked around as the driver deposited his cases in reception. He seemed to have chosen well. For someone who enjoyed exercise, St George`s was no problem to reach on foot. He gave the driver a generous tip and thanked him for his company.

`Welcome to Grenada, Mr Turville!`

The accent was as unmistakably English. The smiling couple behind the reception desk introduced themselves as George and Sally, ex-pats from North London. They promised that his stay on Grenada would be “a home from home”.

“The old country”, as George and Sally described England, was the last thing that Henry wanted to discuss. He complained of tiredness, followed a small bell boy who wrestled his book-laden case to his room and parted with another tip.

The room was chintzy and cramped with knick-knacks but had a pleasant view towards the sea. It was late afternoon. First he cleared the knick-knacks and swept them all into a drawer. Then he showered, changed into shorts, T-shirt and sandals and decided to walk into St George`s and around the harbour to get his bearings. Built on the slopes around the harbour, the town`s pastel-coloured houses with their red and green roofs gave St George`s a jaunty, raffish air. The influence was part French and part Georgian English – a reflection of the island`s mixed history. From the harbour pier, he followed Wharf Road round the Carenaga, the inner harbour festooned with fishing boats and schooners. Along the way he stopped to buy a blue cap to shield his head from the sun.

With a shortage of paving stones to walk on and cracks to avoid, without a moment's conscious thought, Henry converted to merely counting each step. His first aim was to identify the main Government building in which Lou would no doubt work on her return to the island. Up the street from the building, he noticed a small café with tables on the forecourt. There he stopped and bought himself a Carib beer. Seated under a shade, he confirmed that it was indeed the perfect spot to watch comings and goings.

Heat and jet lag, possibly enhanced by the alcohol, hit him and he hired a taxi to take him back to his hotel. Unusually, he had taken none of his punishing exercise that day. Instead, he flopped on the bed and fell fast asleep for eight hours.

In the morning, he found breakfast not at all to his taste. He asked for muesli and had the feeling that the waiter had rummaged on the back of a long-forgotten cupboard to find it. It tasted stale. In turn, that reminded him of Jean. Suddenly, he felt the need to throw himself into hard exercise. He put on his bathing shorts and a top and jogged down the beach. It was so vast and the number of sunbathers and swimmers so small that he felt he had the place almost to himself. After his two mile jog to the end of the beach and back, he kicked off his shoes, flung off his top and ran into the Caribbean for a quick thousand back strokes. Perhaps it was his imagination, or maybe the frigate birds and gulls swooping overhead really were laughing.

Back in his room, he became anxious about his books in the suitcase. They needed to be lined up somewhere. He looked round the room but it afforded no opportunity. He was also worried about supplies of extra strong mints. He hadn`t stocked up before leaving London and was down to his last packet.

Over the next few days, Henry devoted himself to researching the extent of the reported Communist infiltration of the island and seeking a retailer who could supply his favourite brand of extra strong mints. After his search for the mints ended in failure, he hired a car, took his binoculars from the suitcase and drove out to Point Saline where a second airport was being built on a peninsula two miles south of St George`s.

What he found there conflicted greatly with Mariowitz`s briefing in London. Mariowitz had implied that the new airport was being constructed as a military airbase. From a vantage point overlooking the building works, Henry saw that there was no security fence. That surprised him. If the site was going to be a military base, the first thing he would have expected was a fence to keep out prying eyes such as his own.

Over the following days he sought different points from which to observe the site. He found that he was noting not so much what was going on as what wasn`t. His experience with the Ministry of Defence and special forces had taught him what a military airbase should look like. Yet everything that would have been needed was missing. There was no parallel taxiway for military aircraft, no arrangements for dispersed parking, no hardened aircraft shelters, no secure set of underground fuel tanks...Not one of the elements required for a military airbase was even outlined on the building site foundations.

Of course, it was possible that some of the requirements could be built later. But there was no evidence, not the slightest sign that they would be.

After a thorough scour of the terrain through his binoculars, Henry concluded that what he was looking at was nothing more than a new commercial runway, much closer to St George`s than the one outside Greville into which he had flown. It was probably being prepared for an invasion of tourists, not Communists.

Through his binoculars he could clearly see paler skinned Cubans helping the islanders move earth and lay foundations. But it was hardly an army of Cubans out there and, even if it was, so what? He let his binoculars drop and concluded that Marcus Mariowitz and his friends in the CIA were paranoid nutters who had convinced Sir Geoffrey of a trumped-up fairy story.

In the harbour, there was no evidence of a build-up of Cuban or Soviet vessels. There were, in fact, none at all, but Henry was impartial enough not to make a judgement on the basis of just a few days` observation. He would be around for at least a few more weeks and could keep a daily watch.

Every evening he ate and drank in the same restaurant, a small one off the harbour. Jeb the owner seemed to do most of the work while Jaime, his teenage son, spent most of his time leaning on the wall or a broom. The food was good – curried lamb and shrimp crepes; lobster and grilled turtle – and to follow, nutmeg ice cream. Henry tipped well, drank the Carib beer and stayed late.

When he was the last diner in the place, lingering over his beer while Jaime swept slowly under the empty tables, Henry signalled to Jeb to join him in a beer.

"It`s very quiet here. What`s all this we hear in England about Cubans, Soviets and East Germans all over the island?"

"We don`t see anybody much. If dey here, dey sure ain`t spending money in my place."

Jeb settled down on a chair at Henry`s table.

"Is the Bishop government improving things for the ordinary people?"

Jeb thought for a moment, watching his son leaning on his broom and nodding sleepily.

"Bishop is a good man," said Jeb slowly. "We all like him. He`s one of us. But some of the others around him…We get notices all over the island telling us what to do. Some of the people even have to go to political education meetings. They`re all meetings about…"

"'bout Communism," said Jaime angrily and suddenly awake. He pulled a face as if bad fish were under his nose. "How`s it going to help me sweep these floors?"

Jeb shrugged and spoke directly to his son.

"Well, just carry on man." Jeb turned back to Henry. "This island`s still the best place in the whole of the Caribbean."

Henry said he would drink to that and bought Carib beers all round.

Back at his hotel, Henry showered and climbed into bed. At his bedside lay a political biography of Lord Grey, Britain`s Foreign Secretary during the First World War. It stayed unopen. Instead, Henry folded his arms behind his head and mulled over the bogus evidence he`d uncovered on which the British Government had axed aid to Grenada. Perhaps he should write a report – that would rock Washington and London. What would they think of him then?

Next morning, after an invigorating jog, swim and push-ups, he breakfasted on fruit and coffee before showering and setting off for the market. There he bought one post card – a simple photograph of St George`s. Back in his room, in a neat script, he wrote to his wife.

Dear Jean,

I am at a small hotel in St George`s but find it expensive and not to my taste. My research is going well. I am looking for a small apartment to rent and will let you know how that develops, address etc. Please forward any relevant financial papers.

Henry

He read it and wondered whether it sounded a little curt. He considered asking her to send a supply of his extra strong mints but decided not to. He knew that he had to cut the link with Jean. So he added:

`PS Weather excellent.`

Chapter 13

If Henry had been seriously intent on exposing as a sham the alleged Soviet and Cuban military takeover of the island, he would have booked onto the next plane *to* London and written his newspaper article or report. Instead, he waited for the next flight *from* London and began to plan how he and Lou should meet in St George`s.

He envisaged himself strolling through the town when Lou, coming from the other direction and perhaps on the other side of the street, stopped in surprise and waved to him.

`Hi Henry!` She would run smiling across the road, her hair hanging loose the way he liked it. `What are you doing *here*?`

He would grin and glance around him to ensure they were not being overheard. Just to be on the safe side, he would lean close and smell her perfume again.

`It`s a rather secret project. Best not to discuss it here. Perhaps over a drink? Somewhere quiet?`

She would nod intently.

`I know just the place.` As they walked through the town – perhaps in the direction of a little café towards the Grand Anse beach – she would give a tiny giggle of pleasure and squeeze his arm. `This is so exciting Henry!`

Over glasses of cool white wine, he would explain the outlines of the Turville Report.

`There`s a lot of media interest already. Of course, I`ll be taking on the Foreign Office so they`ll fight dirty. But I know their tricks!`

Lou would squeeze his arm in admiration. And then they would stroll down the beach, arm in arm.

Henry opened his eyes with a start. Would he look silly in that blue cap? Would a straw hat look more racy? No, a straw boater smacked too much of an elderly pensioner.

Now wide awake and increasingly anxious, he jumped from the bed worrying that he had not given enough attention to unpacking his clothes. He removed them all from the wardrobe and chest of drawers and laid each item carefully on the bed. With great care, he smoothed out the creases with his hand before replacing them, matching trousers with shirts and stacking underpants and socks in neat piles.

Feeling less anxious now, he touched his toes 30 times, following through with his exercise regime.

Later, back on the bed, sweating and red faced, he allowed himself to sink once again into fantasy. He saw himself hiring a car and driving out to meet Lou at the airport. He saw himself standing in a corner of the terminal building watching her arrival and then – as she stood amid her suitcases, looking for a taxi, her fingers touching her face in anxiety - he would step forward.

`Hi Lou!` He would reach down confidently to pick up her cases. `Let me put those in my car for you.`

`Oh Henry, how wonderful to see you! How on earth did you know?` Perhaps she might even peck his cheek in gratitude. In the car on the drive to St George`s, she would touch his hand. `How kind you are, Henry.`

Eyes suddenly open and staring at the ceiling, he decided that he preferred the option of meeting her at the airport. As he would be in the terminal building, he would not need to wear a hat and, in turn, this avoided having to take a decision on whether to abandon his blue cap and invest in a straw boater.

Later, standing under a cold shower, he ruled out the airport scenario and accepted that he must arrange a more casual meeting. For all he knew, there might be someone at the airport waiting to meet Lou. Perhaps a relative. Or a friend. It scarcely troubled Henry that the friend might be a man. He drew endless comfort from her ringless fingers and, more importantly, from her failure to mention to him in the pub garden that there was a man in her life.

The variations on the theme of how he and Lou might meet were almost endless but had one constant in them. Lou`s look of surprise always melted into a welcoming smile.

When Henry`s watch told him that there were two hours left before Lou`s plane was due to land, he decided on his plan. The meeting would be casual and romantic. He would not wear his cap. Nor would be buy a boater. His head would just have to take its chance in the sun. He would explain to Lou that the Turville Report would require her help before it could be published. On his bed, he looked at his watch again and ran through his mind the scenario he would set up: a casual meeting; Lou`s grateful smile; the drink in the café; the walk along the beach where he would stop with a sudden look of anxiety on his face. She would put a hand on his arm.

`What is it Henry?`

`I need your help, Lou.`

`But what?  How can I help?`

`The Turville Report. It needs an insight on what is going on in your Government.`

She would smile and they would walk on again.

`Of course, Henry. What is it you want to know?`

Lou, of course, had not given Henry a moment`s thought since leaving him at the table in the garden at the Pharoah and Ferret. If Henry was filed anywhere in her mind, it was with everything else she disliked about London:  the cold, the rush hour, the filth in the streets, the overcrowding, the capital`s impatience and bad temper. As the day of her departure neared, she couldn`t wait to get back to her island home.

Chapter 14

On the café table lay a biography of Prince von Metternich, Austrian politician and leading figure in European diplomacy after the fall of Napoleon. Henry had not looked at it much that afternoon. From where he sat at the table under the green umbrella, he had a perfect view of the steps leading up to the Government building and wanted to concentrate on the comings and goings. Particularly the goings..

He could have been mistaken for a tourist, dressed for the tropics in shorts, short-sleeve white shirt and socks and sandals. Not that there were now many tourists on the island. The advent of Communism in Grenada had virtually halted the island`s expanding tourism industry.

Without shifting his gaze, he took another tiny sip from his glass of Carib beer. A Government car pulled up outside the building and disgorged a black man whose face he recognised. It was Bernard Coard, the island`s Finance Minister. As he walked towards the entrance, Lou stepped out of the building. She was dressed in a white dress and white sling-back shoes. Henry could only see Coard`s back and Lou`s smile. A few words were exchanged. He saw her laugh rather than heard it and then she was giving a little wave to Coard and hurrying down the street away from the café as her boss disappeared into the building.

Henry took a gulp of the remaining beer, put the glass down and, book in hand, began to follow Lou into the town. He popped into his mouth his final extra strong mint, the one he had been saving for a stressful moment. Twice he stopped and pretended to look in a shop window or examine a market stall while Lou greeted islanders who welcomed her back to St George`s. Lou disappeared for ten minutes into a women`s clothing shop and came out with a carrier bag. She looked at her watch, then walked, faster now, towards the town`s commercial sector.

Behind her, Henry strolled comfortably. His gaze never left her back. Automatically he was counting his steps under his breath and avoiding anything that resembled a crack or tiny impediment. There was little chance that Lou would turn to look behind her but he remained wary. Dawdling tourists occasion-ally got in his way. While the islanders seemed to know where they were going, the tourists wandered aimlessly and got under his feet. Though he wanted desperately to talk to Lou again, he maintained his discipline. He told himself that he had plenty of time and that it was important first to establish her pattern of daily movements in the town.

He enjoyed a sense of exhilaration when trailing her. He justified it by his belief that he was casting a net of protection over her. It was the same feeling he had experienced on the streets of South London.

Henry assumed that he was following Lou home. When she turned off sharply into a doorway, he paused and loitered for a few moments to allow her time to get her key from her handbag and go inside. Then he walked past. What he expected to see was the entrance to an apartment. Instead, he saw a tarnished brass plate by the side of a wooden door. Henry ambled to the street corner, looked around him to see if anyone was watching him, then turned back. He quickly read the words on the plate: "Dr Winston Roy, Psychiatrist." He frowned and walked on, looking at his watch. For half an hour he strolled, walked back and loitered. After an hour of waiting, Henry gave up and turned for his hotel.

In Dr Roy`s consulting room, Lou gave her psychiatrist a brief smile as she made her way across the wooden floor to the old leather couch. She put her handbag down on the rug in front of the couch and looked up expectantly at Dr Roy. He nodded and she slipped off her shoes and lightly swung herself onto the couch. She wriggled to get comfortable and with one hand carefully brushed her dress down over her thighs.

All this was observed by Dr Roy without comment or expression. He stood by his desk dressed in white slacks and open necked dark blue shirt, a smart figure in a bare, entirely functional room. From her vantage point, Lou observed that in a corner of the ceiling hung the same cobweb that she had seen before she left for London. Nothing had changed since her last visit. Against one wall were cheap shelves filled with Dr Roy`s books. From his desk, Dr Roy picked up a clipboard and pen and sat on the wooden chair at the head of the couch. He spoke quickly and confidently to his patient.

"So tell me, Miss Hope, are you pleased to be back in your island home?"

Lou sighed, as if settling more comfort-ably on the couch.

"Oh yes, Dr Roy."

"And are you glad to see your psychiatrist again?"

"Oh yes, Dr Roy."

"Then why did you not come here immediately you returned?"

She fidgeted slightly before replying..

"I had to go straight to the office."

"To Finance Minister Coard?"

"To his team."

"So how long is it since you saw your lover?"

Lou frowned.

"Nearly four months."

"And during your time in England you have enjoyed

no other…relations?"

Lou lifted her head a little, as if seeking in her surprise to see the psychiatrist who remained out of sight behind her.

"Oh no, Dr Roy."

"And have there been any relations that you had but perhaps did not enjoy?"

Lou smiled at the ceiling.

"Absolutely none at all, Dr Roy."

The psychiatrist stood up and began to prowl the room, clipboard in hand and staring at the ground.

"And this absence from your lover. What feelings does this arouse in you?"

She gave a tiny gasp.

"Lust."

He moved towards the window and spoke with a new thoughtfulness.

"I see. But can you be sure? Miss Hope, can you more fully describe this emotion?"

The psychiatrist paused to make a note on his clipboard and then moved to the window and its half-closed blind.

Lou looked down the couch and noticed that her red-painted toes were squirming. She took time before she replied.

"It`s a deep, unsatisifed longing – a yearning that makes my flesh burn with desire and makes my breath come in gasps."

Dr Roy looked up sharply and his voice became serious.

"Miss Hope, I am afraid this is very serious."

Lou turned her head to him and spoke quickly and anxiously.

`Oh Dr Roy, can you help me?`

He pulled a gap in the blind and peered out of the window. An English tourist in a blue cap was standing awkwardly down the street as if waiting for something to happen. He knew the tourist was English because he wore socks under his sandals.

"You are almost - but perhaps not quite - beyond help. If I am to help, I must not delay.`

He let the blinds snap back into place and turned sharply towards the couch.

Lou had slipped off her dress and lay on the couch in white bra and panties.

The psychiatrist stood for a moment, a smile on his lips, as he looked at his patient.

"Miss Hope, I fear that there is only one way that I can assist you."

He stepped quickly towards the couch, unbuckling the black belt on his trousers. From Lou came an earthy, throaty giggle as she seized Dr Roy`s neck and pulled his head down to hers.

Chapter 15

The waiter at the café near the Government building had carelessly put down Henry`s beer. Now he had to mop up the spots of spilled drink with a paper napkin. His biography of Prince von Metternich lay on his lap until the cleaning was finished. He found he wasn`t getting through his books as quickly as he once did. Somehow he seemed unable to concentrate for so long.

Henry called the waiter back and asked him if he knew where he could buy extra strong mints. The waiter shook his head and briefly stopped chewing.

"I use de mint gum."

Henry was outraged.

"I`m not American!"

The waiter shrugged and walked away.

The sun was sinking fast. A couple squeezed past him to sit inside the café from where the smell of spicy cooking briefly filled the air. Fish, he guessed. He looked at his watch again. Perhaps Lou was working late. An American couple dressed in shorts and gaudy floral shirts sat down at the next table.

"Hi!" said the man. "We`re from Boston."

Henry smiled briefly and picked up his book.

"Excellent. Excellent."

The man leaned towards Henry, deter-mined to strike up a conversation.

"My daughter is studying in the local medical college."

Henry gave him a brief nod, then looked down the street and realised that he had nearly missed Lou. She was already walking quickly away, dressed in a pink short sleeve top and white skirt.

He rushed past the Americans and kept to the opposite side of the street to Lou. When she approached the market square, now deserted, he moved ahead, turned and cut back diagonally across the road. He threaded through the traffic so that he headed towards her. He tried to maintain the fiction that it was all an amazing coincidence.

"Hello, Lou."

He tried to make his smile easy.

She stopped and took half a step back in her white shoes. Her jaw sagged.

"Mr Turville?"

It was the first time she had thought of him since leaving the garden of the Pharoah and Ferret. Henry`s smile broadened to a beam.

"Come, come. In London, you got to call me Henry. And everything is so much more informal out here! Why don`t we have a drink?"

He motioned towards a café on the other side of the road. Lou looked round, as if seeking help. She found his sudden appearance on the other side of the world – on her island – as baffling as it was irritating. She followed him to the café, reluctant and frowning.

Before they reached a vacant table, she caught his eye and held his gaze. He thought she looked angry.

"Are you following me?"

He ignored the question.

"I`d forgotten how early and quickly it gets dark out here." He sniffed the air. "And the all-pervasive smell of spice." He pulled the chair from the table for her so that he could lean over to soak up her perfume. The café was busier and noisier than the one he had left. Henry was beaming again. She found his smile infuriating. A waiter approached and hovered. Henry leant forward to Lou.

"And what would you like?"

"Perhaps a chat with Mrs Turville?"

The smile froze on his face.

"I am afraid that Mrs Turville could not escape the responsibilities of running Kiddies` Swear, South London`s finest children`s clothing shop." Lou made a sound that he thought sounded like a hurrumph and told the waiter she would have a glass of white wine. He ordered another Carib beer for himself. "I thought that we might go on somewhere for a spot of supper." He was too pleased to see Lou again to notice her body language. She was taut and the painted fingers of one hand were drumming a tiny tune of irritation on the white table cloth. "It`s quite up-market here, isn`t it?" He picked up a menu. "What`s the food like? Can you recommend this place? Or somewhere else? Last week I found somewhere off the beaten track, so to speak…"

She cut in frostily.

"Why do you assume that I am free to have supper with you? Even assuming that I wanted to?"

The smile on his face imploded and that gave her small pleasure. She wished that she had told him in London that she was living with a man. That wasn`t strictly true. She still kept her own tiny apartment along the beach, usually rented out to tourists. Mostly she was with Dr Roy in his apartment. Or occasionally playing games in his consulting room. She must have smiled at the recollection of the previous evening because Henry thought he detected a thaw.

"Perhaps another evening? Tomorrow?"

Lou shook her head briefly and put a hand to her forehead as if to help her think. She looked hard at Henry and felt again the mild distaste she had experienced at the table in the Pharoah and Ferret. She rubbed her forehead with a painted finger nail and wondered if she had been a bit hard on Henry. No, she decided, even if he were the last man in Grenada, she would still find it difficult to have supper with him.

"Look Henry…"

"You seem to be deep in thought."

"No, not really."

His meeting with Lou was not going as he planned. He had imagined her being more welcoming – almost pleased to see him. Always in his fantasies there had been her welcoming smile. Instead, she had plunged into what, from the look on her face, were very black thoughts. He gave up trying to be fun.

"I`m sorry if I surprised you."

Lou pulled her handbag on the table in front of her, as if protecting herself from him.

"Look Mr…Henry…I don`t like being followed."

"Oh no, I`m not following you."

He shook his head in emphasis. Lou was becoming exasperated and raised her voice. People on other tables were turning their heads.

"Look. I was in London. You followed me when I was there. I fly half way across the world to come home. You turn up. Ergo – you are following me."

"Not at all. Not at all. I`ve been here for more than a week!"

Lou hit her handbag with the palms of her hands.

"OK. So you arrived here early so as to be ready to follow me!" She realised that she was making a scene and dropped her voice to a hiss. "I don`t like it!"

The stew in Henry`s brain bubbled furiously. He fell back on his old excuse.

"I`m here doing some research on British aid to the island, the implications of it ending and so on. I wondered if you can help me with information on your Government`s view on how the stop in aid is affecting the island."

He looked at her untouched glass and calculated that he had at least a few minutes more in which to talk to her, to persuade her.

"Henry, ask my Government if you want help. But leave me alone! Please! Just leave me alone. Look, I have to say this. Goodbye."

She picked up her handbag and walked out, her glass untouched.

Henry looked at his watch, left the café and walked quickly back to his apartment. He felt in his pocket for his extra strong mints and remembered that there were none left. He changed into his jogging kit and raced up and down the Grand Anse beach. When it was dark, he returned to his hotel room and performed a hundred of each of the components of his exercise regime. The pain of it all blotted Lou – and everything else – from his mind. He ordered a plate of sandwiches and ate them lying on his bed, trying to get back into the biography. He had given up on Prince von Metternich and returned to the unfinished book on Lord Grey. He kept getting to the bottom of a page and realising that he had absorbed none of the words. Only something about Grey, his wife, Dorothy, and birdwatching. He let the book fall to the floor and jogged out to the beach again. It was now nearly midnight and even the jogging couldn`t stop him thinking of Lou and how much he loved her.

There was no way that Lou could have spent a moment longer in the cafe with Henry, even if she had wanted to. For she knew that all the time Henry sought to detain her, Winston Roy was standing over a hot stove in his apartment preparing a welcome home dinner for her. He was an excellent cook. As a medical student in the US, he had quickly tired of burgers, chips and the rest of America`s fast food. So he taught himself to cook. In his apartment that evening, he lit the candles on the table ready for the three-course meal: crab crepes with a puree of callallo and lobster a la Creole.

Later in his double bed, Dr Roy felt mellow. He sat up against the headboard smoking one of his occasional cigarettes. Lying down next to him, her hands behind her head on the pillow, Lou gave a small shudder.

"He`s so…so tight-arsed English. Yet he`s also like, like putting your foot in something squishy on the beach."

Dr Roy took the final puff of his cigarette and leaned over to stub it out in the ashtray on the cheap plastic laminated bedside table.

"So no competition there then."

She took her hands from behind her head, turned and snuggled up to him.

"You can`t be jealous?"

Unseen by Lou, he smiled arrogantly and stroked her hair.

"One can never wholly trust an Englishman. After all, the first ones to come here made slaves of us all."

She looked up sharply at him.

"There`s English blood in me!"

He turned his ebony black head and looked unblinkingly down at her.

"None of us is perfect."

She punched him on the shoulder, called him a beast and lay back again.

"I don`t trust him, let alone like him."

Dr Roy became thoughtful.

"Does he know about us?"

Lou thought for a moment.

"No. Why should I tell him? He`s married."

Dr Roy began stroking her hair again and then caressing her shoulder.

"Well, I think you should see our Mr Turville again."

She looked up in astonishment.

"But I`ve told him I`m not!"

Dr Roy reflected a little on the personality of this strange Englishman.

"Oh, I`m sure you`ll be seeing Mr Turville again. He hasn`t come half way round the world to take one No from you for an answer. And you could always invite me along…" His face beamed with a big, false smile as he adopted a parody of a West Indian accent. "I can play de back man for the Englishman!"

He leant down and kissed Lou briefly on the lips.

Lou put on her sulky face. Dr Roy adored it. That sulk was so sexy yet he could never tell her the effect it had on him. She might use it against him.

"Why, Winston? What have you got in mind?"

He shrugged. Dr Winston Roy was still hard up thanks to Maurice Bishop and his Marxist-Leninist Government. He was so hard up he felt he had to explore any opportunity that came along, no matter how curious. And Henry Turville certainly sounded a strange case. Just as a psychiatric case, it would be worth meeting Mr Turville.

"I honestly haven`t got anything in mind, Lou. I`d just like to meet the man. Just don`t tell him about us. And trust me. Haven`t you always trusted me?"

She nodded and snuggled up to him.

Chapter 16

Dr Roy was correct in his interpretation of the mind of the Englishman he had yet to meet. For when Lou stepped out of the Government building the next evening, Henry stood up from the table at the café up the road and began to follow her. All day he had looked forward to this moment. Just being close to her was enough to stave off the misery of her earlier rejection.

For much of the night, he had lain awake trying to produce new justifications for talking to her. He even got out of bed at 3am to jot down a series of questions for her on the effect on the island of the loss of British Government aid. When he fell asleep as the sun rose, he had convinced himself that she would listen attentively to his questions and want to help.

He slept late, skipped breakfast and listened to the BBC World Service on his tiny portable radio. Mrs Thatcher had won a second successive General Election. He snorted and turned the radio off.

He liked the small hotel less and less. Every time he walked through reception, the owner or his wife tried to reminisce about "the old country", as they insisted on calling it, and particularly about London. England in general and London in particular were the last places that Henry wanted to think about, let alone discuss. If his thoughts began to return to his previous life and Jean, he acted to head them off. Counting was a good distraction device. He would count numbers of licence plates. Or people in the street. Or the floor tiles in his bedroom from where he sat in the armchair reading.

While out jogging he had noticed a block of four small apartments along the Grand Anse beach that were available on long rentals – a minimum of three months. From the board outside, at least one seemed to still be available. He had imagined that after his reunion with Lou he would feel ready to sign up for the apartment. But he couldn`t bring himself to sign up now. Not after she had so misunderstood his intentions. All he had wanted was information on the effects of the loss of British aid.

He curtly cut the hotel owner that morning (the damned man had the impertinence to ask where Henry had worked before retiring). He angrily performed 110 of each of his exercises on the floor and jogged down to the beach for a swim, passing a group of giggling piccaninnies kicking a ball on the sand.

A rational part of his mind told him he should explore the island, perhaps hire a car, until it was mid-afternoon and time to take up his post at the café along from the Government building. But emotions bubbled up hot as steam and swamped all rational thought. After a shower, he arrived at the café in time for a steak lunch and sat there, blue cap on his head, for the rest of the afternoon, occasionally picking up his book and generally putting it down again quickly. .

As the time neared when he expected Lou to leave, he put his cap on the table and raised the book to his eyes, as if reading but in fact peering over the top. He followed Lou into town, surprised at how many people she waved to or acknowledged.

When she stopped at a dress shop, he strolled farther on down the street and loitered in a tobacconists` ready to cut diagonally across the street and meet her as if by chance.

He saw her head down the street towards him, a large shopping bag now in one hand and her handbag in the other. He prepared in his mind a short speech on how important it was that she co-operated with him in his research. He fixed a serious look on his face and crossed the road.

Lou saw him coming, stopped and recalled Dr Roy`s words in bed the night before. He was right. She really had not seen the last of Henry Turville. Winston was a really good reader of men`s minds.

Henry looked anxiously and then fearfully at Lou`s face. Her features broke into an entrancing smile.

"Hi Henry!"

His surprise turned to glorious delight. The woman he loved was beaming at him.

He remembered the short lecture he had prepared.

"I am very serious about the need for a well-researched document on..."

She put her attaché case on the ground and cut him off.

"Sure thing, Henry. I was thinking about what you said. I`ve got a friend I`d like you to meet. We can discuss it all. Over dinner?"

Henry nodded vigorously, too stunned for words.

They fixed to meet the next evening at a restaurant along the beach.

Henry walked back to his hotel as if on air. Lou was a changed woman. She had smiled at him – just as in his fantasies! All was well in his world. He looked at his watch and rushed to the apartment rental office off the market square. The young girl was about to close for the day when he put his foot in the door. She had to phone the owners to put to them his demand for ten per cent off the asking rental. They agreed and he signed the papers. He went back to the hotel and took great pleasure in asking for his bill as he was checking out.

In his room, he wrote a second card to Jean. He decided that this one should be simply a notification of his change of address. He had little doubt that a letter from Jean urging him to return home soon was already somewhere between London and Grenada. He didn`t want to do anything that might stimulate further outpourings of reproach from his wife. The fact was, he told himself as he banged the stamp on the card with the side of his fist, that he didn`t love her. He felt that he never had. He had loved only one woman in his entire life and would love only one – Lou Hope.

On the morning before his meeting with Lou and Dr Roy, Henry exercised more gently and jogged more slowly. After a lunchtime snack in the town, he felt an unusual tranquillity settle on him and he dozed on the bed in his hotel room. Later, he even found himself able to enjoy and finish his biography of Lord Grey.

Lou and Dr Roy were waiting at the table when Henry walked into the restaurant. Lou introduced the men to each other and sat between them. Henry thought that Winston seemed an affable, casual young man. Dr Roy took in Henry`s blazer, white shirt, cravat and immaculate white slacks and noted his unconscious habit of looking at his watch. So this was the man who had followed Lou half way round the world.

The table was prettily dressed with a cheerful cloth, candles and a bowl of flowers. Henry had not noticed. He had eyes only for Lou. She looked particularly good that evening in a white dress that hugged her figure. Her hair glistened in the candlelight. Dr Roy insisted that Henry try the restaurant`s rum punch.

"It`s a particularly mean punch, Henry. Of course, they`re all different all round the island but here it`s real famous."

Henry said he would prefer a Carib beer. Dr Roy ignored him and ordered the punch. When the psychiatrist noticed that Henry was happily sipping the punch, he nodded to the waiter to bring another.

"Winston is a psychiatrist," said Lou.

"Ah!" said Henry. So this was the Winston whose name he had seen on the brass plaque in St George`s. Why did Lou visit a psychiatrist? It seemed a strange business to Henry, a lovely, well-balanced girl like Lou visiting a psychiatrist. Sometime he would have to find out what it was all about. But his head was reeling from the second rum punch and another had mysteriously appeared on the table.

By now he had finished his Grenadan caviar – roe of the white sea urchin – and was dissecting his baked stuffed rainbow runner fish. Dr Roy was entertaining him with snippets from the history of the island.

"Of course," said Dr Roy, "I`ve come straight down from the black slaves." Henry nodded and took another sip of rum punch. "Whereas Lou here has English blood in her. It could be French, of course…"

"No," said Lou firmly. "It`s English."

"Excellent. Excellent,` Henry murmured.

"And I hear you`re doing some research," said Dr Roy.

Henry looked up sharply. He felt troubled. He wondered whether Lou talked about him in her psychiatric sessions with Dr Roy. He didn`t like that.

"I want to help the island," said Henry, his voice slightly slurred.

Dr Roy showed his perfect, white teeth in a smile.

"Well that`s just great, isn`t it Lou?"

Lou smiled with her eyes. Henry thought she seemed quite radiant tonight. She put out her hand as if to touch her lover`s but he withdrew his hand smartly.

Henry asked how long Lou and Dr Roy had known each other.

"Four years," said Lou quickly.

"Well," said Dr Roy, "on an island as small as this, pretty well everyone knows everyone else. To a greater or lesser degree, that is. I mean, how many people are there in London, Henry?"

Henry thought for a moment.

"Oh, about seven million."

"Seven million! Why the whole of Grenada has less than one hundred thousand."

"Excellent, excellent," said Henry. "And how did you come to know each other."

"Chocolate mocha cheesecake!" exclaimed Dr Roy. "You must try it for desert."

Henry said he was too full. Dr Roy insisted.

"It is divine, Henry," said Lou.

"For you," he said to her with what he thought was an adoring look. "Anything."

Lou thought that Henry looked even sillier drunk. She shot a grating smile at Dr Roy.

"How sweet," she murmured as she sipped her white wine.

All agreed that the chocolate-mocha cheesecake was quite heavenly.

When the dessert plates were cleared, Henry – as if absent-mindedly – gathered two unused forks and a spoon and lined them parallel with each other in front of him. Dr Roy raised an eyebrow as he watched the move.

The coffee was on the way when Dr Roy leaned forward on the table.

"So what did you do and where did your career lead you, Henry?"

"Best bit was with the Special Forces."

Dr Roy raised an eyebrow again.

"You actually worked with the Special Forces?"

"Best years of my life."

"Did you go on operations with them?"

"Oh, I was in London most of the time. But I got out to their base. Watched them training and so on. One day I was down there and an officer I`d got to know well said `Look Henry, a chap`s going to come through that door in a moment. For God`s sake, just do what he says` Then a soldier burst in with an automatic weapon and screamed `Freeeze`. So I did. Well, you do when someone`s shouts like that with a gun." Dr Roy and Lou nodded. "Then the soldier blasted away with the gun for about five seconds. Straight at me. I was…well, bloody terrified. Then he stopped firing and ran out. The officer appeared and said

`OK, you can move now.` So I did and when I looked back, there was the complete outline of my body in bullet holes on the wall."

The trio sat in silence for a moment then Dr Roy spoke.

"Well, Henry, that`s a conversation stopper if ever I heard one."

Lou pretended not to understand the story.

"But what did this man with the gun have against you, Henry? I mean, five minutes blazing away and you`re sitting here apparently quite well."

Dr Roy guffawed and Henry realised it was some sort of joke. So he laughed and rambled on.

"I was on the inside track on all the planning and sometimes had to make snap executive decisions at various points. I knew all the details of military actions and had to liaise with foreign governments. Depending on the Foreign Office and Government view and so on. Of course, the SAS was not so well known then. They were working all round the world."

"Not here surely?" said Dr Roy.

"Oh no! It was all quiet here in those days. But not so quiet in recent years eh? In fact, I was hoping that you two could give me the low-down on Grenada`s real politics." He smiled at Lou. "Of course, it`s Lou who`s got the inside track working as she does in the Government."

Henry quickly switched the three pieces of unused cutlery through ninety degrees, each remaining parallel with the other.

Lou was getting tired and wanted to go home with Dr Roy.

"Henry," she said wearily, "you can`t expect me to tell you my Government`s business. Would you have told a stranger what was going on in your Foreign Office?"

"Actually, surprisingly little went on in our Foreign Office. And then again…" He smiled at her…"we are hardly strangers." He looked quickly at his watch.

Dr Roy leaned towards Henry and spoke softly and as if in confidence.

"You OK for time, Henry?"

Henry looked embarassed.

"Yes. Oh yes."

"Only I thought we might take a walk." He put down notes for the bill. "Somewhere quiet. Where we can talk about these things without being overheard."

Chapter 17

On the beach, the sand was almost white under the full moon. There had been a downpour earlier but now the skies were clear and the air fresh from the rain. The trio walked in the soft sand where their foot prints left a deep impression. Lou was between the two men, her dress now a ghostly white. With one hand, Lou gripped her handbag and with the other her shoes. She walked bare foot, feeling the sand between her toes. Down where the Caribbean gently lapped the sand was firmer. Dr Roy ambled in the surf, his lightweight linen jacket over his shoulder. Henry cursed inwardly as sand came over the sides of his casual, fawn shoes and into his socks.

Dr Roy bent down to pick up a conch shell, then ran to catch up with the couple. He walked alongside Henry, handing the shell to him.

"Beautiful? No?"

Henry glanced at the shell without great interest and agreed. It seemed rude to chuck it back on the sand so he held it in the palm of his hand.

"So, Henry, you want to know about the politics of this island. I guess there isn`t much new I can tell you about the military Government – what with you being in the British Foreign Office. But Lou is no friend of Prime Minister Bishop. Or her boss, Coard…"

Lou interrupted.

"Coard is not so bad." She gave a small laugh. "He`s a man of contradictions. He`s more of a hard line Communist than Bishop. Yet he is an extraordinarily able Finance Minister. He`s very ambitious – there`s always been tension between him and Bishop. But Coard lacks the charisma that you need in the West Indies to be a big political leader. Whereas Bishop has the charisma but he lacks the ability to be a good Prime Minister." They walked on in silence while Henry considered her analysis.

"Excellent. Excellent," he murmured.

Lou added a bitter after thought.

"It`s Bishop I hate."

Henry looked up sharply. The word sounded strong and poisonous from her lips. It wasn`t a word that Lou used easily. Her upbringing, her Roman Catholic education – both had emphasised love and not hate. Yet hate was what she felt.

Henry kicked a shell on the sand.

"But they`re not hard-line Communists are they? I know the island is splattered with ridiculous posters but…"

Lou interrupted again.

"It`s not just the posters. Everyone who works for the Government has to attend political education classes." She spoke with a sneer in her voice and made the "education" sound contemptible. "I just pick my nails and pretend to listen."

Henry and Dr Roy laughed.

"Henry, old man, you`ve got to understand this island," said Dr Roy. "In fact, to understand what`s going on here, you`ve got to understand the whole West Indies. You see, this ain`t Russia. It ain`t the huge, geographical mass of the Soviet Union. Here, we pretty much know each other and if we don`t, then we think we do. It`s a small community – they`re all small communities, in comparison to what you know in Great Britain, Europe and the Soviet Union – and we like to be happy under the sun. In fact, we *are* happy under the sun. Because of the slave trade…" He turned and grinned at Henry. "Now don`t take this personally...it`s a fact that we came through that with the living shit knocked out of us. And today, we all make up for that. By being happy. So all this Communist claptrap does not make any difference to the ordinary man and woman. We are not all going to become Commies. No more than we are all going to become raving right wing lunatics, like those who run your country and the United States."

Henry liked what he was hearing. It supported his view that the British Government had been duped by the Americans.

"And what about the Cubans, the East Europeans and Russians who are supposed to be crawling all over the place?"

Dr Roy shrugged and called across to Lou.

"What do you say about that, Lou?"

"The Cubans are helping build the airport but beyond that…" She shrugged. "We have exchange visits."

Henry asked her whether there were secret plans to turn the new airport into a military airbase for the Soviets.

"Not that I`ve heard of," she said. "I think I probably would have heard, given the work I do and the people I know." She turned to look at him. "Does that help?"

Lou was about to ask Henry whether he had been given enough answers for him to now go back home to England but Dr Roy cut in quickly.

"Lou`s the expert but to me it all seems gesture politics. Is that right, Lou?"

She nodded in agreement. She was wondering why Dr Roy was walking on the other side of Henry. She wanted him next to her. She was tired, bored and wanted to climb into bed with him. She tried to wrap up the conversation.

"The Soviets don`t take Bishop and Coard seriously. Even the Cubans don`t."

Dr Roy laughed.

"And we certainly don`t."

The trio walked on in silence. Dr Roy yawned ostentatiously.

"Well, I think I`ll turn in for the night. I`m whacked but I can see you two love birds might want to be alone." Henry turned to Dr Roy who, with a huge theatrical wink, whispered conspiratorially. "You go ahead, Henry. I`m gay!"

With that Dr Roy turned on his heel and ambled back towards the lights. Lou spun round, trembling with fury, and teetered on her toes as if about to run after him. Henry put an arm gently round her bare shoulders. He felt that Dr Roy`s admission of his homosexuality explained everything. Dr Roy and Lou were friends – women often felt that they could enjoy friendships with gays because they knew that there was no sexual intent. He sighed as he pulled Lou closer to him and felt great sexual intent coursing through him. He had never been able to understand homosexuality.

Lou, the rum punch and the stars all combined to induce in him a sense of well being and romanticism that he wanted to share with the woman he loved. He stopped and pointed upwards.

"The sky. The stars. So different. Did you notice in London how the light pollution has increased so much that we can't see the stars as well as you can here?"

Lou shook her head. She didn`t want to think of anything but what she was going to say to Winston Roy when she got back to his apartment.

Later that evening, lying in the double bed in his apartment, Dr Roy heard Lou put her key in the front door lock. He remained sitting up, back against the headboard, reading his book on Jungian psychology and smoking another of his occasional cigarettes. From where he lay, he faced the bedroom door. It opened with such force that it banged back against the wall. He slowly lowered his book and peered over it. Lou stood just inside the bedroom, handbag in hand, shaking with anger.

"You bastard!" She hurled the handbag at Dr Roy, who smartly ducked. The bag hit the wall behind him and landed on the white sheet. "Don`t you ever do that again! He groped me!" Dr Roy calmly climbed from the bed, hoisting his sliding pyjama trousers with one hand and removing the handbag from the bed with the other. He carefully widened a space between the bottles of Lou`s make up on the dressing table and put the handbag down very gently. With a small, caring smile planted on his face, he padded slowly to her side, put his hands on her shoulders and moved to kiss her. She turned her head away sharply. He looked hurt and spoke as if he had been wounded.

"Didn`t I tell you to trust me?"

She looked at him, her lips pursed. Her voice was loud and serious.

"Didn`t you hear me, Winston? The man *groped* me!"

"But I told you to trust me."

She took a deep breath, turned and looked up at him reluctantly and still coldly.

"Yes, but I expect you to..." He skilfully slid a hand round Lou`s back and unzipped her dress as he gently kissed her lips and then her forehead.

"Well, trust me then. I think he can help us."

Lou pouted and shrugged her dress off her shoulders until it fell to the floor.

Her lip curled dismissively.

"A creep like that? Help us? How?"

"I`m working on it. I haven`t cracked him yet."

He kissed her on the forehead again to calm her. "He`s clearly an obsessive personality. He has to make everything tidy." Gently, he began to manoeuvre her towards the bed. "And he`s got a fixation about looking at his watch."

Lou pushed him gently back with the palms of her hands on his shoulders, then stood with her hands on her hips.

"Winston – his obsession is getting his sweaty hands on me!"

With a deft flick, he quickly pulled the sheet back on her side of the bed and continued to whisper.

"Tell me everything he said on your walk. I want to know everything he talked about."

He kissed her lightly on the lips again but she stepped back in shock.

"Talk? What talk?" She fixed him with a stare. "Winston, he nearly had me down on the sand!" Dr Roy put his hands round her waist and gently eased her down so that she sat on the edge of the bed. She reluctantly swung her legs up onto the bed and he saw sand still between her toes. She shuffled up so that she rested against the headboard, her hands on her lap. He padded round the bed and climbed in his side. "Winston Roy!" He stopped as he prepared to climb into bed. "You are a seducer!"

Dr Roy pulled a face in mock horror.

"Me? A seducer? I was the one who was seduced. An innocent young psychiatrist seduced on his own couch by a shameless woman." She threw his pillow at him. He picked it up and climbed into bed. "Now tell me all about it. All that he said."

Lou was wide-eyed.

"I`ve told you – it`s not what he said. It`s what he tried to do!"

"Well, I hope you weren`t too hard on him."

"Winston!"

There was a laugh in her voice and Dr Roy knew that he had turned her round.

Lying in his arms, she told him that it was not just Henry`s groping on the beach that made him so spooky. She was convinced that he was following her.

"He must be following me. Otherwise, how does he keep on turning up in front of me?"

Dr Roy reasoned, quite logically, that if Henry turned up in *front* of her, he couldn`t be following her because to do so he would have to be *behind* her.

Lou found the explanation reassuring and persuasive. She purred. She always found him reassuring and persuasive when he ran his hands through her hair and over her back like that. Dr Roy waited until she was purring some more as he ran his hands down the back of her legs. Then he put his idea to her.

"What we need is just one more threesome with old Henry."

Under his touch, he felt her body tauten.

"I really don`t want to see him again, Winston."

"Oh, you will. You will." Now his hands were stroking farther and wider. "You will."

Chapter 18

In Kiddies` Wear a young mother with a brittle face and dyed blonde hair to match ignored her two small, unruly boys who were pulling jumpers from a shelf. She continued to flick desultorily through matching trousers and jumpers hanging on a rail. A tiny sweater fell on the floor and she stepped over it without a downwards glance. The shop floor was littered with boxes containing yet more outfits, too numerous to fit on the rails. Behind the counter, covered with receipts and plastic bags, Rose rang up the till and examined the contents. She pulled a face and shut the drawer. Rose, still just in her teens, leant on the counter, resting her head on her hands and scratched just below the ring through her nose. Her hair stood up like stalagmites. In the gloom at the far end of the shop, Jean leaned wearily on a door jamb, watching the mother and her children with ill-concealed indifference. Over Jean`s white blouse, a cardian sagged untidily. Her tight brown skirt, which finished below the knee, served only to emphasise her bulges. As the mother and children headed for the exit, Jean called out to them wearily.

"Thank you!"

The door shut behind the trio without acknowledgement.

Rose spoke in her Cockney tones.

"Rude cow!"

Jean walked slowly down the shop to the door, slid the CLOSED sign across and sagged against that door jamb.

"Thank God for early closing."

Rose pulled herself off the counter and stuck her thumbs in the top of her jeans.

"Would you like me to make some tea?"

Her employer shook her her head and remained motionless against the door jamb.

"I`d say Yes to a large gin and tonic but the bottle`s empty and it`s only one o`clock."

Rose moved to the centre of the shop, folded her arms across her ample breasts and sized up her employer. Jean seemed to have been despondent, on the brink of weepiness over the last few weeks. Business was not good but not that bad surely?

"Jean? Are you all right?"

Jean shook her head, stuck a tired smile on her face and finally pulled herself upright.

"I`ll make the tea."

She walked out to the back room. She filled the kettle, pushed the switch and examined the stains inside two chipped mugs. She shrugged, tossed a tea bag into each mug and reached for the milk carton standing on the draining board. On the narrow ledge below the window stood an empty gin bottle and two unwashed glasses. She took a deep breath and shouted to Rose.

"It`s easier to say this without looking at you, Rose..." Back at the counter, where Rose had resumed her slouch, she stood up sharply. Was she going to get the sack? In the tiny back room, Jean`s eyes were filling with tears. "Henry`s left me."

She left the kettle and mugs and walked back into the shop. Rose ran down from the till and gave her a big hug.

"Why didn`t you say so before?" She stood back, looked at her and administered another hug. "Oh I`m so sorry – but he might come back. Mightn`t he?"

Jean spoke through her sobs.

"But he`s...gone...to...Grenada."

Rose stood back.

"Grenada? Blimey – that`s...that`s somewhere on the other side of the world. Isn`t it?"

Jean nodded.

"It`s in the Caribbean. We went there on holiday."

Rose knew all about holiday romances. They never lasted.

"He`ll get over it, you see. It`s just some little holiday fling. It`s different when you meet someone on holiday."

Jean looked up.

"No! You don't understand. We went there 15 years ago. Now he`s sent me a card from a hotel there and says he`s thinking of moving to an apartment. That sounds permanent doesn`t it?"

Rose was confused. She pursed her lips and felt that offering a handkerchief was a safe thing to do.

"Look, Jean, you`ve got to be positive. I mean, my dad went off with another woman but he came back."

Jean looked up in interest.

"And are your parents happy together now?"

Rose turned away.

"Well, no. Mum divorced him but at least he came back..."

Jean burst into a new flood of tears. She knew that if Henry came back she wouldn`t want to divorce him. Rose administered more hugs before Jean thrust herself away and threw her arms out as if to the shop and the wider world.

"It`s all a mess. Look at the shop!" She indicated the contents with a sweep of her arm. "And I`m a mess! Just look at me!" She burst into fresh sobs.

Rose decided to take a grip. She might be young but she had seen her girlfriends go to pieces like this over the loss of a man. Men just weren`t worth it. She spoke firmly.

"Now look here. You listen to me. Whether he comes back or not, you`ve got to get yourself into today`s world.

And get this shop into it, too! But first in line is you!"

Rose walked towards the back of the shop and into the clouds of steam emerging from it. She came back empty handed.

"The tea! Where`s the tea, Rose?."

Rose didn`t turn round.

"I poured it down the sink." She swung behind the counter to grab her handbag. "Come on, we`re off. We`re having a quick lunch. And I`m going to take you in hand."

Outside in the street, Jean turned the key in the shop door and carefully put it in her handbag. Rose took her by the arm and they marched together past the front display window. If the clothes on display looked tired, as if they had been there for years, the reason was that they had.

Between mouthfuls of vegetable lasagne, Rose spoke with uncommon frankness for a shop assistant addressing her employer. Jean listened cautiously, anxious that her frankness to Rose was exposing her weakness. After cups of black coffee, Rose patted her employer`s hand.

"So. What do you think? You`re the boss, after all."

Jean felt comforted. It felt easier to agree with Rose`s analysis of the situation than to argue.

"I`ll do as you say, Rose."

"Well then, I`ll keep you to it!"

That evening Jean walked to the local gym and waited at the front counter to register. Joe had a scratch and then from under the counter produced two different forms.

"Temporary or regular membership?"

Jean spoke with determination.

"Regular."

He filled in the form. When he asked her surname and she said "Turville", he looked up.

"Hey," he said, "you ain`t the wife of that…" He quickly shut his mouth again. He hadn`t seen Henry Turville or Lou Hope for a good few weeks. He spoke a little more gently. "That`s fine Mrs Turville. I`11 take you through and show you around."

Jean had invested that afternoon in a pair of trainers and threw herself onto the walking machine, the rowing machine and everything else that was available.

"Hey!" shouted Joe as he strolled around the gym on her first evening. "You be careful you don`t overdo that!"

Next day, she ached all over. Over mugs of tea in the shop, Rose made her promise to keep going. Joe seemed to be taking a personal interest in her progress. As he walked through the gym, he shouted encouragement.

"Hey! You take care of that Mrs Turville. She`s my very good friend!"

After ten days, she stopped aching and, with her new diet, began to lose weight. Some of the neighbours noticed that Henry was no longer around and invited her in for drinks. She always drank fresh orange juice now. Some evenings she would take Henry`s post card from the kitchen drawer – it upset her too much to leave it out – and sit there re-reading the few lines. The absence of any expression of love at the end of his card made her weepy. She tried not to sit in the lounge because the empty bookshelves still made her cry. She couldn`t believe Henry had taken all his books just for a few weeks` holiday reading.

A fortnight later, on Kiddies` Wear`s half-day closing day, Rose accompanied Jean to a beauty salon. Jean spent the afternoon being massaged and lying on a couch with a facepack and cucumber slices on her eyes. She emerged red-faced and radiant and with her eyebrows plucked and her nails painted.

Emboldened by her progress – the weight was simply falling off her – she agreed with Rose that the time had arrived for a visit to the hairdressers.

"Have it re-styled," Rose insisted. "Get rid of that fringe and the way it sort of goes on round your head just hanging down."

Jean felt the criticism unnecessarily brutal but she took the point. She arrived at Kiddies` Wear next morning with her hair cut in a soft, fashionable and layered bob with a scattering of highlights.

"Oh yes," said Rose appreciatively. "Very trendy."

Jean had lost a stone in weight. When she stood naked in front of the long mirror in the bedroom, she looked almost trim.

There was just one more stage in Rose`s plan for her employer and that had to wait for the next early closing day. After another low-calorie vegetarian lunch round the corner from Kiddies` Wear, the two women set off down the high street on a shopping expedition.

"No!" Jean exclaimed at every shop that Rose stopped at. "That`s much too young for me!"

"You`re just refusing because of the music," Rose protested.

Jean nodded vigorously.

"I can`t hear myself think with that pop music blaring out."

Rose tugged her away from what she called the "frumpy" dress shops.

"You`re not that old!" Rose shrieked. "You`re not a fuddy duddy! Just take a look at yourself."

Eventually, the pair compromised on a clothes shop that seemed upmarket and smart. Vivaldi`s Four Seasons played softly in the background while Rose riffled through a rack of skirts. Young shop assistants bustled round Jean. Occasionally Rose looked up and shouted encouragement.

"Go on Jean – try it! There`s nothing to lose."

Jean swiftly pulled the changing room curtain across but hesitated before pulling it aside. She stepped out in a pastel blue above-the-knee dress that showed just a trace of her décolletage.

"Er, Rose, I`m just not sure about this…"

Rose swung round to look.

With one hand she threw the brassiere she was examining into the air and with the other hand punched the air.

"Yes! Yes!"

Over the following weekend, the shop was refitted. When Jean and Rose arrived for work on Monday morning, fitters were removing their ladders and picking up tool boxes. From the back of the shop, Rose wheeled down the new mobile racks and positioned them in front of the stark new shelves and hanging spaces highlighted with bold chrome spotlights. Jean followed her assistant, pushing containers of jumpers and other children`s wear with which she stacked the shelves and drawers.

As Rose passed by with the final rack, the smart and trim Jean looked up and whispered out of earshot of the fitters.

"I wrote to Henry over the weekend. I feel ready for him now."

Rose pulled a face that indicated indifference.

"Well, I hope he comes back. But you just keep your options open. Someone better might turn up – you hear?" Jean looked doubtful. "You hear what I say?"

Jean nodded reluctantly.

Chapter 19

Henry woke up with a start, his mind leaping-frogging out of unconsciousness. Immediately, he was aware that his head was throbbing. With sudden horror through the pain, he remembered the night before: his hands sliding down Lou`s back: his hands grabbing Lou`s arse. He knew that it should be a memory to savour. Instead, it sent him leaping from his bed and onto the hotel bedroom floor, groaning. It was not yet dawn and the darkness matched his mood. He began frantic press-ups to drive away his demons.

His watch told him it was not much past 3am. He was suffering from an old problem. Too much alcohol in the evening would find him awake with a clear mind in the early hours. Except that now he wished his recall was not so clear.

Gasping and heaving himself up and down on the carpet with grim resolve, he pieced together the events of the night before. Clearly, he had drunk too much of the rum punch. He resolved not to drink another glass. He rolled over and, hands behind his neck, began raising his legs from the floor, feeling the tightness across his stomach and the sweat pooling at the centre of his back. How did he drink that much when he distinctly remembered telling Dr Roy that he did not want the wretched stuff? A curious chap that Dr Roy. Amiable and very hospitable. But what was Lou doing with him as a friend? He pulled a face in the dark. Then he remembered. Lou had told him that Dr Roy was a homosexual.

That was where it had all begun to go wrong with Lou, along the beach when Dr Roy left them alone after his confession. Now another piece of memory returned. He saw Lou running along the beach. Away from him. And his groping.

He pulled his legs up faster and higher, his stomach muscles going for burn, but still he couldn`t erase the memory. Clearly, he had upset her. It was such an adolescent, misguided, mistimed mistake.

He saw Lou in the moonlight struggling in his clumsy embrace. He dropped quickly back onto the carpet. With his back to the floor and his hands behind his neck, he began raising his shoulders from the ground. Again and again. That was better. That was the exercise that really hurt. That made him forget. After doing it 40 times, he stopped. And then again he remembered Lou`s arse. His hands were not just idly resting on it. They were exploring. It was a wonder she hadn`t slapped his face, or screamed for help, or reported him to the police. He was lucky that she had just run off.

He put on the light, changed into his jogging gear and set off to run the length of the beach and back again before first light. For the first time, he saw the sun rise over the Caribbean. It was such a magnificent sight that he should have been transfixed in wonder. Instead, he just ran on, still trying to blot out the awfulness of the previous night.

What stopped him in his tracks was the thought that he might have to try to cancel the three month rental on the new apartment.

Would Lou ever speak to him again?

On his way back to the hotel, a crowd of local children picked up their ball and ran after him, shrieking and chattering in the local patiois. In his room, he dawdled over breakfast, eaten on his lap in bed. He was grateful for the black coffee and lay back on his bed. He had to make a decision on the apartment and his future on the island. He couldn`t bring himself to do so.

He was desperate for an extra strong mint. He wondered whether to write to his sister in Leeds, explaining that he had left Jean so could she send him a batch of mints urgently. But how could he? He no longer knew his future on the island.

A leisurely swim in the Caribbean enabled him to count his strokes evenly and deliberately. It was very calming.

Over lunch at a café along the beach from his hotel, he tried to finish the book on Robespierre. His mind refused to concentrate. Somehow the French Revolution just didn`t seem relevant or important. All that was important in his life now was Lou. Again he cursed his stupidity. And the rum punch.

In the afternoon, his feet took him to the café along from the Government building where she worked. He did not want to go but his obsession took him there. He tried to delay the inevitable by mooching round shops but no sooner had he gone inside than he was out again and heading on to the café.

He needed to see Lou one last time before deciding whether to cancel the apartment rental. If it could be cancelled.

He took his regular table on the café forecourt. He had given up on his book, which now lay unopened before him, and read the island`s newspaper. He skimmed it and found nothing of interest. He sipped his coffee - he couldn`t face alcohol that day - and just stared down the road. In his misery he had no clear idea of what he was going to do. Arrange another casual meeting with Lou or simply follow her? What he did know, with total conviction was that to see her and be near her would be enough to help him through the rest of the day.

She came down the steps quickly, looking at her feet. He hadn`t seen her do that before and for some reason he picked up his paper and pretended to read it. Lou looked up the road towards the café and took her usual route towards the town. He stood up to follow her, hanging well back, hugging walls, turning to look in windows. All the time he noticed that today Lou was half looking over her shoulder, as if expecting to see someone. It was almost, thought Henry, as if she expected to meet him.

Henry saw her turn into a shoe shop and he loitered up the street, pretending to look in shop windows. He kept looking at his watch and then down the street. After 20 minutes, she had still not reappeared. People were staring at him. Perhaps Lou had left the shop without him noticing. Or was there even a rear exit? He crossed to the other side of the road and sidled down to try to get a view into the shop.

As he stared directly across the road, Lou emerged with two carrier bags.. They stared at each other. Lou swallowed and remembered what she had agreed with her lover in bed. She smiled, then raised a hand and gave a tiny flutter of her fingers.

Henry beamed and did not so much walk across the road as float towards her. He felt that she was an extraordinary woman, full of forgiveness. Twice he had clearly, palpably upset her, even hurt her. Yet the next day she smiled a welcome at him. What a woman! It was little wonder that he loved her so much.

She offered her cheek. He was profoundly moved by such a gesture of reconciliation. He kissed it with all the gentleness he could muster.

"A drink?"

She nodded.

"But I must be quick. Lots to do."

She gave a tiny, false smile and they walked down the road together.

The nearest bar was noisy and full. Much too downmarket, Henry thought, for such a woman. She crossed her legs and tossed her head so that her black hair swung off her face.

She ordered a white wine and Henry was relieved to see that this time she sipped it, leaving a trace of her pink lipstick on the glass. He began to stammer an apology.

"Lou, about last night. I…"

She waved him into silence.

"You had too much to drink. I blame Winston. Those rum punches are evil."

"Especially when I said I didn`t want them."

Lou looked surprised.

"Really? I missed that. Well, it was Winston`s fault then." She went quiet and looked into the distance. Henry thought she looked sublime, perhaps like a portrait by Reynolds. In fact, Lou was thinking that Winston had a lot to answer for. More than she had thought.

"No," Henry insisted. "I must apologise."

Lou studied him and thought he looked like an overgrown school boy. For the first time, he stirred a tiny emotion within her. Pity.

"Apology accepted." She took another sip of her wine. "Now what Winston was wondering - no, what Winston and I were wondering - was whether you would like to go out on his boat. See the island from the sea."

Henry couldn`t believe it. He could do without Dr Roy joining the party, but in the circumstances he considered himself to be a very lucky man.

"I`d love to. When?"

"We can both do next Saturday. How about you?"

Henry had nothing in his diary for as long as the year lasted.

"Great!"

Thoughts of cancelling the apartment rental vanished. He moved in two days later and in the meantime bought another postcard which he sent to his sister. On the top, he wrote the address of his apartment. Underneath, he told his sister:

> "You may have heard that I have left Jean. I am starting a new life here. The island is idyllic. The

islanders liken it to Eden. However, the extra strong mints which, as you know, have always been my favourite are strangely absent. It would be a great kindess if you could send me some.
Regards
Henry"

He settled in well in his new lodgings. The apartment was cheaply and shoddily built – the walls were thin and he could hear every move that his neighbours made – but he was happier alone. He could establish his own routines in the place. He also slept better than in the hotel, which meant he awoke refreshed and raring for his morning jog. After a quick on-the-spot warming up in the tiny hall of his new home, Henry jogged out into the lobby. He slammed the door behind him and accelerated through the exit just as the postman was entering with a bundle of letters in his hand. The force of the collision bowled the postman onto the nearby wall. Henry Turville slowed to on-the-spot jogging and bellowed.

"Have a care, damn you!" With that, he jogged off for the beach.

The post man dusted himself down and picked up the scattered letters. He walked to the door through which his assailant had emerged and looked at the new slip of paper in the name-plate. He spoke aloud and with disdain.

"Mister Henry Turville!"

He looked down to the letters in his hand and read from one envelope, which had been forwarded from the hotel. This time her hurled the name from his lips with contempt and spittle.

"Mister Henry Turville!!"

He turned to the front door through which Henry had disappeared and shouted.

" Mister Henry Turville! Trash! Trash man!" He slid Henry`s envelope down into his back pocket and slapped it with the palm of his hand. "You`re going in de bin, Mister Turville."

Later that afternoon, when his work was finished, the postman sat in the small living room of his home and retrieved the envelope from his pocket. In the kitchen his wife was cooking for him. Their five children played noisily in the yard.

Slowly and carefully, the postman opened the letter and read Jean Turville`s piteous appeal for her husband to return. Jean`s emotions, which had flowed unrestrained from her pen, were reduced to a slow stutter from the postman`s mouth. Occasionally, he shook his head in disbelief.

"Poor, poor woman. He don`t deserve a woman like that."

In the kitchen, he gently eased his wife aside from the waste bin and tore up the envelope and letter into small pieces.

"Trash, Mister Turville. Trash!"

Chapter 20

The newer and sleeker saloon car pulled up outside Kiddies` Wear and Jack Reardon stepped out. Business was looking up for him and he was enjoying the trappings. He lifted his dark blue hand-made suit jacket from its peg by the rear seat, watched the indicator lights wink as he centrally locked the car and turned towards the shop. In the window, the normal boring rows of children`s clothes had gone. The dusty window display had been replaced by dummies of smartly-dressed toddlers chasing each other and blowing bubbles that had been stuck to the inside of the glass. He nodded appreciatively.

"Neat. Very neat."

He rapped on the glass in the door and peered through at the figure beyond.

Behind the new, elegantly curved counter, Jean looked up and waved from her stool. She was dressed in a smart blue suit with skirt line just above the knee. At her side stood a bottle of wine and a half-full glass. A second but empty glass stood ready by a tall and untidy pile of papers. She slipped down from the stool and unlocked the door.

"Jack! It`s so good of you to come at such short notice."

He smiled and raised his eyebrows as he looked round the refurbished shop.

"So what`s the crisis? Spent all the money refitting the shop?"

Jean laughed and pointed to a stool behind the counter for him to sit down.

"No. Business is beginning to pick up. I`m even doing a bit of advertising. The problem is…Well, you probably don`t remember but the VAT Inspector is due to come at the end of the week and…" She pursed her lips and looked at the floor "I`m afraid I lied to you. I`m in a total mess with the paperwork."

"Oh Jean! That`s not like you. Not at all."

She looked up, shamefaced.

"Well, yes but there`s been so much…."

She perched on the other stool and asked him if he wanted wine or tea. Jack nodded to the wine bottle and she filled the second glass. He took a sip and looked at her over the rim.

"So?"

"I think I should be totally honest about the whole business. It`s not the easiest thing to discuss. You see, Henry has left me."

Jack put down his glass.

"Oh, Jean. I`m very sorry. Really. That`s awful."

"It was six or seven weeks ago. Maybe eight. I`ve stopped counting now. And that must be a good sign." She sighed and sipped her wine, savouring it in her mouth before swallowing. It was her first alcohol since going on her diet. "But I`ve let the paperwork slip. What with having the shop refitted. And everything."

Jack became businesslike, reaching out for the papers and then his briefcase on the floor.

"That`s understandable enough. I`m sure we can soon…"

Jean put out her hand and touched his to stay it.

"No, Jack. There`s more. You see, I haven`t spoken to anyone about this. There isn`t really anyone to speak to. And I need some advice – financial advice." He settled back on the stool and Jean finally let go of his hand. " You see, Henry has taken early retirement from the Foreign Office. Well, they retired him early. And he`s gone abroad. I think there`s another woman. He was in a hotel for a few days and he sent me a postcard with an address he was moving to – an apartment, I think, in the town. Nothing more than that. Just the address. I`ve written to him at the hotel and then at the apartment. Again. And again. But there`s no reply. I`ve even phoned the hotel but they`ve only got the forwarding address to the apartment. And there`s no phone number for him at the apartment. I`ve tried International Directory Inquiries again and again. "

Jack screwed up his face in thought.

"You could ask the Foreign Office to help. They must have someone in Grenada. A representative or something like that – to handle the occasional crisis for tourists. It`s the least they could do."

Jean shook her head.

"No. I would find it too humiliating."

She slid from her stool and began to pace up and down the floor in thought. She stopped when she reached the other side of the counter to Jack and looked unblinkingly at him over the heap of papers. He found the eye contact uncomfortable and looked down to shuffle some papers.

"Well, then, what you need, Jean, is a solicitor."

"I`ve got one. I`m going for separation and then a divorce. What I wanted to talk to you about is his pension. It`s a lot." Jack nodded in agreement and shifted on his stool. He slowly got up and walked round the counter to face Jean. "Well, you`d expect it to be. And it`s going into his bank account but I can`t get at it. At least, not yet. I know I will be able to get at it when the solicitor has sorted things out. Fortunately, I`ve got the shop. So I can live."

Jean absentmindedly stroked a small woolly jacket hanging on one of the racks as she faced Jack.

"So what you`re getting at, I suppose, is what else can

you do to get your hands on his money?"

She smiled.

"That`s a brutal way of putting it."

"We accountants can be brutal people." He screwed up his face again as he tried to remember the financial background to the shop. She wished he`d stop pulling that face. He was so good looking with his dark hair and straight jaw. Jack`s face brightened. "I seem to remember that Henry took out a mortgage on his half of your house to pay for this place."

"That`s right."

Jack beamed.

"Ah ha! In that case, we`ve got him!"

She moved a little towards him. "Is that important? About his mortgage?"

Jack nodded vigorously.

"Tell me something. Just how nasty do you want to be with Henry?"

"Oh – all the way and then some more."

He was surprised at how bitter she sounded.

"Well Jean, you just leave it to me. I`ll show you how to skin him – and that`ll be before your solicitor gets to work on him."

She made a tiny, excited jump right up to him and took his arm.

"I knew you would know how to do it!"

Jean had never behaved this way to Jack before. She was being girlish, affectionate, a little skittish and very cuddly. He knew he had a decision to make. He could become very businesslike again. Or keep following where he thought she was leading. He reckoned she was a good 15 years older than him but that didn`t prevent him feeling excited. He had never made love to an older woman but had often fantasised about it. The decision resolved itself for him and he took her arm, looking into her blue eyes.

"I knew something had changed in you. You look better. Younger."

She laughed.

"There`s nothing like losing a husband for shedding a few pounds."

Jack put both arms round her and found she was waiting, almost anxious, for him to kiss her. He was surprised by her passion.

"You`re a very attractive woman, Jean."

He gently steered her towards the back room of the shop, kissing and fondling her, until they were by the toddlers' nightwear range. Jean`s sexual experience, though limited, told her where he was leading her.

Later, as she shyly dressed, she felt a sense of quiet wonderment at what she had allowed to happen. Watching Jack refill the wine glasses, she asked herself whether this was the beginning or the end. She had read a lot in the women`s magazines about "flings". Was that it? All over. Just like that.

Jack handed her the glass and kissed her on the lips with a gentleness that she considered appropriate to her feelings, which were unusually delicate.

"I`m going to have to be quick," he said. Jean tried not to smile. By the clock on the wall, he had taken four minutes. "I`ll get someone at the office to sort the papers. No trouble there. I`ll phone you – but not about the papers. In case you want to see me again. He kissed her again but quickly and was gone.

Next morning a bouquet of flowers arrived at the shop addressed simply to Jean and with nothing to identify the sender.

"A secret admirer!" said Rose, excitedly.

Three evenings later, Jack phoned her at her home. She had no hesitation in inviting him round. Jack was relieved. Business was good but he didn`t want to lose a customer.

Chapter 21

The power boat leapt over the smooth waters of the Caribbean, zig-zagging between the moored schooners and fishing boats of all shapes and sizes. Above them but disappearing fast from view was Fort George, on high ground above the harbour.

Dr Roy was at the wheel, dressed in T-shirt and jaunty naval-style cap. Lou was leaning against the deck rail. Her skimpy white shorts reminded Henry of how he felt in Joe`s gym when he first caught sight of the tantalising outline of her thighs hugged by a white leotard. On her head, she wore a white cap similar to Dr Roy`s.

Henry felt correctly dressed, for once, in his white slacks and white short-sleeved shirt. He shivered in the wind and pulled his blue cap down harder on his head as Dr Roy fully opened the throttle. He edged along the rail to stand close to Lou. Tentatively, he put out his arm. Immediately, she swung round and pointed.

"Look – that`s Point Saline. Where the new airport is being built." She made her way along the rail and away from Henry. "And look, from here the view of the island is wonderful. It`s one of my favourite spots."

Henry nodded. At the stern, he noted the boat`s name, Karl Jung, under specks of foam being whipped away in the wind.

"Strange to name a boat after a psychiatrist," he shouted to Lou.

Lou corrected him with a smile.

"A psychologist. Winston believes that Jung`s system of analytical psychology – and Jung himself – are very under-rated."

Henry looked out to sea where dolphins were playing, skipping in and out of the low waves. He turned to Dr Roy and shouted.

"Hey Winston! This is some boat." Dr Roy just smiled. Henry crossed the deck and stood by him. "You know what puzzles me Winston?" Dr Roy just smiled lazily again. He didn`t care what puzzled Henry. He was enjoying the wind on his face. "What I want to know is just how much call there is for a psychiatrist in Grenada?" Dr Roy knew that the answer was "Not enough" but said nothing and kept smiling. "It`s such a happy island. Isn`t it?" Dr Roy felt forced to nod. "I haven`t come across anyone here who looks like they need a trick cyclist!"

Dr Roy thought that Henry Turville was a certain case for psychiatric treatment. He just turned to Henry, nodded and shrugged. Lou leant on the rail and grinned at her lover`s discomfiture. She caught Henry`s eye and shouted, the wind almost whipping the words from her mouth.

"Henry! Ask Winston to tell you all about Jung!"

Henry took a step back and put up his hands.

"OK. I get the message. Sorry I asked. And Winston, please – not Jung!"

Dr Roy took a hand off the wheel and held it out to Henry.

"Do you want to take over? Have a spell at the wheel? You`re quite safe out here now we are in open water."

"Great!"

Dr Roy dropped a sly wink to Lou as he stepped back and gave her waist a quick squeeze. He decided it was time to come clean with Henry.

"OK Henry. I`ll give it to you straight. The boat came with the good times. Before the coup and Bishop and Coard. Under the old Government, you could make plenty, plenty money."

Henry nodded as he gave the wheel a gentle turn this way and then the other and felt it respond to his touch.

"Ah! Of course! I should have guessed. How did you make it? Drugs?" Dr Roy said nothing, just stared out to sea at the dolphins disappearing over the horizon. Overhead flew a frigate bird. "Don`t worry, Winston. I don`t give a damn. When I was a British diplomat I had to toe the British Government`s line. But do you know what I believe?" He stole a quick glance at his wrist watch while pausing for a response. Dr Roy remained silent. "If people want to blow their minds with drugs, let `em!"

Dr Roy took the few steps down to Henry at the wheel to speak more easily to him.

"Listen, I never ran anything hard. A bit of coke in one direction. Some marijuana in the other. We all have to earn a buck. Or two. Take Lou. She gets paid by the CIA."

The look of quiet amusement on Lou`s face vanished and she jumped from the rail as if it were electrified. She shrieked.

"Winston!"

The boat swerved violently as Henry spun round, first towards Dr Roy and then back to Lou. He was incredulous.

"You work for the CIA?"

Dr Roy took the two steps needed to reach the wheel, grabbed it and took control. He looked hard at Henry.

"Hey, steady man! I think we found your raw nerve there!"

The boat steadied. Henry stepped back and took Lou by the shoulders, staring into her eyes with an intensity that frightened her.

"You really work for the CIA? How? How did they recruit you?"

Lou tried to wriggle out of his hold, wincing.

"That hurts!"

He let go and she rubbed her shoulders, looking from one man to the other.

"What`s up with you guys today?" She looked angrily towards Dr Roy. "Winston! I hate you!" He shrugged as she turned back to Henry. "It was while I was in the States studying. Long before I went to London." She turned theatrically towards Dr Roy. "It was supposed to be a secret, Winston!"

Henry was still intense.

"So what do you do for them?"

She smiled sweetly at Henry.

"Much like what you did at your Foreign Office. Not a lot!"

She turned her back on him and stared out to sea.

Henry paced up and down the deck alongside the rail. Eventually, she turned and looked at him as he shouted into the wind, "What`s your front?"

Dr Roy turned his head in surprise and called out.

"Hey man, don`t get personal!" As an afterthought he added quietly. "Not that it`s anything to do with me."

Henry had forgotten that Dr Roy existed. His mind was in turmoil. After acting like boiling stew for weeks, his emotions churning, his brain was unused to serious thought. Then he formulated his questions and almost spat them out so fast was he thinking.

"For how long? How do you deliver? What do you deliver? Who recruited you? How often…"

Lou removed her cap and flapped it in front of his face.

"Cool down Henry!" She leant back on the rail and thoughtfully rubbed her thigh. "I can`t remember how long it is that I`ve been doing the work." She looked across to Dr Roy. "How long – four years maybe?" Dr Roy nodded. "I`m paid for what the CIA call research work. I report to a research company based in Switzerland. That`s where the money comes from. I don`t tell them much. There`s not much to tell. Is there?" She pulled a face and put the cap back on her head. "Oh, and if you must know, it was a lecturer who recruited me. Not long before I left college in Florida."

Henry began prowling the deck again. Dr Roy shouted over to him.

"Henry! You forgot the why!" Henry looked puzzled. "Why, Henry? Why?"

Henry nodded. His brain must be slowing in retirement.

"What made you start work for the CIA? Did they have some hold over you?"

Lou explained.

"No, the CIA had no hold on me. I started the work after daddy was killed. I felt so bad. I wanted – want - revenge."

"Smart lecturer," Dr Roy shouted.

Henry began prowling again. It wasn`t the lecturer he was thinking about. It was the other word Lou had used. Revenge. He began to stalk in small steps on the deck, performing a perfect square, intense in his thoughts. He stopped and then briskly walked back to Lou, beaming.

"Lou, you don`t know how happy you have made me."

She was taken aback. Henry, filled with happiness and love, saw her standing momentarily speechless, her lips slightly parted. He took the opportunity to lean forward, take her by the shoulders and kiss her on the lips before she could resist. Dr Roy, his back to the couple as Henry pressed his lips remorselessly against hers in the hope of a response, called out.

"Hey Henry, what have you got in mind?" He turned just in time to witness Lou retrieving her poise and struggling out of Henry's embrace. "Well, I mean I know what you`ve got in mind. But what`s with the CIA?"

Henry didn`t answer. He was lost in his thoughts and

remained so, on and off, for the rest of the day. As the boat headed back to St George`s after a round trip of the island and a stop at a tiny harbour for lunch, Henry said he thought he had a plan. He would refine it in his head over the rest of the weekend.

"I`ll explain it to Lou early next week. Over supper."

Lou smiled to hide her grimace.

Chapter 22

Dr Roy knew that Lou was in a bad mood. She had woken him in the night with her turning and huffing and puffing. He had lain next to her silently, breathing evenly and gently, staying calm and not letting her rile him. He was doing much the same now at the breakfast table.

As if emphasising to her lover that she was sulking, Lou pulled her short, white dressing gown tighter round her and firmly re-tied the bow. Dr Roy smiled and offered to make more coffee.

"I`ll do it," she said.

Instead, she sat kicking her bare feet under the breakfast bar.

`Sure thing,` said Dr Roy, standing up quickly and putting water in the kettle. He reached for a book on the working top, sat back at the breakfast bar and began reading.

"Winston!" He looked up. "It`s anti-social. Reading at the table."

Dr Roy replaced the book on the working top, resumed his seat and with it a look of expectancy. She just kicked her feet. The water in the kettle boiled.

"Shall I do the coffee?"

His voice was solicitious. Lou stood up slowly as if the effort were exhausting and her thoughts were elsewhere and eventually poured the water into the coffee pot.

"Winston…" Her voice trailed off but Dr Roy knew from the slight whine in the tone that she was about to crack. "Winston, I can`t go on with this. I mean…"

He leant forward quickly, as if in surprise.

"There`s not something wrong is there, darling? Why didn`t you say earlier?"

Lou wasn`t listening.

"… the man is now kissing me. And you`re egging him on."

She carried a cup of coffee to the table and slammed it down next to him, spilling much of the contents in the saucer. She stood back, hands on hips.

"I have to hide my relationship with you. I have to scurry from my flat to here as if I`m some – some sort of criminal." She waved her hands wildly. "I have to tell him I`m staying with my aunt when I`m here. I have to dodge around and take detours to make sure he`s not following me." Now she was shouting. "For God`s sake, I`m having to act like I was a real CIA agent!"

Dr Lou put a finger to his lips, as if reminding Lou of the secret. In turn, Lou began pushing through the gap in his dressing gown with a long finger, emphasising her words with every shove at his hairy chest.

"Don`t…you…talk…about..secrets." She ceased shoving him and shouted instead. "It was you, Winston. You told him about the CIA!" He remained calm, almost unmoved, occasionally making a facial movement to demonstrate that he was listening to her. "And I know exactly what you are thinking." She began waving the finger at him. "And I am not doing it. I am not sleeping with that man. And if you make me, we`re finished!"

Dr Roy smiled soothingly and patted the stool next to his, indicating that she should sit down.

"Lou, darling…"

She sat down making a show of her reluctance. He put his hand on hers on the breakfast bar. She snatched her hand away.

"Don`t you darling me! I`m not – repeat NOT –

going to have sex with that man. That`s it. Final."

"I`m not saying it will be necessary."

She stood up. Her eyes widened and she threw her hands in the air.

"It may not be necessary! There we are. Thin end of a psychiatrist`s wedge." She again waved a finger at him. "You`re the only man I`ve ever slept with. Aren`t you proud of that? I`d have thought you would want to treasure that. But no. `It may not be necessary.` In other words – it could be necessary!"

"Darling, he`s clearly got some plan to help us bring down the Bishop Government.

What sort of treasure is that?"

She crossed her arms deliberately and turned her back on him.

"Clearly more of a treasure than I am to you."

Dr Roy stood up and spoke in a voice that was the nearest he ever came to loss of temper or impatience.

"OK. OK. Let`s call it all off." Lou turned round to face him, her arms still folded. "We throw away our chance to get rid of Bishop. You lose the chance to get revenge for the death of your father. I have to live with this God awful government. I have to live with its Communist aversion to drugs. I have to live off what I can earn as a psychiatrist, which is diddly-squat. OK. That`s it. Fine. Fine. We`ll just dump Turville and go on as before." He opened his arms wide to Lou. "For you, anything." Lou unfolded her arms and moved sweetly into his embrace before peeking up at him.

"You mean that?"

"Absolutely."

"You love me that much?"

He dropped his arms from around her and his face became serious. He stood back from her in the tiny kitchen.

"Lou. Lou. Now let`s get real. Remember the rules. We don`t do the love thing, do we? It`s just an empty concept. Right? Trust. Kindness. Tenderness. These are concepts that we can understand." He smiled. "OK! And the sex!"

Lou felt chastened. The love word had just slipped out.

"But I don`t have to sleep with him?"

"In fact, *I* have never even suggested it."

She snuggled up to him and looked thoughtful.

"If it is so important…" She peeked up at him again in the way that he found so endearing. "And, of course, it is. I do want to see the end of this Government. So perhaps I could just play him on a bit. Until we know just what it is that he can do for us. What do you think?"

Dr Roy smoothed her hair with his hand and resumed his calm tone.

"Well, just play for time." He kissed her on the nose. "But only because you want to."

She smiled again.

"Sorry about the love word, Winston. Sometimes I, I…" She couldn`t find the words – not without using the love one.

He pulled her to him.

"I understand, Lou. I do. I know your feelings. I have the same feelings for you." He held her by the shoulders and gently pushed her away enough to look into her eyes. "I`d do anything for you. I`d die for you."

She looked up.

"Really? Really die? For me?"

"Of course."

She snuggled back into his arms. She didn`t like the thought of him dying for her. But it was sweet to say it. A start, she thought.

After showering and dressing, they drove across the island to a tiny bay on the west coast for a day with friends. The Levitts both worked in the island`s medical university and had a house that overlooked the sea and a jetty.

On the verandah, the two couples ate lobster, watched the pelicans and in the late afternoon swam in the bay. It was an idyllic afternoon and Lou did not think once of Henry or Maurice Bishop. She thought a lot about Winston, watching his strong back and arms power him through the azure water.

On the drive back, Lou fell silent in the passenger seat as darkness fell and the walls of forest seemed to close in on the small car as it headed back to St George`s. Dr Roy turned to look at her and put her quiet stillness down to tiredness. In fact, Lou was thinking about her slip of the tongue that morning. Her use of the love word. Dr Roy heard her sigh heavily.

"Anything wrong, darling?"

"No. Just tired, I suppose."

"Try to sleep."

She pulled her feet up and rested them on the dashboard, encircling her knees with her bare arms. The trouble was, she realised, that she did love Dr Roy. She might not be able to define it and he may be able to pull her words to pieces when she tried. She knew how viciously logical he could be when he wanted. All done with a smile and a purring voice, of course. But she knew that what she felt for him was love. And that, in time, she would want a baby. Or two.

It made her feel an enormous yearning. She sighed heavily again. And she had always believed that love was supposed to make you happy.

Chapter 23

Henry was waiting at the café along the street from the Government building but this time as Lou came down the steps, he stood up, called and waved. He felt a new confidence, born of his belief that fate was throwing together him and the woman he so desperately loved.

The morning on Dr Roy`s boat had changed the way he saw his future. Until now, he could not see beyond the next day. Dare not look beyond it. Now, as he waved his newspaper at Lou, he was looking to a future in which they shared each other`s lives. Endlessly.

The shout took Lou by surprise. She walked towards him slowly, swinging her attache case and looking down at the ground.

"I had to wait for you," he explained. "I haven`t got your phone number or address." Lou said nothing. "To fix up for us to have supper."

What Henry had in mind was supper at his apartment. He visualised the best of what he had eaten in St George`s – starting with that Grenadian caviar, moving on to the Lobster a la Creole and with the finest wines. He had even been out and bought an island cook book. From what he had seen, his previous lack of culinary skill did not seem to be a handicap. He was an intelligent man with a degree. All he needed to do was to follow the steps. Armed with his cook book, he felt confident that his love for Lou would help him to prevail when it came to tackling lobsters.

He noticed that Lou was shaking her head as she sat down next to him.

"Winston will have to come, too."

Henry could see no good reason why that man should continue to get in the way of him and his beloved.

"Winston`s a great guy but…"

She cut in quickly.

"But you owe him a supper. And he took you out on his boat. Most of the day. Round the island."

Henry had bought their lunch but he took her point.

"I think that you and I need to get together. We need to keep this close. It`s not good to have too many in on my plan. Winston doesn`t figure in it. It`s secret work."

Lou looked sourly across the table. She knew exactly what he had in mind. And every detail of his plan.

Henry ordered her wine as she stared defiantly at him.

"Henry, you`ve got no choice. You`ve got to keep Winston on side. He already knows everything. He knows that you`ve got a plan to do something about…"

He cut in quickly, leaning forward and frowning.

`Don`t say anything here! That`s the first rule. You could be overheard.`

Reluctantly, he conceded that Dr Roy had to be kept on side – or `in the loop`, as the Foreign Office described it. He sat back and thought of cooking for Lou and Dr Roy. That riled him. He certainly wasn`t planning on cooking a romantic meal for Winston, too. He decided that he would postpone – not abandon – his plan for a tete a tete dinner with Lou at his place. With a sense of relief, he suggested taking them both out to dinner. (Despite his best efforts with the cook book, he couldn`t quite make out what he was supposed to do with the lobster before the a la Creole bit.)

The next evening the trio gathered round a restaurant table in a smart and expensive hotel along the Grand Anse. Lou wore the same white dress that Henry remembered glowing in the moonlight. Henry felt strong and in control. He also stayed clear of the rum punches. Dr Roy amused Lou and Henry with stories from his time as a medical student. And then Dr Roy drove them all back to Henry`s apartment.

Henry had beers and a bottle of white wine lined up on the cheap chipboard sideboard in the lounge. Out of politeness, Lou took a glass of wine but resolved to pretend to sip it. Dr Roy accepted a beer and tried to settle down alongside Lou. It was difficult. The sofa was small and uncomfortable.

On the wall Henry had pinned sheets of paper. On the uppermost was written, in Henry`s fine, neat writing

PLAN

Dr Roy nodded to the pad.

"So, Henry. What is it? The plan?"

Henry finished pouring his beer and strolled to the centre of the room.

"In fact it took very little planning. Everything became clear – at least to me – the moment that Lou said she does a little freelance work for the CIA."

He picked up a pencil lying on the sideboard and began to jiggle it with his fingers. "First, we must all agree on secrecy. Absolute secrecy. OK?"

Dr Roy and Lou nodded and looked at each other. They spoke in unison.

"Agreed!"

Lou giggled. It all seemed so silly. She remembered Henry`s lecture at the civil service college and how seriously she had taken him then. Henry looked reproachfully at her and she pulled herself up and tried to look serious as he coughed and resumed his presentation.

"At a time like this, I work best with paper." He moved to the pad of papers pinned to the wall and tore off the top sheet to reveal another word:

OBJECTIVES

He walked around the room, tapping the pencil on a thumb nail. "Our first objective is to get the Bishop government out. Agreed?" Lou and Dr Roy nodded. "To secure that objective, we will have to secure another objective." With a dramatic flourish, he pulled the top sheet of paper off, revealing under it:

PLOT INVASION BY USA

Dr Roy turned to Lou and saw her eyes widen. Lou turned to Dr Roy and saw his jaw sag. Dr Roy regained his composure first and broke the stunned silence.

"Holy Dr Freud!"

Then Lou spoke.

"Henry, you`re mad. Off the wall."

With all the force he could find in his right arm, Henry hurled the pencil to the floor. It landed soundlessly on the small red rug and lay there infuriatingly intact. He wanted to stamp on it but controlled himself with a huge effort and a lot of deep breathing. As Henry stood gulping at the air, Lou wondered whether he was hyper-ventilating. Dr Roy began to rise from the sofa and spoke soothingly.

"Hey, Henry old man. Take it easy now!"

Dr Roy had seen worse behaviour in the Crazy House, the locals` name for St George`s mental institution, but not often outside. With an immense effort, Henry pulled himself together.

"Look, are you two serious or not?"

Dr Roy padded back to the sofa and raised an eyebrow at Henry. It all seemed a bit extreme. Provoking the world`s greatest superpower to drop its military might on little old Grenada. But if it got the Bishop Government out and opened the way for a resumption of his free enterprise, he was willing to listen.

Lou just shook her head in disbelief.

Henry stared at the floor and began to pace, talking fiercely and loudly but almost as if to himself rather than his audience. Dr Roy leant forward, not so much in expectation of what Henry was going to say, but with interest in Henry as a medical case.

As Henry talked, he paced a small but perfect square on the floor.

"On and off I`ve worked for half my life with the security services."

He completed the first leg of the square and turned into the second leg.

"I can help you do this if you want."

He turned into the third leg of the square.

"I know how the tiny minds of the CIA work."

He turned into the fourth leg of the square.

"I know the words that turn them on."

He was again facing Dr Roy and Lou. Dr Roy settled back on the sofa and forgot just how uncomfortable it was.

"Hey, that`s real interesting."

Dr Roy was talking profesionally. Henry looked up at the clock on the wall and pointed at it with a finger.

"I even know the exact time their spy satellites are overhead this little Spice Island of yours." Henry looked again at his audience. Dr Roy and Lou turned to each other, their eyes widening again. "So it`s make-up-your-minds time." He caught Lou`s gaze and held it.

"Lou – are you with me? All the way?"

Instinctively, Lou turned to Dr Roy for help and Henry again wondered what hold this psychiatrist had over the woman he loved. Dr Roy thought for a moment.

"He`s right, Lou. Are you prepared to go along with Henry? All the way?"

Lou looked down at the floor before returning Dr Roy`s stare. She didn`t like the way he had phrased his question. She repeated it and stared apprehensively at Henry. "All the way?" She turned to Dr Roy again. He was nodding seriously. She picked up her glass and drank heavily. Dr Roy answered first.

"Sure thing! Count me in, Henry."

Henry ignored Dr Roy. He had no part to play in his plan. Instead, he kept staring at Lou. She shifted uneasily on the sofa and not just because the cushions felt so lumpy.

"Well…OK. Yes."

Henry bent down, picked up the pencil and took a step to the wall to reveal the next sheet of paper. The words he exposed were

CIA WEAKNESSES.

He turned back to Lou, smiling.

Lou sank back on the sofa and groaned inwardly, asking herself what she had let herself in for and why she had agreed. The answer, she knew, was that she had agreed for Dr Roy. She always did. Since her first therapy in his surgery, he had increasingly towered over her intellectually and emotionally. She was not only in love with him but in thrall to him.

For an hour, Henry expounded on the rank stupidity and naiveté of the CIA. He revealed management charts and lists of names until the pad of paper on the wall was turned into a pile on the floor. Most of what he said simply swept over her. She wanted to take Winston`s hand but knew that she could not. She needed to go back to his apartment and lie in his arms to be reassured and comforted. Finally, there was no more paper on the wall and Henry was smiling at her.

"Now Lou, I can`t stress just how much you and I are going to have to work together very closely on this." He looked at his watch. "You`re at work tomorrow?" She nodded. "Let`s fix for us to get together here as soon as possible to get down to the details of what you`re going to do."

Lou had what she thought was a stroke of genius.

`It`s my turn to buy supper!`

Henry looked stern.

"Security, Lou. Security. Nothing about this must be said in a place where it could be overheard. No, we`ll meet here."

She turned to Dr Roy. He smiled slightly and nodded in agreement.

As Henry let Lou and Dr Roy out into the warm night air, he felt not just content but a little smug. He foresaw Lou and himself working ever more closely on the plot to bring down the Grenadan Government.

He strolled into the bathroom, a small smile of satisfaction playing on his lips, and reached into his toilet bag for his toothbrush and toothpaste. Out jumped a cockroach, clacking and rattling onto the tiles and then into the lounge. He pursued it with one of his slippers but lost it as it scuttled under the sideboard. For two hours, he sat on the sofa, turning the light on and off in the hope of encouraging the cockroach to show itself. Finally, he went to bed and slept badly.

Chapter 24

Henry looked anxiously at Lou, uncertain of just how much she had enjoyed his cooking. Was she just being polite? He felt that he had lived a large part of his life with the three courses they had just eaten. In fact it was only an entire day that he had spent in the kitchen.

Lou perched in the middle of the sofa. It seemed safer not to allow Henry room to sit next to her. Outside in the kitchen were the remnants of Henry`s first serious attempt at cooking.

Henry was confident that the Grenadian caviar had been a success but then there wasn`t much he could do to destroy that. He had given up on the lobster and opted for baked stuffed rainbow runner fish . Until he got them home, he hadn`t realised that he had to gut them before stuffing them. Perhaps he had been too severe with the gutting but after he had finished the job, there seemed little left to stuff. So he had gone back into town to buy more runners. The nutmeg ice cream wasn`t bad but not the same as in the restaurant. He wondered whether the ice cream had been changed by having to refreeze the runny mess it had become on the short journey from the shop to his apartment.

Lou felt humbled by Henry`s culinary efforts and, against her better judgement, thought him quite endearingly sweet. But not sweet enough to move up the sofa. After complimenting him on his skill and declining a second glass of wine, she had wondered whether to offer to help with the washing up. While he was out of the room, she peeked into the kitchen and changed her mind. It was a disaster area. Amid the chaos, she noticed on the draining board what appeared to be the remains of two lobsters seemingly ritually ripped to pieces by a mad man. She would mention this to Dr Roy.

Over coffee, Henry said he needed to debrief her. Lou swallowed hard but relaxed when she realised that he merely wanted her to give him the details of how she worked for the CIA. Seated as she was on the sofa, he felt compelled to pull up a hard-backed dining chair, which he placed in front of her. He paced a little round the room and then sat on the chair. Slowly, as he droned on, she felt a familiar sense of weariness and boredom descending.

"So how many times have you called the CIA via the Swiss research company?"

"Henry, I can't remember. Once a month? Once every two months. When the CIA money goes into my bank account, I feel guilty and try to think of something to tell them."

"Such as?"

"Oh, I don't know. If I saw a foreign ship in the harbour, I'd remember its name and tell them about that some time."

"Not any information from within the Government?"

She shrugged.

"A bit I suppose but no-one ever really tells me the sort of things I imagine the CIA want to know."

Henry laughed.

"Bloody CIA! But you must have some idea of what they want from you?"

"Henry, I'm a trained economist. Not a trained spy. And anyway, I'm too busy to take any real notice of their requests."

Henry grinned and thought she was wonderful. He

imagined Mariowitz's requests for information being passed to Switzerland and Lou's phone calls. From what he could gather, she ignored what they wanted and simply gave them whatever nonsense she thought up on the way to the bank to withdraw the CIA money.

"OK. So tell me more about the information you gave them."

"Oh, I told them when I heard that Cubans were beginning work on the new airport. And if a trade delegation was over here. That sort of thing." She looked intently at him. "I do have other things to do, you know!"

"Of course. Now let`s try to get a bit more detail on the information you sent."

Lou became exasperated.

"Henry! I`ve been through all this."

She sighed wearily and looked at the clock on the wall. Henry stared at the floor and began again.

"OK. I`ll go through it. You pass information about once a month but it`s low grade information and you pass it by phone to a controller at the end of the line." Lou nodded and he shook his head as if in disbelief. "This is almost medieval. Hasn`t your Government learned how to tap its civil servants' phones?"

Lou sat up sharply.

"You don`t have to be rude about my country."

"I`m sorry." He leant forward and put his hand on hers. "I was thinking of the risk the CIA was exposing you to." Lou removed her hand and patted his, as if he were a child.

"That`s very kind of you, Henry. But can we just get on with this? I`ve got to go to work in the morning."

Henry became businesslike.

"Of course. I`m so sorry. Anyway, our first step is to establish your credibility with Mariowitz. Get Marcus to rely on you. And then Marcus`s chums to rely on you. Get you into a routine of dropping information. Establish a style. Establish your authority."

"Who? Who`s this Mariowitz? Who's this Marcus?"

Henry looked up.

"I beg your pardon? Marcus. Marcus Mariowitz. He looks after this part of the Caribbean for the CIA. He is your ultimate boss. I've told you. I went through the management structure when you were here with Winston!"

"I see. It sounds like you know him. This Mariowitz."

Henry stood up quickly and began to prowl the room.

"A little."

Lou leant forward on the sofa.

"Should I get the feeling, Henry, that all this is a bit personal? I mean what are you doing all this for?"

As soon as she had asked the question, she wished she had not. She knew exactly why Henry was doing all this. Henry sat down and looked intently at her.

"Lou," he said a little wearily, "I am a professional." He took a deep breath. "I also want to help you. My feelings for you are very…"

Lou cut in hurriedly.

"OK Henry, let`s stick to business. What more do you want to know?"

He felt a little unsettled, preparing as he had been to tell of his great love. But Lou had her alert and businesslike face on, and clearly wanted to keep all talk between them strictly about the CIA. He sighed and resolved that a little later he would again seek to demonstrate to her the depth of his feelings.

"So tell me if any Soviet or East European specialists are due to come here." Before she had opened her mouth could answer, he snapped at her the thought that had streaked into his mind. "Well, what if it is personal between me and Mariowitz? It`s personal between you and Bishop!"

Lou nodded. She couldn`t argue with that.

"A few East Germans are coming. But they`re nothing special."

She could see that Henry was interested.

"I`ll decide if they`re special. What are these East Germans?"

"It`s just a goodwill visit. Political tin pots. Very low grade."

"And when will they arrive?"

"August 12, I think."

"Good. Check that date. Then pass it to the CIA. Say it`s a top-level, secret dele-gation and you don`t know its purpose but you`re trying to find out."

"OK."

He was staring into her brown eyes, excited by the way her knees peeked from below her skirt. He again took her hand from where it lay on her lap. She made no move to take it away.

"Two days after your first call, you phone your CIA number again. And you say the secret visitors are arms specialists. Very high level arms specialists."

"OK."

With his hand over hers, Henry began gently to rub her thigh through her skirt. All the time she held his gaze.

"You see, the first piece of information you pass on will prove correct. East Germans will arrive when you said they would. Then, because the first piece of information proves your credibility, the CIA will believe that the East Germans really are high-level arms specialists."

"That`s very cunning, Henry."

As she spoke, she looked down pointedly at Henry`s hand.

"We`ll wind up old Mariowitz wonderfully, darling."

"It all seems too easy."

Henry turned his head to look up at the clock on the wall, a second hand ticking. He spoke in time with the ticking hand.

"This…will…go…like…clockwork."

As he back to her face, he leant forward to kiss her. Slowly, his head moved closer and closer to hers. Her eyes remained wide open and she made no move to stop him. She simply raised her head at the last moment and kissed him on the brow. When she spoke, her voice was soft.

"Oh Henry. I know how you feel. But it`s just not quite, well, the right time…"

He stood up quickly.

"Absolutely. Understood. No problem."

She stood up, stretched and yawned.

"I need the bathroom."

He stepped back and threw out an arm to direct her. She giggled. He looked like a traffic policeman in London.

"Absolutely. Understood. Straight through the bedroom."

He was pointing to the door and then looking up at the clock as if to time her absence.

Lou stifled another giggle.

"I won`t be a moment," she said.

On the way through his bedroom, she stopped by the bedside table and looked at the coins, piled by size with the Queen`s head up, and pens in parallel rows.

She called to him.

"It`s all so neat and tidy here. How sweet – all the coins in neat little rows."

She heard him calling back.

"You`ll find a new bar of soap and a clean towel on the shelf over the wash basin."

In the bathroom, she found a large bar of apparently untouched soap and a fresh towel on the rail.

"It`s OK," she called. "There`s soap in the basin and…"

He shouted sharply.

"No – that`s mine! Use the new stuff on the shelf."

She shrugged and did as she was told.

"Whatever you say, Henry."

On her way out the front door, she slipped out quickly, turning only to giive him a quick wave with the fingers of one hand.

After she had left, Henry felt suddenly depressed and knew sleep would not easily come. He needed to think, and to keep himself alert he sat down on a chair in the lounge. In one hand, he was armed with his slipper. From time to time, he would get up and turn the light on and off. He rest of the time he sat still and watchful, his eyes fixed on the gap where the wainscoting met the floor. He was intent on luring the cockroach he knew was bound to scuttle out for its nightly forage around his flat. He broke off his vigil only to rearrange his books on the sideboard. First he lined them left to right in descending size but found the appearance displeasing. Then he arranged the books so that they descended in size from both ends, making a pleasant dip in the middle. He sighed with satisfaction. At least not all his time had been wasted. At 3am he gave up his unproductive cockroach guard and went to bed.

Chapter 25

Marcus Mariowitz kicked his new waste bin and it completed a satisfying curve over the room, finishing by the bookcase. He was happier now. Not only did he have a bin again but it had been returned with a hygienic plastic liner. He crossed the room, picked up the bin and put it down by his desk. From the outside pocket of his jacket hanging over his chair he took the afternoon`s banana ration.

Life was looking up for Mariowitz. Not only had his bin been returned but he had been put in charge of the bins on the entire floor. It was now his responsibility to check the contents of each bin every evening to ensure that only authorised material had been deposited in them.

He took the final bite of the banana and threw the skin over the room. It landed in the bin with a satisfying clunk.

Checking everyone's bin was a responsible job. The memo on his computer instructed him on what was and was not authorised bin material. Cuttings from newspapers and magazines and even entire newspapers and magazines were unauthorised material that had to be shredded. If the enemy knew what the CIA was reading, it could give them an insight into what the Agency was thinking. A hastily written postscript at the end of the memo stated that, while on the subject of what should and should not go through shredders, staff should refrain from trying to shred soft fruit.

Mariowitz sighed. It was hard work shouldering all this responsibility now he was back on the Agency`s UP track. He also had a new secretary. All to himself. Miss Hoover had got herself a new job. In her place was Ann-Marie Shuttle, early twenties, long blonde hair, legs that went up forever and a husky, breathless voice over the intercom that brought him out in a sweat. Not that Mariowitz had time for lingering in the evening with Ann-Marie. For a start, he was too busy with Grenada. The island was beginning to move up the Agency`s agenda. And Ann-Marie was moving up his wife`s agenda.

He took his reserve banana from his jacket`s inside pocket and munched as he thought of his wife. Dolores was from Alabama in America`s Deep South. Though the USA was supposed to be the world`s most mobile nation, with people from one state cheerfully fitting in with those of another, Dolores had never got along with the Washington women with their lunches, feminist meetings and general bitchiness. Now Dolores was becoming jealous of his secretary. Well, not so much his secretary, whom she had never met, but her voice.

Mariowitz took the last bite, wondered whether he should pay for a therapist for Dolores. He scored another bullseye with the skin in the bin. It seemed a good omen. He looked at the clock. Five minutes to go until his review group presentation in the conference room. He picked up his papers and slides and opened the door.

As he stepped into the corridor, his intercom buzzed. It could be an important call. He was getting more important calls these days. He turned back and flicked the switch down. It was his secretary. Husky yet urgent, she sounded as if she had just come back from doing what Mariowitz knew he would like to do to her.

"It`s your wife." Anne-Marie gave him no chance to say that he didn`t have time to speak to her. So he told Dolores himself.

"God Damn it! I haven`t time!" he snarled and flicked the switch up. It was the fifth call from home that day. The kids, the plumbing, his secretary, the snooty bitch next door, some Washington fag who had cut Dolores dead in the street. Mariowitz picked up his papers and slides and marched up the corridor with the confidence of a man who knows that he has the correct code number for the conference room.

As Mariowitz entered the room, the bald gum chewer (who was responsible for part of Eastern Europe) looked the other way. Immediately, Mariowitz stepped onto the dais and checked the lens in the projector. It looked clear. Life was like that in the CIA headquarters. You couldn`t trust anyone. No-one trusted you. And a CIA man knew he was on top when he stopped trusting himself.

Hurlingham walked in, followed by the Valkyries. He bestowed a generous smile on Mariowitz. He stepped onto the dais and called the meeting to order. The Valkyries looked at each other and their facial skin stretched horribly as they raised their freshly painted eyebrows. Hurlingham on the dais with Mariowitz?

Mariowitz flicked on his first slide. A great grey mush filled the screen. Mariowitz fiddled desperately with the controls. Hurlingham said he had seen clearer pictures through cloud at 20,000 feet while bombing those Commie bastards in Vietnam. Irritably, Hurlingham stepped onto the dais and waved Mariowitz aside. He tried unsuccessfully to get a good picture. He gave up and turned on the audience.

"I don`t know who`s doing this but it`s got to stop!" He ordered the bald gum chewer to go down the corridor and fetch the spare projector. He then apologised to Mariowitz. The Valkyries shot knowing glances at each other. Hurlingham put his hands behind his back and addressed the room. "Marcus has been producing some real interesting intelligence from Grenada, haven`t you?" Marcus smiled. The gum chewer pushed in the projector and Mariowitz began flicking up his slides. The first slide read:

HIGH-LEVEL EAST GERMAN
DELEGATION VISITS GRENADA

Mariowitz turned to his audience.

"We were told that an East German delegation would arrive on August 12. Later information was that the delegation comprised arms specialists. The delegation duly arrived on the appointed date. Of course, it took a while for the contents of the East Germans` meetings with the Grenadan Government to reach me – that is, the Agency."

As if by way of the answer, he flicked up another slide on the screen and stepped back while the audience absorbed the implications of the single word he had displayed.

MISSILES

A voice in the audience said "Jeez". The Valkyries stirred as if preparing for take off.

"As yet," said Mariowitz, "we do not have precise details of the missiles that were discussed or the decision reached. I hope to have those details shortly."

He flicked up more slides, all showing the work underway at the island`s new runway.

"Of course, we have had concerns for some time that the new airport on Grenada could have a military dimension. We now have details." He flashed more slides of the runway were flashed on to the screen. "Of course, it looks deceptively like a civilian runway. At the moment. But the intelligence we have received is that as soon as the runway itself is completed, work is to start on…"

In quick succession, slides appeared on the screen, each with just a few words on it in capital letters.

A PARALLEL TAXIWAY...DISPERSED PARKING...RADAR...HARDENED AIRCRAFT SHELTERS...SECURE UNDERGROUND FUEL TANKS...UNDERGROUND WEAPONS STORAGE...SURFACE–TO-AIR MISSILE SITES

The bald gum chewer was still smarting from pushing the projector.

"That all fine, Marcus, but what is the status of your intelligence source or sources? Is there confirmation?"

Marcus shuffled his feet a little.

"We are talking of one source. In the circumstances, I do not consider that confirmation is necessary – or possible, given the access that this source has." Hurlingham nodded in agreement. "We are talking of an intelligence source right at the heart of Government."

One of the Valkyries fluttered a hand up, but then let it fall back. She knew when she was beaten.

Hurlingham rested his hand on Mariowitz`s shoulder.

"OK. Thanks Marcus. Thank you all. We have to raise our game. With the State Department. The Defense Department. And the White House. From here on, Marcus, we need to meet on an as-needs-demand basis. Well done."

Mariowitz inclined his head modestly. His colleagues filed out, unusually silent and subdued.

Back in his office, he punched the code into his computer and sat back as he waited for the screen to clear. All CIA agents were known by code numbers but Marcus had his own pet names for the ones he looked after in the Caribbean. There was HOPELESS, TRIES TOO HARD, JUST GOSSIP, BLACK MAGIC and HOLE IN THE HEAD. For the agent who had just come alive in Grenada, he had the pet name BEAUTIFUL LADY.

The screen showed that there was no new intelligence data to be analysed. Mariowitz switched off the machine and looked at the date on his desk diary. He expected more data from BEAUTIFUL LADY around now. The agent was getting into a regular reporting pattern and was picking up on his requests for information.

Marcus set his computer screen on standby and reached out automatically as the phone rang.

`What are you doing with that secretary, Marcus?`

Marcus regretted that the answer was in the negative but bit his tongue. He felt that Dolores was becoming paranoid. She complained that Ann-Marie sounded indecent over the phone. He was wondering whether to suggest that she got help when his screen came alive.

`Sorry, Dolores. Got to go. I`ve got to deal with my Beautiful Lady.`

In St George`s, Lou had just put down the receiver in the red telephone box. Outside, Henry paced up and down as if waiting to make a call. As Lou turned to step out of the box, he walked on quickly. Lou ran to catch him up and walked alongside as they headed for the beach. It was Saturday and Henry wanted to discuss the next steps in his plan. He looked over his shoulder to ensure that no-one could overhear him.

"Did you tell your Swiss contact what I told you to say?"

Lou nodded, giggled and involuntarily grabbed his arm. She teetered for a moment as she tried to stop laughing. She felt slightly hysterical.

"Oh Henry! This is so silly!"

He hurried her along towards the beach.

Chapter 26

Henry was finding Maisy a bit tiresome. He had never met the old lady, felt he never wanted to and blamed her for his never being able to see Lou for long. As he walked along the beach with Lou, he sighed as she explained that she must – once more – get back to her step-mother.

As Lou walked beside him, listening to Henry propounding the next step in his plan, she felt pressured and she was not coping with it very well.

For a start, Dr Roy didn`t seem to mind too much that she was spending time with Henry. Sometimes he would put his hands round her waist and murmur that he really missed her when she was seeing Henry. Yet increasingly she found herself wondering whether such tiny signs of affection and jealousy were, in fact, fabricated for her benefit. That made her uneasy. It added to the tension she already felt over sending bogus information to the CIA. Over-riding this complex scene was the pretence, for Henry`s sake, that she and Dr Roy were just good friends who met from time to time.

Then there was Lou`s lie that she regularly stayed with Maisy out at the plantation house when in fact she spent most nights in Dr Roy`s apartment. Her constant need to check whether Henry was following her added to her jumpiness. Some evenings, when she wasn`t sure if she had thrown him off her trail, she walked back to her own apartment, got in her jeep and headed out of St George`s as if she really were going to stay with Maisy. Then she would turn back, park and skitter through the streets to arrive back at Winston`s place, like a furtive fugitive.

Henry did not blame Lou for having so little time to be with him. After being forgiven twice by the woman he loved, she could do no wrong in his eyes. It was Maisy whom he blamed. She seemed to be a very demanding and selfish old woman. He felt like telling Maisy just what he thought of her. If he ever had the chance.

In Henry`s first days and weeks in St George`s, Lou had simply told him that she owed Maisy a great deal. That was true and the implication was that she had to go home to her step-mother. Now Lou found herself having to tell outright lies and that made her feel uncomfortable.

Lou stopped on the beach, kicked off her shoes and carried them so that she could feel the sand between her toes. Henry took her hand and to his surprise, she let him keep it. Somewhere inside her, Lou gave a little shrug and thought that if the gesture kept Henry happy, why not? Dr Roy wasn`t going to mind.

Henry sought to build on the milestone.

" Why don`t we go for a trip round the island? Let`s make a day of it."

The corners of Lou`s mouth turned down. Henry knew what was coming.

"That`s a lovely idea, Henry, but it`s Maisy. She`s not as well as she might be."

Lou felt a new twinge of conscience. Her Roman Catholic upbringing rebuked her. Not only was she lying about her step-mother. Now she was making the poor woman ill.

Henry tried to smile. "Perhaps another day." He made a superhuman effort and continued. "I hope she is soon feeling better."

Such a wave of guilt overwhelmed Lou that she stopped and took Henry`s other hand.

"I promise you. I will take you on a day trip round the island. Soon."

Henry`s spirits lifted. He returned to the point of their meeting as they resumed their stroll.

"We need to move to the next stage of the plan. We have to precipitate a coup within your Government."

Lou looked sharply across at him and stopped again.

"Why didn`t we do that in the first place? Why all this US invasion stuff?"

It was a good question. So good that Henry didn`t want to answer it. For while Lou would be content just to see Bishop toppled as Prime Minister, he wanted a full-scale invasion. Nothing less than a US battle fleet at sea, planes in the sky and troops in St George`s would satisfy him. As he could hardly explain this, he sought to divert her.

"Look, I thought we all agreed that I`m in charge of strategic planning. OK?"

Lou pursed her lips and softly mouthed OK. She began to walk on and Henry found he was no longer holding her hand. As so often with Lou, the day was not going as he had hoped.

"Right," he said. "Next step. I want you to get writing paper and envelopes from the offices of Bishop and Coard. Can you do that?"

She pulled a pained face.

"Why?"

Henry looked exasperated.

"Lou, are we going to do this properly or not?"

"OK," she said wearily. "I`ll get writing paper and envelopes."

"And I want you to identify two secretaries, one working for Coard and the other for Bishop."

"Why?"

"Trust me."

She raised her eyebrows and gave a tiny snort.

"Where have I heard that before?"

Henry chose to ignore her.

"Just give me some names. Please."

Lou thought for a while.

"Well, there`s Mary…And there`s Joyce."

Mary was in her early forties, a round and jolly lady whose official job was to work for Prime Minister Bishop. Initially, she had been employed as a typist but was so slow that she had been switched to take over responsibility for delivering mail and making coffee, not just for Bishop but for other Ministers, including Finance Minister Coard. She enjoyed going into Bishop`s office best of all. He always had a smile and a friendly word or two. She liked Coard least of all. He was always grim to the point of rudeness.

Joyce was in her early twenties, petite and pretty with a sparky personality. She worked as a secretary exclusively for Finance Minister Coard. In fact, she had never worked for anyone apart from Coard. She therefore didn`t appreciate just how mean a boss he was. Just married, Joyce`s new husband was the envy of many men in the building.

Henry heard all this office chatter as Lou and he walked back towards St George`s but he cared nothing for what she said. Instead, he was wondering where on the island he could buy a second hand typewriter. After Lou pecked him on the cheek and said she must rush back to her step-mother, he strolled in the back streets of the town until he located an ancient portable Olivetti in a junk store.

After Lou slipped him the notepaper and envelopes on a beach walk, he typed two letters, put them in the envelopes and went out for a jog. As he passed the post box, he slowed and dropped the envelopes through the slot before accelerating away towards the beach.

Some days later, he and Lou met again for an update. Lou walked at the water`s edge, letting the warm foam tickle between her bare toes. Henry interrupted her reverie. He outlined more bogus intelligence he wanted her to send to the CIA. He had noticed in the harbour a

Cuban ship, the Vietnam Heroica. This had set his imagination racing.

Forced once more to stop concentrating on the delicious sensation of cool water on her toes, Lou asked what he had done with the official notepaper. Henry gave a curt, formal reply that made Lou think he was patronising her.

"It`s a well-established rule in the civil service," he said, "that people need to know only what they need to know."

Lou reacted furiously. Maybe it was the tension she was under.

"I`ll tell you what I need to know! I damned well need to know what you did with the notepaper! Otherwise, you and your CIA plan can go hang!"

Henry was aghast at her outburst and turned round hurriedly to check that no-one could overhear them.

"OK! OK! Just keep your voice down and I`ll tell you. Well, there`s Mary and she works for Bishop." Lou nodded. "Well, to all intents and purposes, she has just written to Coard telling him that Bishop is organising with the army to oust him and put him in jail." He saw the incredulity growing on her face and carried on. Speaking rapidly so that there was no space for her protests, he added: "And Joyce works for Coard and she`s written to Bishop telling him Coard is organising the army to oust him."

Lou had stopped on the wet sand. Henry decided it was best to behave as normal. He walked on as all the anger that had been building in Lou burst forth.

Her first shoe hit him in the back. The second caught him on the head, the heel scoring a wound in his scalp. He put his hand to his head and felt blood. Lou saw the red smudge on his palm but didn`t care. In anger, she stamped the sand with a bare foot.

"You did what? Those are my friends! Anything could happen to them! What the Hell do you think you are doing?"

Henry found his handkerchief and pressed it to his head.

"Honestly, Lou. Don`t be silly. They`ll be fine."

"Fine? They could be sacked! For pity`s sake, this is a military government. They could be shot!"

Henry waved his bloody handkerchief dismissively.

"They`ll be all right. You see."

"Henry, this is not Britain. It`s Grenada."

Henry laughed.

"Politicians are the same the world over. I guarantee you that I know how they`ll react. I know what interests politicians, what motivates politicians. Your friends will be OK."

Henry was talking to her back. She was stalking down the beach, back to St George`s. She turned once to shout at him.

"They`d better be OK, Henry Turville. Or you, me and this whole exercise is over."

He ran after her.

"It will be all right. I promise. Really!"

They walked on in silence. Eventually, she stopped.

"Let me have a look at your head." She pulled his matted hair aside. "You`ll live."

While Lou agonised in the Government`s economics section over the safety of Mary and Joyce, the two envelopes worked their way through the building to Bishop and Coard.

In his office, Coard despatched his correspondence with his usual brisk efficiency. In the bottom of his mail tray, he found an envelope marked "Private and Confidential: For the personal attention of Mr Coard." His brow furrowed as he opened it and quickly read the brief letter inside.

"Jesus!" He snapped sharply at his secretary and told her to get out of his office, picked up the phone on his desk and dialled a number. "We gotta meet fast. Bishop is trying to organise the army against me."

In the Prime Minister`s office, Bishop`s smile faded as he opened his letter marked "Private and Confidential: For the personal attention of Mr Bishop." He pulled out his red handkerchief and mopped his brow as he read it. As Mary walked in with his coffee and expected the usual cheery greeting, she was curtly told to wait outside. Then Bishop picked up his phone and whispered into the mouthpiece.

"We gotta meet. Coard`s organising the army against me."

Out in the corridor, Mary felt deeply troubled. Bishop had never acted like that before – throwing her out of the room with the tray and coffee pot still in her hands. She shook her head. Coard was usually the rude one.

Outside the door marked `Bernard Coard, Finance Minister`, Mary knocked and then entered with her tray.

Coard`s eyes opened wide when he saw her.

"Mary!" he said with a big smile. "Well, if it isn`t loyal, reliable Mary!" She looked round to make sure no other Mary was behind her and then set the tray on his desk. Coard stood up. "That was wonderful." He beamed again.

Mary looked at the coffee tray. It was just the same as she always brought in at this time of the morning. There weren`t even any biscuits. The revolutionary government had banned biscuits as too bourgeoise. She thought it best to humour him.

"That`s OK Mr Coard. It`s the very least I can do to help a man like you!"

Coard had stood up from his desk and was edging close to her. She felt very uncomfortable. "I would very much appreciate it if you could keep on helping me like that. Could you?"

Mary decided it was time to get out of this lunatic`s office. Clearly the man had been working too hard.

"Sure thing, Mr Coard. Any time you like. It`s nothing at all to me."

"Promise?"

"Oh yes! Oh yes!" She hurried from his room, eyes widening. Outside,

she stood shaking her head. "Dey can be nice to you for years and then turn on you. And then the one who ignores you for years is suddenly all over you!"

She walked off, shaking her head.

That night in the Prime Minister`s Residence, Bishop met with his closest allies. He looked around the table and calculated that Coard probably had more supporters than he did and was probably the favourite to win the support of the army. He tried to be philosophic but the sweat soaking his shirt betrayed his fear.

"We can`t do any more. It`ll all be down to the army."

One voice at the table tried to sound positive.

"We need more intelligence on what Coard is doing. Names. Details. Can`t you get more? What about this source you`ve got?"

Bishop nodded his head slowly and decisively..

"I`ve thought of a way to handle that."

What Bishop`s plans involved was sending a letter to Joyce, his loyal confidante. The trouble was, thought the Prime Minister as he again mopped his brow with his handkerchief, that the island`s postal service was becoming so unreliable. So much mail was going astray. Only that morning he had ordered an inquiry.

Chapter 27

Marcus Mariowitz hung his jacket on the back of his chair and surveyed his new office. Then he walked round it with big strides. He smiled the proud smile of a man who knew that everything had increased proportionately in size in his new room. The book case was bigger. His desk and chair were bigger. The shredder was bigger. Even the bin. He made a mental note to ask Dolores to buy bigger bananas.

The books from his old office looked lost in the new bookcase. He walked to his desk and buzzed Ann-Marie, who had moved with him as his secretary. She answered with a husky whisper.

"Yes, Marcus."

She had started calling him by his first name when his promotion came through. He didn`t mind but he wished that she hadn`t used his first name when speaking over the phone to Dolores. It made Dolores overwrought.

"Ann-Marie, I need more books."

"Which books in particular Marcus?"

"Heck, I don`t know. Books. Get me books. Just fill the spaces."

"Sure thing, Marcus."

He walked over to the window. Its long, heavy curtain was designed to prevent terrorist bombs sending shards of glass into his room. It made him feel good. You had to be pretty damned important in the Agency to be worth that sort of investment. He tossed the banana skin towards the bin and it fell short. He walked to the bin, picked up the skin and tried again. It fell short. He shook his head. He was missing because the required shot had lengthened. This was serious. It could take hours of practice to perfect the new throw.

This bigger desk had two telephones. One was for all the Agency`s calls. The other was for Dolores. She was becoming a serious problem. Here he was, talked about as the most likely successor to Richard Hurlingham, and his prospects were being hindered by a neurotic wife with an insane jealousy of his secretary. He just hoped that the therapist could turn her round.

The second telephone, allowing Dolores to phone him direct without having to speak to Ann-Marie, had been his idea. Hurlingham had been cautious at first, pulling thoughtfully at the end of his long chin.

"I like a man who thinks laterally, Marcus, but a second phone is strictly off limits. However, as we value you, I`ll see what I can do."

Apparently the request had gone all the way to the top of the Agency. Then the new phone had been installed. It was red. And it began to ring. Mariowitz looked at his watch. It was 9am and Dolores should be with her therapist. He picked up the red phone. Dolores was with her therapist and the therapist had thought it would be a good idea if she went right ahead and phoned him.

"I`m not paying the danged therapist all that money just to waste my time. Waste his!"

Mariowitz slammed down the phone and checked his computer. He saw that Beautiful Lady had called in again and settled down to read the report. Beautiful Lady never disappointed. A year ago, Beautiful Lady had been nicknamed Dunce on his computer. It was as if overnight, Dunce had become a model agent. He felt – though he did not actually rationalise it this way – that Beautiful Lady was giving him everything he wanted, almost as if she could read his mind. Not, of course, that Beautiful

Lady knew who he was. No more than he knew her real identity. He shook his head in admiration and turned his brain to assessing the new intelligence on the suspect ship Vietnam Heroica, now moored in St George`s harbour. He whistled gently and on his screen called up the slides that he was presenting to that afternoon`s meeting. Urgent revision was needed.

In the afternoon Hurlingham stopped by Mariowitz`s new office on his way to the conference room.

"Everything OK for you here?" he asked, looking round the new room.

"Fine."

Hurlingham briefly browsed the big bookcase, filled by Ann-Marie while Mariowitz was out at a celebratory, expenses-paid lunch in one of Washington`s finest restaurants.

"I always say," said Hurlingham, "that I can judge a man by his books." He quickly absorbed the titles. "That`s what I like to see – a man with an eclectic literary taste."

Mariowitz made a mental note to look up "eclectic" in the dictionary.

Hurlingham said he was stepping out for the john and Mariowitz checked out the bookcase. On the shelves he saw Stendhal`s Scarlet and Black, A Plain Man`s Guide to Sciatica, Homer`s Ilyiad, Cooking With Aubergines, Plato`s The Symposium, A Guide To Gardening American-style, Sophocles` Theban Plays and Everything You Ever Wanted To Know About Warts.

Mariowitz buzzed Ann-Marie.

"Are you literary or what?"

There was a pause.

"Am I literally what, Marcus?"

"The books. The books."

"A job lot, Marcus. All within budget."

Hurlingham put his head round the door and Mariowitz stepped out, tightening his new tie. It was a birthday present from Dolores – yellow bananas on an unripened green background. He loved it. Side by side, Hurlingham and Mariowitz strolled down the corridor to the conference room.

On the dais, flanked by Hurlingham, Mariowitz switched on the projector with confidence. No-one would dare sabotage it now.

Hurlingham called for silence and said he would make a short address.

"We meet at short notice for what will be a short meeting. But no less important for that. You`re all aware of Mariowitz`s intelligence on Grenada. And his track, which is very good."

He put his hand on Marcus` shoulder, smiled and handed the meeting over to him.

On the screen appeared

GRENADIAN GOVERNMENT
ABOUT TO SPLINTER

A buzz of excitement went round the room and Mariowitz saw the Valkyries go into a huddle as he began.

"The Marxist-Leninist Government under Bishop is imploding. There are two factions. One is led by Bishop." A picture of Bishop beaming appeared on the screen.

"The other by Coard." A picture of a particularly evil-looking Coard came onto the screen. Mariowitz left it there for a few moments. He had spent a lot of time in the picture library securing a picture of Coard looking as nasty as that. "Each is now preparing to take up arms against the other – inevitably through the army." A picture of Hudson Austin, General of the Armed Forces, appeared. His arms were crossed and he appeared to be sulking. "The time available before the coup is difficult to judge. It could be set off by just one angry word. The best judgement is that we are talking at most of two weeks. It could be much less. And violence could be widespread. Bishop has significant support among the people. They could turn out to support him. And if the army`s on

Coard`s side, then it could be army versus the people. In short, we could have a bloody civil war on our doorstep." In quick succession, Mariowitz flashed up pictures of pro-Bishop Ministers and pro-Coard Ministers. "I can go into details of individual ministers if you want."

Hurlingham cleared his throat and intervened.

"I don`t think that will be necessary at this stage."

"There doesn`t seem to be a Minister in the Cabinet who isn`t prepared to see civil war. It`s all got that intense. It`s very personal. Finally…" Mariowitz flashed up the final slide.

SOVIETS PREPARE TO STEP IN

"At the highest level, we know that the Government expects the Soviets and their allies to move in as soon as any coup there is over. The Commies will offer further support and back-up for whoever wins. In other words, they are in a unique position to strengthen their hold in our back yard."

Hurlingham stepped forward again.

"That`s very good, Marcus. Questions?"

The gum-chewer spoke first. He still hadn`t forgotten or forgiven being made to go out and wheel in the replacement projector.

"Who`s going to win, Marcus? From the pictures, there seemed to be a lot more ministers supporting Coard than Bishop. Is that the score? "

"It`s down to the army. Basically, it`s down to which way General Hudson Austin swings."

A Valkyrie showed her teeth. It was meant to be a smile but the plastic surgeon had left no slack in the skin round her lips. She began to speak without apparent lip movement.

"How the heck has this suddenly blown up out of nowhere? There hasn`t been a hint of this in intelligence until now."

Mariowitz wasn`t rattled now. He knew his support went up even higher than Hurlingham.

"That`s easy to answer. The Coard faction has been

organising in great secrecy. Then Bishop got wind of what was going on."

The gum chewer came back.

"What verification is there for this? How many sources have verified it?"

Mariowitz shifted from one foot to another.

"Good agents are thin on the ground in Grenada. It`s a small place. There are agents who report sightings. All I can say is that this agent knows what is going on."

"In the government you mean?"

"I would categorise the source as A1. Inside track and with a proven record. The agent who alerted us to the plans for the new airport to facilitate the landing of Soviet aircraft."

Hurlingham began to close the meeting down.

"Clearly the Soviets and their pals are positioning themselves to move in if – or when – the Grenada Government collapses in crisis. I am recommending up the Agency that the National Security Council considers taking appropriate action."

The room echoed its approval.

Mariowitz moved towards the projector again.

"There`s just one more piece of intelligence…"

Hurlingham turned in surprise. Everybody making for the door simultaneously stopped. This was unheard of. Mariowitz had been keeping a piece of intelligence back from Hurlingham. The Valkyries went into a new huddle, betting on whether Mariowitz would live or die. It was a brave underling who sprang a surprise on Hurlingham.

Mariowitz smiled confidently and flashed onto the screen a picture of a cargo ship. "Just before the meeting started, I received a piece of intelligence about the Vietnam Heroica – a Cuban ship moored apparently harmlessly in the harbour at St George`s. What we now know is that the ship is unloading under cover of darkness. I cannot give a confirmed intelligence report yet on what is being unloaded. However, the unconfirmed intelligence is one word."

On the screen he flashed one word:

MISSILES

Hurlingham blew air out of his mouth in a long, low whistle.

"Well, thank you Marcus. I believe that confirms our analysis. We were right to agree that we must ratchet this up to the National Security Council."

Outside the room, Hurlingham looked quizzically at Mariowitz, who just shrugged.

"It came through while you were in the john."

Mariowitz ambled off down the corridor. The gum chewer strolled alongside Hurlingham and nodded to Mariowitz surrounded by admirers.

"Even the Valkyries want to know him these days."

Hurlingham looked puzzled.

"Valkyries?"

"Sure. Valkyries. Witches. Harridans. It`s what the whole floor calls them."

The gum chewer thrust his hands in his pockets and sloped off. What an intelligence agency – even the boss didn`t know what was happening on his own floor.

Hurlingham stood, thoughtful, as the Valkyries accompanied Mariowitz back to his room. Hurlingham had read English at college and knew that Valkyries weren`t witches. Slowly, it came back to him over the 30 years since college. Valkyrie – each of the Norse God Odin`s twelve handmaidens who selected heroes destined to be slain in battle. He smiled and walked towards his office. Mariowitz`s peer group had certainly got that wrong. Mariowitz was the Agency`s next star. He wasn`t going to crash and burn.

Chapter 28

In her office in the economics section, Lou agonised over Mary and Joyce. In the corridors, she looked anxiously at their faces for a hint of trouble but saw nothing unusual. What she did sense throughout the whole building was an increase in tension. And then the gossip began to spread. Bishop and Coard, never friends, were said to be at each other`s throats. Or they would be if anyone could persuade the two men to meet each other.

Lou usually lunched with Jackie, her best friend who worked in the section to promote tourism..

Over salad in the canteen, Jackie whispered to Lou.

"Tourism`s getting worse. Everyone here blames me! As if it`s got nothing to do with Communism!" Jackie was always bluntly honest with Lou about everything, including boyfriends. She put down he knife and fork and leant forward. "I keep meaning to ask – who`s that man I`ve seen you with at the café along the road?"

Lou was dismissive.

"Oh, just someone who lectured when I was in London. He`s on an extended holiday here."

"Just wondered if everything was OK with Winston, that`s all."

Lou gave a small laugh.

"Oh no! Everything`s fine."

Lou envied her friend the openness that was denied her by her liaison with the CIA. She hated having to be furtive, and was becoming increasingly uneasy not just with Henry Turville`s secret plans but also Winston`s willingness not only to collaborate but to use her in the process.

That afternoon, Henry sat at the café table and watched Lou leave work without looking in his direction. Most evenings, on noticing him, she would casually walk over to say hello. Sometimes – oh joy! – she would stop for a drink. Since she had hurled her shoes at him on the beach, she had two afternoons in succession looked straight ahead and stepped out fast towards the town without acknowledging him.

Henry could not stop himself following her. Lou guessed that he would try. She deliberately tried to throw him off. She slipped up side roads, twisted back and eventually took a taxi to Dr Roy`s apartment.

On those two afternoons, Henry scratched under his cap where the wound was healing and watched the taxi drive off with Lou. This wasn`t London. And even if another taxi had been to hand – and she made certain there was not another in sight – he couldn`t jump in and shout "Follow that taxi!" The driver would have thought he`d had too much rum punch or sun.

Dr Roy was cooking callallo quiche when Lou got back. He had a light touch with a quiche and was assembling a mixed salad as she put her head round the kitchen door to greet him.

While she changed into a skimpy black top and white slacks, he poured her a glass of wine and a Carib beer for himself. He leant against the door so as to keep an eye on supper while they talked.

"So," he asked, "what goes on in the Government? Are Joyce and Mary still OK?" Lou nodded as she combed out her hair. "Well, that makes it four days now since Bishop and Coard got their letters and old Henry seems to be right. Bishop and Coard are too busy fighting each other to remember how it all even started!"

In bed that night, Dr Roy smoothed Lou`s hair with

one hand and massaged her back with the other. She purred like a cat.

"It`s got nothing to do with me," she heard him say, "but I reckon old Henry knows the minds of politicians. Not that I get to see too many politicians at the Crazy House."

Lou smiled into the pillow. She recognised his tactics. First he would get her really relaxed and then drop an innocent-sounding suggestion.

"Perhaps you ought to start being a little nicer to Henry, honey…"

Winston was manipulating her again.

"OK," she said, "If he`s at the café tomorrow, I might give him a wave."

"That`s right baby," said the psychiatrist as he moved his hands father and wider. "Let`s just keep Henry simmering. You know it makes sense."

Next evening, Lou strolled over to Henry`s table determined to be nothing more than polite. His cap was by his side and as he turned to the waiter to order her wine, she saw the scab in his hair where her shoe met the target. He asked if her two friends were all right.

"Well, for the moment they do appear to be."

"If anything was going to happen, it would have done so by now." He nodded to the building she had just left. "I need to know what`s going on there. Can we take a walk after our drink?"

She nodded.

Along the beach, he recalled that she wanted to take him on a tour of the island. Lou sighed and suggested the next Saturday.

"I`ll hire a car," he said, "and pick you up at Maisy`s."

She waved the idea aside and said she would drive.

"It`ll be easier for me. I know the roads."

It was a lame excuse. The island was tiny even by Caribbean standards. One road encircled the island and three more bisected it. Two minutes with a road map of the island and a driver scarcely needed ever to look at it again.

Henry was boyishly enthusiastic about their trip and Lou found it difficult not to feel awed that such a small gesture by her could generate such pleasure in him. She even felt the tiniest bit fond of him – the way she felt about her nephew. He was just 12.

A couple of nights later, in bed with Dr Roy, Lou said that she had been doing some thinking.

"Being with Henry reminds me of my feelings for Bishop."

Dr Roy put down his book.

"Oh dear. Poor, poor Henry."

Lou sat up and shook her head. She explained how in the three years she had worked for the Bishop Government, she had done everything possible to avoid meeting Bishop himself. She made excuses not to go to Government receptions if she thought he would be there. If she passed him in a corridor, she always dropped her eyes.

"It`s always been deliberate, of course," she explained. "Just about everybody on the island thinks he`s such a fun man, yet I don`t want to see that because I fear that if I get to know him a bit, I might get to like him too. And that would make it harder for me to hate him."

"So what are you saying - that all this getting-to-know-Henry has changed the way you feel about him?" He turned to her and grinned. "You ain`t got the hots for old Henry, have you?" He expected her to punch him or throw a pillow. She normally did when he teased her. Instead, she told him to be serious.

"The point I`m making is that back in London, Henry simply gave me the creeps. And I`m not saying that he doesn`t now. But I have got to know a lot about him and, well, it`s hard to be so antagonistic. So what I`m wondering is this: would I hate Bishop so much if I had to get to know him? Like I now know Henry?"

Dr Roy moved his weight onto an elbow and looked at her.

"Well, I can`t say for sure. I would say, though, that there is a good chance that the more you knew him, the more your hatred would diminish. I mean, that`s why societies put their leaders together in the same room and make them talk to each other. The better they know each other, the less likely it is that they will want to fight each other."

Lou paused for scarcely a second before coming back at him.

"But Bishop and Coard aren`t just in the same room – they`re in the same Government, which makes them pretty close – and yet they`re about to start fighting each other!"

Dr Roy was patient.

"That`s about something entirely different. Bishop and Coard`s conflict has been created by what they perceive – wrongly, as it happens – to be a breach of trust and now they are in a contest for survival. But you are right in your general point about getting to know people." He turned on his side and began caressing her thigh. "My own view is that we should all be much nicer to each other. All this talk is just too heavy for folks in bed. And by the way, this being Friday evening, what shall we do tomorrow?"

Lou had forgotten.

"Oh, I told Henry I`d take him sightseeing round the island."

Dr Roy looked up with his most appealing expression.

"Am I coming too?"

She kissed him quickly on the nose.

"I think he trusts me not to."

When Lou drew up outside Henry`s apartment in her four-wheel drive jeep, he had been ready and waiting for a full half hour. She offered her cheek for him to kiss and headed north along the west coast with its cliffs and pretty bays. Fishing villages clung to the hillsides and Lou pointed out men on the beach pulling nets from the sea.

Farther north, past Halifax Harbour, she took the jeep off the road and onto a steep track that took them past groves of nutmeg trees and then to Concord Falls. They stood, watching the water crashing, and Lou shouted that it was nearly an hour`s walk up to the even bigger falls.

"Shall we leave that for another day?"

Henry agreed and they went on in the jeep, climbing higher and winding high above the coast with its tiny inlets and secret coves. The peaks, which from the air had looked squat, now rose majestically, their flanks swathed in heavy green vegetation. Streams and torrents fell or dripped down their sides. Massive bamboos arched over the road.

Skirting the peak of Mount Nesbit, they headed on past Gouyave and Victoria before entering the intensely cultivated spice-growing area. At Sauteur, Lou suggested a stop for lunch: fresh lobster. Henry wanted to pay but Lou insisted that it was her treat. As she pushed back her plate and Henry sipped a coconut juice, she suggested moving on to Caribs` Leap.

"Ah," said Henry, shifting a little in his chair. "That`s where the Caribs..." His voice trailed off and he looked into the distance over the sea.

Lou thought he looked uncomfortable and finished his sentence.

"It`s where the Caribs – the original inhabitants of the island – all leapt to their death over the cliff rather than submit to the French." She shrugged. "So the French brought slaves in to work for them."

Henry turned back from the sea.

"To be blunt, I`d rather not go there. You see, I`ve always found places of mass death so mournful. I went to Auschwitz once." He shook his head. "And to Glencoe in Scotland where the Macdonald clan were massacred. And then there was…"

She put her hand on his.

"Henry, it`s OK. I understand."

Lou smiled gently and thought what an extraordinary man he was. She had never guessed that there was such hidden sensitivity. So they drove past Caribs` Leap and stopped instead at the nearby St David`s Bay where they walked before their journey turned south past Levera Pond, a crater lake with mangrove swamps. Lou pulled the jeep to a halt and said they had a choice: continue back to St George`s along the east coast or strike inland and through the Grand Etang forest before dropping down to St George`s.

"It`s your call," he said.

She began explaining the advantages and disadvantages but he sat back in the seat and insisted that she choose.

"OK. We`ll go to Grand Etang and I`ll show you some of my favourite places on the island." She grinned. "In fact, if you`re very good, I`ll show you my favourite place on the whole island!"

Skirting round the airport and Grenville, the island`s second biggest town, Lou headed towards Mount St Catherine, an extinct volcano and the island`s highest peak. The winding road ran up from the Great River Valley past villages with names left over from the island`s French domination, and through forests of ferns and plantations of nutmegs, cacao and bananas. She pulled off the road and stopped by Grand Etang, a lake filling an old volcanic crater in the lee of Mount Qua Qua. They got out to get a better view.

"I used to come here after daddy was killed. To do my thinking. So it`s a bit special for me."

Henry gave her hand a quick, sympathetic squeeze.

Back in the jeep, she seemed brighter.

"Now," she announced, "it`s on to Grand Etang itself. If you sit quiet and are lucky, you might see monkeys. Or mocking birds. Or bats and armadillos. Or piping frogs."

While Henry professed himself to be interested in

seeing all the animals, reptiles and birds, he was also interested in Lou`s jeep.

"Some motor, this. Courtesy of your CIA work, I suppose?"

Lou shook her head.

"I inherited when daddy was killed but Maisy was in charge of all the money until I was 21. But my inheritance wasn`t much – not by English standards – though here…" Henry thought that Maisy seemed still to be in charge but he said nothing. Lou shot him a glance and bit her lower lip. "I`ve got a confession to make. The CIA money. It`s just been tripled. I noticed on my bank statement." She smiled. "I suppose I have you to thank for that."

Henry laughed. He found it funny to imagine Mariowitz drooling over Lou`s reports and instructing the accounts department to increase her pay. Lou became serious. "Henry, isn`t this all getting a bit out of hand? The CIA stuff, I mean?"

He shook his head vigorously.

"No. No. Anyway, we`re nearly there. Almost at the end of the campaign. You'll see."

He looked at his watch and leaned forward to adjust the jeep`s electronic clock on the dashboard.

"I want all this to be over, Henry."

He nodded, put out his hand and rested it, as if to comfort her, on the smooth flesh just below her white shorts. Lou felt uncomfortable with his hand on her thigh but the jeep was bumping as they went along a track and she needed both hands on the wheel.

She pulled the jeep over. Lou led the way to a clearing and pointed to two large, smooth stones side by side. Henry guessed she had been there before. They sat down.

"I must admit," said Henry, "it is pretty spectacular out here. I came to the island when I worked at the British Embassy in Washington. But we never got out to see some of the places I`ve seen today."

"You and your wife?"

Henry replied brusquely.

"That`s over."

"Are you getting divorced?"

He shrugged.

"All in good time. I've more important things to think about."

Lou told him to hush and pointed out a monkey. Later, she whispered to him.

"This is my favourite place on the island. It`s real jungle but without anything that can hurt you. It`s a jungle where only people can hurt you."

He whispered.

"And talking of hurting people…I take it that Mary and Joyce are still OK?" She nodded. "So I`m forgiven?

Lou pecked him quickly on the cheek.

"I guess so. As long as they stay safe."

She stood up and beckoned him to follow her into the forest. They stood listening to the mocking birds. She pointed to an armadillo.

On the way back to the jeep, Henry said there was something he had been wanting to ask her.

"Go on."

"Why do you visit Winston`s psychiatric practice?"

She frowned.

"You`ve been following me again. Why all this following, Henry? I know you`re doing it and it doesn`t help!"

Henry looked at his wrist watch again.

"You`ve said yourself, Grenada is a small place. People just come across these things."

Sitting on a fallen log not far from the jeep, she gave him her explanation.

"I told you that after daddy was killed, I came out here a lot. After he died, I was very mixed up. Very depressed. Maisy persuaded me to see Dr Roy. He`s a very good psychiatrist. He was…is…very good for me."

Henry sat down beside her.

"I see." He was still for a moment. "There`s something I`ve been wanting us to talk about."

If Henry had been looking at Lou instead of pointedly looking away at the forest, he would have seen her shoulders sag. She knew what he wanted to say.

"About us," he said. Lou clenched her fists. Exactly what she had expected was happening. Henry was looking at her now in what he hoped was a serious yet romantic pose. "I think you know how I feel about you." Lou, in despair, let out a great sigh and stared ahead. He again put his hand on her thigh. He was beginning to spoil a perfectly good afternoon. Without looking down, she removed his hand. He spoke sorrowfully and she wondered why she kept thinking of him as if he were a child. "I`m sorry."

She decided to be bright.

"Henry, I`ve had a wonderful day. Really. I`ve enjoyed it. Can`t we just leave it at that?" He looked dolefully at her and picked at the bark on the log with his fingers. "Henry, let`s not spoil things between us. Please!"

"But I love you."

"Oh Henry, you don`t!" He looked up in surprise at the challenge. "I like you Henry, I really do. I`ve grown to like you." He believed implicitly that her liking would gradually grow into love but had no time to say so because she had raced on. "And I know that you like me. Like me a lot. Probably quite a lot even. But Henry, you don`t *love* me." She was speaking confidently now because she felt she knew what love was. She felt it for Winston Roy. "What you feel for me is infatuation." She stared at him as he slumped. He let out a small moan, shook his head and took her hand.

"Lou. It`s love. Real love. Tell me that with time you could love me. To live without hope would be life not worth living."

She tried to say the words that would dash his hopes but they would not come out. Instead, she stared speechless at him. He looked so crushed. She felt many things for him as she observed his reactions. Pity. Affection. Care. But not love. She turned merely to smile kindly at him and he kissed her full on the lips. She didn`t respond. She just sat like a rag doll. Eventually, he took his lips from hers.

"Oh Henry! I do wish you hadn`t done that."

She stood up briskly and took his hand, like a nanny leading a small child away from the cookie jar. How could she tell him that what she felt for him was not love but more a mothering instinct?

In the jeep on the way back he sat in silence. As the jeep left the forest, he turned and smiled.

"There`s hope, Lou. Not for nothing are you my Lou Hope."

Then he swiftly moved to small-talk, chatting about the armadillo, their lunch and the lakes. He suggested supper. She shook her head and he showed his disappointment.

"What about tomorrow?"

"Sorry, there's Maisy…."

The jeep pulled to a halt outside Henry`s apartment.

She turned her cheek. He took her head in his hands and she felt his strength. He kissed her again full on the lips. She struggled and he released his grip.

She drove off cursing herself. For being so weak with Henry. For being manipulated by Winston. For hating Bishop.

Chapter 29

After the adventures of the day, Henry fell into an anti-climatic depression. He mooched around his apartment yearning for an extra strong mint. They had such delightfully soothing qualities. He was surprised that no mint supplies had reached him from his sister. He pulled a postcard from the sideboard drawer and wrote her a quick reminder.

Henry made himself some toast, opened a beer, tried and failed to begin his biography of Bismarck, threw the book on the floor and followed it. On the carpet he began his exercise regime, counting and feeling the pain until he forgot about Lou.

He willed himself to change into his jogging gear and set off along the beach. At the far end of the sand, exhausted and able to run no farther, he threw himself in the shallow warm water and lay back looking at the sky.

As he jogged back to his apartment, the picanninnies came after him again. This time they were shouting and trying to race him. Henry strode out, enjoying the challenge, and left them behind but not until St George`s was in sight. He had to turn and walk back to his apartment, exhausted but victorious.

It was the prelude to a night of wakefulness when his brain raced and jeered at the mental tricks he sometimes played to make himself sleep. He tried making his mind a complete blank. He played his numbers and letters games, taking the dates of famous English battles and reducing them to letters of the alphabet. So, the date of the Battle of Trafalgar was 20 10 1805. The individual numbers added together made 17. One and seven equalled eight. H was the eighth letter of the alphabet. He even remembered all the letters that he created from adding together all the dates of all the battles he could recall and tried turning them into words. He got to A HIGH BED, A BIG CAB, but still had one F and a G left over. And he was still wide awake.

He gave up trying to blot Lou from his mind and accepted that he would not sleep. How could he when he was churning with resentment and perplexity because she simply would not accept that he truly loved her? Once more the stew in his brain bubbled and he convinced himself that if only she would believe in his love, she would be compelled to reciprocate it. Such an overwhelming love as he felt was incapable of being ignored rejected. The first rays of dawn threw shadows in his bedroom. It lighted the typewriter in the corner of the room. He thought of a letter. A love letter to Lou. Of course, a love letter could not be typed. He turned on the light, found paper and pen and began to draft his letter.

He cudgelled his brain for the poetry he could remember, made notes and by the time it was fully light he was sitting at the small dining room table finishing the final draft. He re-read it and felt that after reading it, no woman could refuse him. He began by likening Lou`s loveliness and temperate nature to Shakespeare`s summer`s day. He gently moved her, courtesy of W B Yeats, through the coming years to when she was old and grey and full of sleep.

He concluded, via Shelley, by likening his love for her to the vast, carved stone of Ozymandias, king of kings, stretching immortally into the future. By now he felt ownership of the poets` words and so movingly and eloquently did they encompass the width, breadth and depth of his love that he found himself sobbing soundlessly. For a moment, he toyed with creating a fourth dimension to describe his unique love but decided that the single tear drop that had fallen on the paper should suffice.

He went back to bed but still couldn`t sleep. In the adjoining apartment, a typewriter had started to rattle and upstairs a German couple had returned from some all-night foray and were shouting drunkenly at one another. It was past 6am when he eventually fell asleep. He woke feeling so refreshed that he thought it must be at least mid-morning. He looked at his watch and found it was just turned 7am. He saw his letter for Lou lying on the bedside cabinet and the memory of his night`s work sent him leaping lightly from the bed and into the shower. He felt a compulsion to get the letter into Lou`s hands as soon as possible. The sooner she read it the sooner she would understand. Of course, he did not know where Lou lived. Just somewhere in the island`s hinterland. All he knew was that the Hope plantation grew bananas. He briefly considered handing his letter in at the Government building but rejected the idea. He wanted to see for himself the place where she would read it.

Dr Roy would know where Lou lived! He had no phone number for him but knew his private consultancy address. After quickly swallowing black coffee and toast, he walked into the lounge and with one move swept off the sideboard his biography of Lord Randolph Churchill and smashed it down decisively on the cockroach.

Much cheered, he set out on his jog to Dr Roy`s door. Along the way, he passed the postman, who pulled himself sharply out of Henry`s way and hurried into the foyer of a small block of apartments. If Henry had passed closer to the postman or had stopped to exchange pleasantries, he might have noticed the hint of peppermint on his breath. The postman had recently acquired the habit of popping into his mouth an extra strong mint.

At the door of Dr Roy`s consultancy, he banged loudly. When there was no reply, he banged on neighbouring doors. A stark naked man dripping with water opened his door and continued towelling himself down while Henry explained his problem. The man found it very funny. Apparently Dr Roy was hardly ever at his consulting rooms. Business was bad. But he told Henry were Dr Roy lived.

When Henry knocked at Dr Roy`s door, Lou had already left for work. Dr Roy had no appointements until the afternoon.

"Sorry to trouble you," said Henry, "but I need to know Lou`s address."

"Ah," said Dr Roy. He was trying to remember if anything of Lou`s was on show in the living room or kitchen but couldn`t be sure. He pulled his dressing gown more tightly around him. "I`d ask you in but I`m in a hurry." Henry looked on expectantly. "Ah. Lou`s address. You mean out at the plantation house." Henry nodded. "Well, let me see. Are you going to put something in the post or do you want to go there?"

"Go there."

"Right, then what you need is not so much an address as directions."

He then gave Henry detailed directions that were correct in every respect except that instead of turning right off the road to Grenville, Dr Roy told him to turn left.

Henry muttered his thanks and went off to hire a car. On the way, he remembered Maisy, clearly unwell and possibly even confined to her bed in the plantation house. He bought a big bunch of flowers.

Dr Roy phoned Lou at the office.

"Henry`s been here, honey. Wants your address at the plantation house. Driving out there right now, I guess, with something for you. Letter maybe."

Lou snapped at Winston as if it was his fault.

"I knew something like this would happen. You and

your stupid ideas."

She dialled Maisy`s number.

"Look darling, I know this sounds silly but a man called Henry Turville is likely to turn up. He thinks I still live there and will probably want to leave something for me."

"Are you saying you want me to tell him you live here if he asks?"

"Well, yes."

Maisy replied quietly but with a firmness that Lou remembered from her childhood.

"I`m not lying for you, Lou."

It was bad enough that Lou was having an affair with that Dr Roy, nice enough young man though he seemed. But if Lou was in a tangle with another man, she had no intention of getting involved.

Lou appealed to her to at least *try* to help.

"I`m not making any promises."

Henry followed Dr Roy`s directions, driving out past the Annandale Falls and through the Grand Etang forest and then forking left. After that, the directions ceased to make any sense. He tried a worker in the field but the local patois defeated him and the two merely stared helplessly at each other. Eventually, he stopped at a small house that looked to be the sort of place in which Lou and Maisy would live. Certainly the house was in a banana plantation. At the sound of the car, an old man in a battered and dirty straw hat ambled out of a shed and listened to Henry`s problem.

"You mean Lou Hope whose father got killed?"

Henry turned the car round and followed the new directions. As he stopped by the plantation house, the skies turned black. Letter in one hand and flowers in the other, he stood under the porch as the first huge drops of rain fell.

The door opened and Henry said he was looking for Lou Hope`s house. Maisy chose her words carefully because she wasn`t going to lie.

"Can I help?"

Henry assumed that the elderly black woman before him was the maid.

"Perhaps I could speak to Maisy?"

Maisy crossed her arms in front of her and set her face. She`d had this problem before. Strangers seemed to think that she should have the same coffee coloured skin as Lou.

"You`re looking at Maisy!"

By now the darkness of the sky had turned into a cloud burst. Henry handed over his letter and asked Maisy to give it to Lou. He turned to go and noticed the flowers still in his hand. He pushed them at Maisy, who softened. It was a long time since a man had bought her flowers.

"You sure these are for me and not Lou?"

"No. For you. And I`m pleased you are looking so well."

He turned to go and looked for his car. It was just a dim shape behind the sheets of rain. Maisy beckoned him into the hall.

"I wouldn`t put a dog out in that. You`d better come in and wait a while."

Henry accepted a glass of coconut juice. He noticed that every time he tried to speak his hostess moved in sharply with a question.

"Can you tell me about London, Mr Turville? The shops and everything?"

Outside the rain continued to lash down as Maisy inquired about the Tower of London, the Queen, Buckingham Palace, Windsor Castle, Scotland, English weather. Henry found her interest it Britain quite remarkable. She stopped only to produce a cold fish salad for their lunch before launching into more questions – about the British love of dogs, race relations and the Houses of Parliament.

While Henry considered her to have a remarkable appetite for knowledge, he found her unsocialised in that she was incapable of leaving space in the conversation for him to slip in a question. He concluded that he had clearly been mistaken in thinking that Lou`s stepmother was physically ill. Her problem was clearly mental. The poor woman probably suffered from some form of dementia.

Finally, she stopped asking questions and made a statement.

"It seems to have stopped raining."

Henry took the hint, thanked her for the lunch and her time, reminded her to give the letter to Lou and stepped over the puddles to his car. He drove back to his apartment with a headache and the belief that Lou was a saint to go home to that gibbering woman every evening.

Lou phoned Maisy that afternoon to check if Henry had found the house and delivered anything.

"A letter," said Maisy. "He could have used the post."

"Did everything go OK?"

"Very well. He brought me flowers. But if you mean did I lie for you, the answer`s No. But he didn`t get much chance to ask anything."

"What did you think of him."

"Very knowledgeable about his country."

Lou said she would drive over that evening and spend the night at the plantation house.

Over supper that evening, Maisy said that what Lou did with her life was for her to decide. Lou finished the last of the snapper fish and felt she had no choice but to outline her problem.

"Darling, you know what`s wrong. There are two men."

"Well, you just gotta decide which man you love."

"Oh, that`s easy. It`s Winston."

Maisy pushed her plate back and said the problem solved itself.

Lou sat in silence. How could she explain that her own desire for revenge was keeping her in a dishonest and hopeless relationship with Henry?

"When did you last go to mass?"

Lou didn`t answer. She couldn`t remember but felt guilty as Maisy looked at her as if she were still a young girl.

"I`ll come back here on Sunday and we`ll go together."

Maisy brightened. Her faith was so deep and wide that she knew that going to mass would help Lou. At 10 o`clock, when Lou said it was time for her to go to bed, Maisy had still not delivered up the envelope. Lou was forced to ask for it. Maisy pulled open a drawer and handed it over.

"I almost forgot." .

Now that, thought Lou, is at the very least a white lie. She said nothing and hurried into her old bed at the top of the house. Apart from a few adolescent scribblings, this was Lou`s first love letter. She slit it open with the nail file from her bedside table and lay back on the pillow to read it.

She finished and put the letter back in its envelope. As a declaration of love it was elegant and deeply moving. She wondered whether she was right to have challenged the sincerity of his feelings. Did Henry feel more settled now he had put into writing his emotions? For her, the letter had only increased what she came to name her `Turville turmoil.`

Chapter 30

At his desk in his consulting room, Dr Roy opened his accounts book and surveyed the income for the last twelve months. It did not make pleasant reading.

"Down, down, down."

At this rate, expenses would soon be exceeding income and he would be subsidising his private business from his pay for three half days a week at the mental institution and another three at the university. He looked round the dusty room that was long overdue for redecoration and realised that getting rid of it would be more than a business transaction. The room and its couch had a sentimental value for Lou and him. For anniversaries or to make up after tiffs, some couples went to a special restaurant or returned to the place where they met. This was the place to which Lou and Dr Roy returned for The Game.

He slid the accounts book back in his desk drawer and stretched out on his consulting couch. Perhaps old Henry was right and Grenada was just too happy an island for a private psychiatrist to prosper. He closed his eyes and found the couch restful. It underlined the mantra that he was repeating increasingly to himself – regret nothing and stay calm.

Yet he did regret that he had been so complacent during the good times. The cocaine had shipped easily into Grenada and the marijuana just as easily out. Before long, he had been stopping off at other of the Caribbean islands to make drop offs and collections. His associates had set up a consulting room in Florida so that he could justify his trips to and from Florida. He smiled at the memory of that consulting room.

It was real smart – a brand new couch, thick carpets, bookcases and a shared receptionist perched at her desk along the marble entrance hall. At the front door, the brass plate with his name on it was polished every morning.

Instead of using the Florida office to build a new list of clients, Dr Roy had simply used it as a front for his drugs running. On the couch, he groaned slightly at the thought of the clients he might now have in Florida. The state was stuffed with folks who wanted to pay someone to listen to their problems.

He was finding it hard to stay calm. It was not just worry over money, but Lou too. He had never chased a woman in his life and believed that, if he kept a woman happy in bed, she wouldn`t stray. That was why he had felt no fear in encouraging Lou to play along with old Henry. Now he had just the first twinge of apprehension. Lou had been keener to drive half way across the island to get a letter from Henry than spend the night in his arms.

And what had Henry written? All Lou would say was "Poetry". Dr Roy had never written a love letter, let alone a poem, in his life. He climbed off the couch and made an announcement to the empty room.

"Dr Winston Roy ain`t about to start writing love letters and poetry now!"

As he walked back to his apartment, he decided to take Lou out to dinner that evening. He couldn`t afford it but some of Lou`s money helped with the housekeeping and, looking to the future, Bishop and his cronies should soon be history.

He suggested a trip out for supper when Lou came through the door.

"Don`t be stupid!"

He noticed that she didn`t even kiss him.

"Just a thought, honey. Winston will just have to get out his frying pan and…"

Lou leaned against the back of the armchair and looked at him as if he were dim.

"How can we go out to supper when Henry is out there spying on me? Winston, don`t you realise I have to give him the slip when I come here?" She raised her hands in despair. "That is, if he is following me! I don`t know when he is and when he isn`t!"

Dr Roy gave her a cuddle.

"That`s OK honey. We can drive up to Grenville for a meal."

She shook her head.

"Too far and I`m too tired."

"Work, honey?"

She looked up.

"No! Henry! Henry! He was back at the café table today."

"Ah! His letter and poetry. How did you mark it? Five out of ten? Seven? Eight?"

Lou pulled herself away from him and stood facing him, her fists clenched..

"Winston! I feel a responsibility for that man. Sometimes…sometimes…he`s just like a wounded animal. Vulnerable."

Dr Roy thought that wounded animals should be put down but considered it prudent to keep that to himself. She was standing in that slightly pouting, sulky way that he found so attractive and which could be banished with a kiss. He kissed her on the forehead but she remained unresponsive.

"Right!" he said, "A dinner to remem-ber."

He plied her with wine and fed her fillet of fish with finely minced herbes de provence. Lou mellowed with each mouthful and at the end of the meal allowed him to manoeuvre her to bed. She needed comfort. She felt confused and torn.

"I`m having to lead Henry on, so as to keep going this nonsense to unseat Bishop. I`m running a double life because I`m with you but Henry thinks I still live with Maisy. The atmosphere in the entire Government is downright nasty with everyone either for or against Bishop or Coard. And that`s all because of me. Somewhere out there, for all we know, the Americans are planning an invasion. It`s all got so much that I don`t even know any more whether I want Bishop to go!" She looked despairingly at him and began to cry. "And there`s us!"

Dr Roy calmed her, ran his fingers through her hair and told her to hush.

"It won`t be long now, Lou. Not long. Henry says it won`t be long until it`s all over, doesn`t he?" She nodded and dried her eyes. "Let`s just let it roll out for a bit more. OK?" She smiled weakly. Dr Roy leaned over and picked up his book. "Y`know how it is. If I don`t read for five minutes I can`t get to sleep."

Lou remembered that he hadn`t answered her properly – hadn`t addressed the problem of `us`.

"But what about us, Winston?"

"We`re fine, honey. Just fine."

He didn`t even take his head out of his book.

When he did turn out the light, she lay awake thinking about what he had said and matching it against what she had wanted to hear. She took a very deep breath, made a resolution and eventually fell asleep.

In the morning, Dr Roy awoke to find that she was already up and dressing for work. He was not due at the mental institution until after lunch and lay back expecting Lou to bring him coffee as usual. When he heard the front door slam, he realised that he was not only missing his coffee but a goodbye.

At her office, Lou announced that she would take a late lunch. She returned to Dr Roy`s apartment that afternoon and piled her clothes into her jeep. She drove to her apartment, empty of tenants since tourism had dried up following Bishop`s death. She dumped her clothes and belongings in the hall and got back to work late. No-one noticed. And if anyone had noticed, they wouldn`t have cared. In the Government building, little work was being done. Everyone was waiting for the Bishop-Coard battle to enter its final round.

People were jumpy. Especially Joyce, Finance Minister Coard`s secretary. That morning she had seen the postman walking towards her kitchen door waving a thick envelope. She lived with her husband on the outskirts of St George`s. As the postman approached, the island was under another downpour and the rain sounded like stones falling on the tin roof. From the simple kitchen in which she was finishing the washing up, she dried her hands on a towel and opened the door.

The postman pointed to the first line written on the brown envelope.

"It`s your first letter that says you are the Missus!"

She laughed and shut the door. The envelope was heavy, sealed with tape and her name and address had been typed. She needed a small knife to cut through the tape. When she got her thumb inside and ripped the envelope open, a bundle of one hundred US dollar bills tumbled to the floor.

She screamed and stood transfixed, her hands on her mouth. Then she bent down and scooped up the notes, slamming them into the drawer under the working top.

Chapter 31

When Dr Roy turned his key in the lock and opened his front door he could see straight down the hall and into the bedroom. The doors of Lou`s wardrobe hung open. He strode down the hall and saw that only empty hangers remained on the rail.

With a conscious effort, he carefully shut the wardrobe doors and left the apartment. He strolled as slowly as he could make himself to the courtyard bar in a nearby hotel. He wanted to be alone and he knew the bartender there was morose to the point of dumbness. He drank several shots of Bourbon in quick succession and told himself that he was wrong to be in the bar. He should be continuing his life as normally as possible. Sticking to his routines. That, he reflected, was what he would have advised a patient.

It was dark when he opened the front door for the second time and the first move he made after turning on the lights was to look for a note. There had to be a note. There was always a note. Except that he couldn`t find it. He gave up and opened the refrigerator and then shut it quickly. Like all excellent cooks, he enjoyed cooking for someone else. He could not face cooking just for himself.

It wasn`t until he threw back the bed cover that he found the note. It was on her side of the bed. He nodded appreciatively. That was a nice touch. The note was placed just where he missed her most. He could see from the size of the folded paper that it wasn`t going to take long to read.

"No love letter or poetry for lil' old Winston," he said aloud. First, he skimread it.

> Dearest Winston
> I explained to you what is wrong with my life – last night and earlier. Staying with you as things are will not solve my problems. So I have gone back to my apartment.
> All my love
> Lou

He looked up and considered that the letter wasn`t too bad. She was gone but not necessarily for good and there was no mention of Henry. Then he sat on the edge of the bed and gave it closer analysis.

"OK," he said aloud. "Where`s the hidden meaning?"

> "*Dearest Winston*

(That`s good. "My dearest" would have been better but at least it`s not plain old Dear Winston.)

> *I explained to you what is wrong with my life – last night and earlier.*

(She`s under a lot of pressure, torn this way and that, but I told her it would soon be over. But what`s with the *earlier* bit? Could that hark back to the old love word? Winston, that is not good news.)

"Staying with you *as things are* will not change my problems."

(What`s with the *as things are*? Clearly, she ain`t going to change things or she wouldn`t have walked out on me. That means it`s down to me to change. Hey! This is serious.)

"So I have gone back to my apartment."

(That means she`s waiting there for me to collect her but only on her terms as set out above. Winston, this is crude blackmail!)

"All my love"

(It`s that *love* word again. Worse than that, it`s *all* of her love. Which is good in a way `cos it means that old Henry ain`t getting any of it. But as Lou and me don`t believe in love – or at least, I still don`t – that hardly matters.)

He threw the note on the floor and spoke aloud and angrily.

"That`s worse than blackmail. That`s emotional blackmail. And even worse, it`s sneaky!"

He noticed that he hadn`t screwed up the note, just thrown it on the floor. He found that worrying. As worrying as realising that he had counted the three times he had talked aloud to himself that evening. He put the note in the drawer in his bedside cabinet and went to bed with Jung.

"At least you know where you are with an analytical psychologist! Shit! That`s four times this evening."

He woke early and went to the breakfast bar with a note pad to scribble his reply.

"Darling Lou

(Smart! Nice word *Darling* but no sense of possession about it.)

Of course, I understand and want to help you.

(That`s what psychiatrists are for. To *understand* and to *help.* That`s what I did after she started visiting me for consultations)

The place just isn`t the same without you.

(Factually correct. She isn`t here so it`s gotta be different.)

I`ll be at the consulting room every evening after you leave work.

(It`s where we always go for anniversaries, after tiffs etc. It`s a positive sign that I want to make up with her.)

You are my dearest treasure.
Winston

(Last bit was bound to be hardest but I ain`t going down the love word route. It`s true! I do treasure her! Or I would if she were here. What woman could resist being a man`s *dearest treasure?)*

He put the note in an envelope and pushed it through the letter box of her apartment.

Lou went home lunchtime to see if there was a letter from Dr Roy. She bent quickly to pick up the envelope from the mat. Tearing it open and removing the small square of paper, her eye went straight to his sign off.

She scoffed.

"Dearest treasure!"

She walked back to work fuming.

Late that afternoon, Henry was sitting like a silent sentinel at his usual spot at the café table as Lou left work. She strolled up to him. Tentatively, he asked if she would like a drink.

"That would be nice. Or, I have a better idea. Why don't we eat out? Let's have an early supper," she said. "I am famished. I know a little place where we can eat al fresco."

She could see how ridiculously happy she had made him. That made her feel guilty because she knew she was being deliberately hypocritical. On Sunday she would need to go to mass with Maisy. She sighed. She had so much to confess.

The place to eat that she had in mind was on the corner where Dr Lou would pass on his way to his consulting rooms, whether he was heading from his apartment or the mental institution.

Lou settled down at the restaurant table with a drink in her hand. Henry was so pleased with himself that he ordered a rum punch with lots of nutmeg on top. She found him curiously solicitous about Maisy. He suggested that Maisy suffered from dementia and wanted to know about the island`s facilities for caring for the elderly mentally infirm. She chose to ignore him by burying her head in the menu.

She was ordering roast duck with port wine when she looked up from the menu and saw Dr Lou ambling down the street. She kept her gaze on the menu card long enough to ensure that Dr Roy had seen her before she put her hand on Henry`s.

"It`s so sweet of you to take me out. I`ll regard it as a thank you for my little treat taking you round the island."

She kissed him on the cheek.

Henry caught his breath and leant forward to say how much he had enjoyed their day out. From the corner of his eye he caught sight of Dr Roy. He was walking up the street, his head turned back to stare at them.

"Was that Winston?"

She shrugged.

"Possibly. I didn`t see." She chattered on to cover the incident. "I`m going to mass on Sunday." Henry was the atheist son of Baptists. "Maisy thinks I`m becoming a heathen and that I need to confess my sins." Henry straightened up, alarmed. "It`s all right. Don`t worry. I confess in generalities." She sipped her wine. "Otherwise, I`d be there all night."

Dr Roy continued his walk to his consulting room. Behind his desk, he drummed his fingers on the old blotter that he had inherited with the office equipment.

Two hours later, when it was clear that she wasn`t coming, he went to the courtyard bar in the hotel and drank more Bourbon.

Chapter 32

On Sunday Lou collected Maisy to take her to the tiny Roman Catholic church where, as a child, she had worshipped regularly. Inside it was cool and comforting. Everything – the altar, the flowers, the pews, even the priest – looked the same. It was just Lou who had changed. She didn`t believe any more in the liturgy and the responses. Or the ritual of confession. Let alone the blood turning to wine and the bread to Christ`s flesh. She believed in something but knew that it had been largely lost somewhere in the Holy Land tens of years or even a hundred years after the crucifixion. Yet going to mass made Maisy happy. Maisy was even happier when Lou told her that she had moved back into her own apartment while she sorted herself out.

Next morning Lou chose her clothes with care. She put on the same white dress and sling-back shoes that she had worn when she had lain on Dr Roy`s couch after her return from London.

During her lunch break, she had her hair trimmed and washed. After work, she stopped off by Henry`s café table but told him she couldn`t wait. She promised to join him for a drink later in the week then walked off. She didn`t bother to check whether Henry was following her. She then headed for Dr Roy`s consulting room. She walked up the two steps to the door and knocked as he had before, more times than she could remember.

"Come in!"

She smiled politely at Dr Roy sitting behind his desk. He stood up and collected his

clipboard and pen from the desk top.

"Good evening, Miss Hope."

He directed her to the couch and gestured for her to lie down. Perched on the edge, she kicked off her shoes and swung her legs up onto the leather. With a hand she adjusted her hair before lying back and smoothing down the white linen over her thighs.

Dr Roy sat on the wooden chair positioned at the head of the couch.

"Miss Hope, you have not been keeping your appointments. I have waited and you did not come." She did not answer. "How long is it since your last appointment?"

She answered briskly.

"I can`t remember. A lot has happened since then."

"Why do you keep me waiting, Miss Hope? Why?"

"Henry has been very demanding."

Dr Roy pursed his lips.

"In what way, Miss Hope?"

"I have to make telephone calls for him. Among other things."

"But you can make time, surely, for your appointments?"

Lou`s voice was taut.

"I said Henry is very demanding."

"We are not discussing Henry Turville."

"If I am to continue these appointments, then I must discuss Henry."

He stood up and made his way with his clipboard to the window where the blinds were half closed.

"Miss Hope, do you associate any emotional feelings with your missed appointments?"

She paused.

"Yes."

"How would you describe these feelings?"

"I find it hard…I can`t…"

Dr Roy tweaked the blinds to look outside.

"Come, come Miss Hope. Just think of your earlier appointments. Are the feelings you had then similar to those that you have now?"

Her voice became anguished.

"No."

By the window, Dr Roy`s crisp, business-like manner wilted into anxiety. He fiddled nervously with the string on the blinds, then took a deep breath. Lou heard it and her mouth tightened.

"Miss Hope, let`s start again. Is there within you yearning, lust, desire?"

He turned towards the couch, waiting for her answer.

"Well…."

She left the word hanging.

Dr Roy sensed success. He dropped the string on the blinds and they fell back, rattling gently.

"Well what, Miss Hope?"

"Well…Yes."

He smiled into the blinds and turned round slowly. According to the long-established rules of the game, Lou should now have slipped out of her dress. She should be lying on the couch in her underwear. Instead, she was still fully clothed.

He turned back to the blinds, tweaked them open again and pretended to look outside. He knew that he had no interest in what was going on out there, only what was happening on the couch. He turned back to the couch. She had not moved.

He spoke quietly.

"Your dress, Miss Hope. Your dress."

She replied primly.

"I`m quite comfortable as I am, thank you, Dr Roy."

He shouted so loudly that he saw her flinch. She had never heard him shout before.

"Take it off!"

"Not while I`m involved with Henry."

He swallowed hard and turned back to the blind, not bothering to so much as twitch them."

"It has come to that, then?" Then she heard him speaking, as if to himself. "We must remain calm." She smiled at that and deliberately misunderstood him.

"I am calm."

He dropped the clipboard to his side and the pen to the floor where it lay untouched. He stared at the blinds because he could not bring himself to look at her.

"So Henry…Henry, old chap. Is he…? Are you…Does he…?"

She answered briskly.

"Your questions do not have their usual point and polish, Dr Roy. If you want to know whether we`ve been in the sack, then I must say that a lady never kisses and tells." Dr Roy bent down and collected his clipboard and pen. She knew she had scored a direct hit because she could hear his pen tapping on the edge of the clipboard. "What I can say, Dr Roy, is that Henry`s very sweet and protective. I have to thank you for bringing us together."

He swung round and spat the word at her.

"Bitch!" He flung clipboard and pen to the floor. "Undress!"

Lou sat up and turned sharply on the couch, slipping her toes neatly into her shoes on the floor.

"Not while you are so keen to see my relationship with Henry work!"

She walked to the door, opened it and began to leave. He strode over and stood watching her.

"Miss Hope!" She stopped but did not turn. "In view of today`s events, there will be no consultation fee." She walked on. He called again. "Lou!" She heard the pleading in his voice and again stopped. This time she turned and looked enquiringly at him as he struggled to find the right words.

"What do you want to say, Winston?" He shook his

head and she threw her hair back with a toss of her head. "OK, Winston. The game`s over. At least for now."

She walked out, turning only to shut the door softly behind her.

Chapter 33

Joyce was carrying a bundle of files in her arms, on her way to leave them in Bernard Coard`s office when she saw Prime Minister Bishop walking towards her from the far end of the corridor. Joyce`s friends in her office thought her particularly nervous that morning though she said nothing to indicate why. Her manner was understandable. The entire building knew that either the Prime Minister or the Finance Minister was going to be imprisoned in one of the island`s ancient forts when the army decided which man to back and which to sack.

Joyce stepped aside, her back to the wall, to let Bishop walk by to the door at her side on which was written "Prime Minister". The civil servants who looked after Bishop had found him unusually unsmiling over the last few days but it was the old, grinning Bishop who Joyce saw as he stopped at her side. He gave her a wide smile. She saw flashes of gold fillings among his white teeth. Glancing over his shoulder to ensure that the corridor was clear, he leant towards her and whispered.

"You've got something for me?"

She looked down at the files in her arms and shook her head.

"No Prime Minister I`ve got…"

Her voice trailed off. She dare not mention Coard`s name. Civil servants knew that to mention Coard`s name to Bishop or Bishop`s name to Coard was to risk an instant dressing down and, in the longer terms, sharing the same fate as the man who lost the power game. Bishop kept smiling as he opened his office door and beckoned.

"You come on in."

She didn`t know what to say but thanked him anyway and stepped inside.

In the room, he stood close to her, more as if they were friends than Prime Minister and civil servant.

"Joyce, I know you can help some more."

She hesitated.

"I`ll do what I can, Prime Minister."

He looked serious.

"Come back here any time you`re ready. Y`know, you and I have got to stay real close." He suddenly looked very serious and put his hand on her arm. "Joyce, you`re my best hope."

She nodded and edged for the door. While she didn`t know exactly what he was getting at, she remembered how, before she was engaged to be married, some of the men had tried to get her into the stationery cupboard. He gripped her arm fiercely to stop her leaving.

"No, don`t go."

She wasn`t reacting as he had expected. Suddenly he remembered his misgivings about the capital`s postal service, currently the subject of an inquiry into lost mail.

"You got the money?"

She shrieked and he let go of her arm.

"It was you?"

"Of course! There`s plenty more. The more you do for me, the more you can have."

She dropped the files, opened the door and fled.

He jumped to the doorway and shouted.

"Come back!"

He heard her squealing voice.

"I`m only just married!"

As she neared the turn in the corridor, she heard the sound of boots marching. For the second time that morning, she pulled herself against the wall. This time she recognised the lean and mean face of Hudson Austin, General of the Armed Forces, in full dress uniform. Behind him marched four of his tallest, smartest soldiers, each with a rifle on his soldier. They passed her without a sideways glance.

In his office, Bishop heard the boots approaching and looked round in panic, as if seeking to flee. Then he sagged into his chair and called his private office on the intercom. He instructed his staff to stay in their offices until the army told them to leave and asked that the order be passed on to everyone in the building. He was still sitting behind his desk when Hudson Austin appeared in the doorway.

"Well," said the outgoing Prime Minister calmly, "I see that you have made your choice." Hudson Austin nodded to the soldiers who gestured with their rifles for Bishop to stand up. They slipped on the handcuffs and led him away.

Word soon spread of other arrests. From her window, Lou could not see the army jeeps and trucks but Jackie gave a running commentary over the phone from her office in the tourism section and told her when Bishop had been driven away.

"Great!" said Jackie with heavy sarcasm when the last soldiers had driven off. "No-one considers my problems. Tourism is really going to be helped when all this goes out on television in the US and Europe."

Lou replaced the receiver and sat motionless at her desk. She was responsible for Bishop`s removal and his almost certain execution. It was cold revenge. But she did not feel as elated as she had expected.

As Lou left the office that evening, she got another shock: Henry was not at his usual table. It was empty under a green umbrella shade fluttering in the breeze. Henry, wandering around the market that morning, had returned to his apartment the moment he saw army trucks on the streets. In the Foreign Office he had read enough diplomatic telegrams to know that when a coup is launched, the safest place to be is at home. Especially in a country as unstable as Grenada and with such an ill-disciplined army. When word of the coup reached the medical school, Dr Roy continued giving his lecture but was keenly aware that he had scored a new record by losing the attention of the entire room for a full hour.

In the island`s hinterland, the news that Bishop had been arrested did not go down well. To the men and women who laboured in the fields, on tiny boats and in processing plants, Bishop was a popular figure. He had always sought to make himself an island personality – one of the reasons why Coard and his acolytes, all ultra-left machine politicians, despised him. Importantly, the islanders knew that while Bishop was a Communist he was also a pragmatist who was prepared – unlike Coard and his cronies - to cut ideological corners to keep the ordinary islanders happy.

Since the days of French and then British rule, political unrest on the island had always organised itself in the market square in St George`s. It was there that Lou, less cautious or worldly-wise than Henry, went to watch the growing demonstration at Bishop`s arrest. From within the island, villagers poured into the square to vent their anger. She watched pro-Bishop men whip the crowd into a fury. One after the other, firebrands vied to outdo each other with rabble-rousing speeches.

Finally, the square was brimming with islanders chanting the same slogan.

"Free Bishop! Free Bishop! Free Bishop!"

As if at some command she did not hear, the crowd became a mob and poured out of the square and through the streets towards Fort Rupert, the town`s military base in colonial days. Now it was Bishop's jail. Lou followed the tail of the mob, through the streets and out of town towards the fort, perched on a cliff edge over-looking the calm sea.

Outside the fort, the soldiers who patrolled or stood guard lacked the sharp-eyed discipline of the men whom Hudson Austin had picked to arrest Bishop. As the sound of the mob`s fury reached the soldiers` ears, they turned to each other and waited for orders that did not come.

The sight of the soldiers` rifles slowed the mob momentarily as the leaders at the front of the phalanx watched to see how the army would react. Some of the soldiers pulled back. Others took their rifles from their shoulders but, instead of pointing them at the mob, left them dangling weakly at the ground.

Like a big, hungry animal, the mob sensed weakness and began to advance cautiously as it judged the soldiers` reaction. The mob abandoned caution when the unseeing mass at the rear pressed blindly on, forcing the leaders faster and faster towards the soldiers.

Lou hung to the very back of the mob with men and women who, like her, were tagging along to see what happened.

She moved from one side of the street to the other, standing on doorsteps trying to catch sight of what was happening. A triumphant cry from the mob signalled that the soldiers, lacking orders and unable to bring themselves to fire on their fellow islanders, had been overwhelmed.

The shout from the men and women at the front of the mob became a chant as it spread back towards Lou.

"Bishop`s free! Bishop`s free!"

Lou felt numb. All the emotional turmoil she had suffered with Henry and Dr Roy to secure Bishop`s downfall was wasted. Faces in the mob turned towards her, excited and jubilant. Momentarily she felt the fear of the outsider who is suddenly exposed.. A young man shouted to her that the soldiers had thrown down their rifles. She nodded and felt sick.

Then Lou became aware that the mood of the people at the back of the mob had changed. More and more of them were turning and looking past her. An army jeep and trucks were racing up the street towards her.

Within seconds, the mob faced two ways. The front towards Fort Rupert. The back towards the army jeep and trucks.

At the front of the crowd, Bishop was lifted aloft and she saw his head bobbing, his arms waving. The cheers from around Bishop mingled with the growing jeers from the back of the mob where everyone had now turned to face the jeep and trucks. The soldier driving the jeep tried to push the vehicle into the throng of people but gave up, waving his arms in despair at the young officer by his side who urged him on. The driver leant on his horn. The mob jeered and drowned the sound.

The officer jumped from the jeep and shouted orders to the soldiers in the trucks. Drivers climbed out. The tailgates came down and soldiers poured onto the street. Beside his jeep, the officer shouted to the crowd to make way. By way of reply, he was met with a barrage of booing and spittle. He took out his pistol and waved it. The booing stopped but the cheering from around Bishop continued. The officer shouted again but nothing happened. Lou realised that the crowd was now jammed so tightly in the street that those who wanted to move were, in effect, trapped.

The officer stepped back and put his pistol back in his holster. A murmur of relief rippled through the crowd. He turned to the soldiers and shouted an order. Lou did not hear it. She just saw the soldiers put their rifles to their shoulders and point them over the heads of the crowd.

A volley of shots rang out.

As the rifle shots echoed and faded, the entire mob began to scream in panic. Instinctively, it surged away from the line of soldiers, their rifles still on their shoulders, and towards Fort Rupert. Lou caught sight of Bishop, still held aloft and gesticulating wildly. Then he suddenly disappeared into the mob.

From the front of the crowd she heard shouts, then cries and, finally, screams. It was the hysterical screams of men, women and children hurled over the cliff edge by the sheer pressure of the surging crowd behind them.

Lou pressed herself into a wall, her fingers clawing at the stone, as the fringe at the rear of the mob broke away and ran past the line of soldiers, the jeep and the trucks. Then entire chunks of the mob raced past her. The file of trucks, led by the jeep, began to inch forward and then gather speed towards the fort as the crowd thinned. Gripped by the panic, also Lou turned and fled, stopping only once to pull off her shoes so as to run faster. Back in the market square, she began to understand the enormity of the human tragedy. Those who were not weeping or comforting the bereaved were telling of the bodies hurled over the cliff edge.

Lou felt impelled to walk back to Fort Rupert to see if she could help. She knew it was a hopeless journey. The islanders who had been pushed over the cliff edge had been as doomed as the Caribs who had voluntarily leapt to their deaths to escape the French. But she had to try. She half walked, half ran back, passing abandoned bags and shoes. Before the fort was in sight, a woman friend from her office grabbed her arm.

"The fort is surrounded by the army. Don`t risk it!"

Again, she turned back to the square. On a corner she saw a weeping child, a girl aged no more than eight. Lou bent down to ask her what was wrong. She looked up and said that she had lost her mother and father.

Lou took the child`s hand and walked her towards the square. She couldn`t bring herself to ask how or where the child had lost her parents. Eventually, a young woman villager sitting on the ground in the square recognised the child and said she would look after her.

Dr Roy sat in his office, his chair pushed back and his feet resting on the desk. After his lecture at the medical school he had tried to phone Lou but couldn`t get through to the Government building. He assumed that the army had cut all telephone lines.

It had seemed natural to make his way to his

consulting room to wait for her. It was to the dusty room that the couple always returned at times of crisis or celebration. He knew nothing of the mob, which had not come close to his office, or the massacre at the cliff by the fort. From his chair he heard rifle shots and assumed that Bishop was being executed.

With his hands behind his head, he whistled a little and smiled at the thought that even now old Henry was working to get rid of Coard, too. A small US invasion and

the restoration of a more freedom-loving government would pave the way to the resumption of his little business sideline.

His whistling became cheery and louder as he thought that a trip with Lou to Tobago, where he had friends, might be very congen-ial while the Americans cleared the Commu-nists out of Grenada.

He heard footsteps outside the door and lifted his feet from the desk and onto the floor. Picking up his pen, he made as if to write on the fullscap paper on the blotter.

The door burst open and Lou ran in sobbing. She threw herself on him. Dr Roy stood up and gathered her into his arms. He whispered to her.

"Hey! Take it easy babe!"

This was not what he had been expecting. He gently sat her down in his chair and settled on his haunches, looking into her eyes.

"Oh Winston, it`s ghastly. Awful. Bishop was freed by the crowd. Then recaptured. And now shot. Executed."

Dr Roy felt it would be unseemly to celebrate openly and Lou clearly had more to tell. He looked impassively at her.

"So our wish has come true."

Lou began to stand up, gulping and weeping.

"People fell – were pushed over the cliff edge – by the crowd - in the…."

"Where?"

“At Fort Rupert. Where Bishop was. Children…everybody. Over the cliff.”

Dr Roy stood up. This was not what he had expected. He knew the cliff and the drop to the beach.

“Wasn`t it a philosopher who said that Hell is being given what you wanted?”

The two stared at each other until Lou spoke.

“What I wanted.”

Dr Roy walked to the window, peered out through the half-drawn blinds and turned back to Lou.

“I`ve got to go and see what I can do to help.”

He bent down by the side of Lou and pulled from a drawer a black medical bag. He drew a finger through the dust on it.

“It`s hopeless, Winston. People don`t survive that fall. What we`ve got to do is to stop this invasion madness. If we don`t more people could be killed. More people will be killed. Why is Henry so obsessed with an invasion? We`ve got what we wanted though…”

She began to cry again. Dr Lou walked past her with his medical bag.

“Later. Later.”

Chapter 34

It was a busy day in Kiddies` Wear. Mothers rifled through the hanging rails or sifted through shelves. Rose helped a customer try a coat on an unwilling toddler. Children wailed and snivelled and rushed around.

At the counter, Jean looked up at the queue of customers. She couldn`t remember trade being so brisk. She rang up the cash in the till, put the toddlers` suit in a bag and turned to the next customer.

A woman in her early thirties, petite, blonde and pretty but with a pinched face, joined the queue and irritably pulled her three year old boy closer to the push chair in which a baby whimpered mindlessly.

The mother moved closer to the counter. Jean looked down at the pushchair as the woman handed her a blue romper suit to wrap. Jean slipped it into a carrier bag and laid it on the counter.

"Oh! That`s a lovely baby!"

The customer smiled and rummaged at the bottom of her handbag for a credit card. Jean thought it was a weary smile and processed the card. The woman bent over the counter to sign the transaction slip. Jean glanced at the name on the card as she handed it back.

"Thank you." The tiniest shadow passed briefly across Jean`s face. "Thank you, Mrs Reardon."

The woman smiled again, no less wearily.

"Are you Jean?"

"That`s right."

"My husband handles your accounts, doesn`t he?"

She put her card back in her handbag and reached over to grab her son as he tried to pull a dress from a nearby rail. Jean began to deal with the next customer.

"Jack? Oh yes. Jack`s…been very helpful." She glanced down quickly at the child, now standing beside his sister in the pushchair. "Oh, they are lovely. Two boys?"

Mrs Reardon nodded.

"Boys! How lovely. I`m pregnant myself, you know."

"Oh, that`s wonderful! Do you have other children?"

"Oh no!" She patted her tummy behind the counter. "Bit of a surprise really. Especially at my age."

"Well, there`ll be no shortage of baby clothes! Good bye then."

At her home early that evening, Jean sat in the lounge and sipped a glass of pure orange. Jenny Reardon. So that was Jack`s wife. She remembered her face and felt that it explained a lot about her affair with Jack.

She had never asked if there was a Mrs Reardon and Jack had never offered any details of his personal life. Of course, she had guessed that there was someone else in his life. He had always said he needed to get back to his house to sleep.

"I`ve never been able to sleep in a bed with anyone else in it," he had explained. "I think it`s got something to do with sleeping in the same room as my brother until I went to college."

Jean had nodded understandingly, though his explanation scarcely made sense. Anyway, she didn`t really want him sleeping over at her house. It would have made their arrangement seem permanent. Instinctively she knew that, whatever the affair grew into, it would not be permanent.

Even when he wasn`t with her, she scarcely thought

of his domestic arrangements. What was important was that they were both were having fun. The fun was the sex.

Jean had no experience of how to manage an affair with a man, married or single. She had gone up to university just before the days of the pill and female sexual emancipation. So she had come down from university in the same virginal state as she went up. Henry had been the only sexual partner in her life.

She and Jack had made love in the spare room – it had a double bed – at her house. It seemed wrong to think of having sex with Jack in the room she had shared with Henry. Anyway, there were only single beds there.

It all seemed quite irrelevant as Jack seemed to revel in making love in unusual places.

As their love affair blossomed, she realised that though Henry had been a long-distance jogger round the streets of South London, in bed (and he only made love in bed) he was a hundred yards man. Jack was now her marathon man. She used to call him that.

The neighbours stopped inviting her in for drinks when they saw Jack`s car parked on the drive three times a week. But she didn`t mind. She was having a fling. And she did not care what the neighbours would think. They could twitch their curtains all they liked. .

She had never expected love from Jack. Initially, she had gasped her love for him at what seemed the appropriate moment. Occasionally he had puffed his love for her.

It could not last long. She knew she would feel no surprise when it ended. What did surprise her was her pregnancy. She kept wondering whether the pregnancy test could be wrong. Or that she had perhaps misread the instructions. Or that the colours had got mixed up. She bought three test kits before she was convinced.

By her calculations, she must have fallen pregnant very early. She was delighted with the news. Finding herself expectant brought back with a rush all the repressed yearnings for a family that she had been forced to stifle throughout her married life.

She glanced at the kitchen clock. Just enough time to get to the gym. She wanted to have a quiet word with one of the trainers about how long she should continue with her exercises and which ones she should avoid as her pregnancy developed.

In the gym, as she stepped out vigorously on the walking machine, she heard Joe shout to her trainer.

"You look after that Mrs Turville! She`s a very good friend of mine."

As she left, Joe was leaning on the counter picking his teeth with the end of a straightened paper clip.

"Good night!" she trilled.

"Joe`s a good name," he said. She stopped and turned. "You see, you can have it with an `e` or without an `e`. Depending on whether it`s a boy or a girl."

"That`s very sweet, Joe. I`ll remember that."

As she walked up the drive, she heard the answering machine in the hall bleeping faintly. It was Jack, saying he was sorry she wasn`t there and he`d try again later in the week. She made a note on the pad by the phone to call Jack at work the next morning.

Suddenly she felt tired. She had been told to expect fatigue. An early night was called for. In bed, she thought again of Jenny Reardon`s pinched, weary face. It was easier to understand Jack now that she had seen his wife. Little Jenny was not very good in bed with Jack. Not adventurous enough. Whereas she, Jean Turville, was a veritable strumpet. She laughed out loud. All those years and Henry hadn`t known that he was married to a wanton woman.

Chapter 35

Lou shook her head at Henry and told him she didn`t have time to stop for a drink.

"No, I`ve got to get home." She didn`t want to drink with him. "I`m too exhausted." She nodded back along the street to the Government building. "With Coard now Prime Minister, no-one knows what they`re doing or where they are."

Henry was anxious to delay her.

"Will you be working for Coard? Or staying where you are?"

She shrugged.

"Henry, I`ve got to go."

She felt a weary depression now that Bishop was dead. She needed a new beginning and she knew that Henry was not going to be part of it. Henry was in the past. It was just that he didn`t recognise it yet.

He became insistent.

"You can`t go. We need to walk." He looked round conspiratorially. "One more phone call." He patted to the seat for her to sit down. She turned and walked off.

"Sorry, Henry."

It wasn`t that Lou had simply switched the Off switch in her life for Henry. She felt much the same weariness with Dr Roy. She couldn`t be bothered to play either of their games. She rubbed her forehead as she walked towards the town. Perhaps she was really getting depressed. She pulled her shoulders back and swung her attaché case to try to lift her spirits. If she were depressed, she would sort it without the help of Dr Roy.

Lou reached the front door of her apartment without remembering how she had got there. She looked at her watch. The walk had taken her the usual fifteen minutes but she couldn`t recall a step of it and for the first time, she hadn`t taken evasive action to throw Henry off her trail. She was too depressed even to think about that. And anyway, Henry was now in the past tense so far as she was concerned.

She pulled out of her case the few bits of shopping that she had bought at lunchtime, packed them in the refrigerator and decided on an early night in bed with the one luxury she always yearned for when she was low: chocolate biscuits.

Down the road, sheltered by a coconut tree, Henry watched the door close behind Lou. So she did have somewhere to live in St George`s. Why hadn`t she mentioned it? Why had she pretended to live outside St George`s with Maisy? Was there even someone living with her?

He felt tricked and betrayed. For more than an hour he loitered to see if anyone called or came out. After a drink and salad in the town, he returned and stayed until late in the evening. He saw nothing.

On the next evening, Lou walked out of the Government building and gave Henry a wave. That, she thought, is all he`s getting from me today.

Henry attempted no subterfuge, nor made any pretence at bumping into her. He simply strode up beside her, seized her arm below the elbow in a fierce grip and spoke softly and menacingly.

"We`re going for a walk on the beach."

She walked on, struggling to escape his grip.

"Let me go!"

"The beach! Or I don`t let go."

He was marching her along now. She was frightened and gave in.

"Let go and I`ll come with you."He let go of her arm but stayed close to her and said nothing until they reached the beach. She turned on him and demanded to know what he thought he was doing. He was standing, glaring at her.

"Your apartment. You`ve got an apartment."

Lou remembered that she had walked straight home the previous night without diversions to throw Henry off her trail. But why not? She no longer lived with Dr Roy. She hissed at Henry.

"Because it`s my home now. I used to let it to tourists. Now I live there myself. By myself. But more to the point, why do you keep following me?"

"Grenada`s a small place. You come across…"

She slapped his face. He was so surprised that he put his hand to his cheek and stood on the sand looking helpless. She felt much better though her hand stung a little.

"You are invading my privacy. Stop it. Will you stop it?"

He nodded.

"I`m sorry. It`s just that I love you."

She stamped a foot on the sand.

"You do not love me! Infatuated – yes! Obsessed – yes! Love – no!"

He grabbed her hands.

"I do! I do!"

She sagged.

"Oh, I give up!"

He seemed to interpret her words as a victory and grasped her unwilling hands in his.

"You will understand. You will."

She shook her head.

"It`s you who doesn`t understand. I am very low, Henry. Probably depressed. There are a lot of things wrong with my life and you are one of them."

He was no longer listening.

"One more phone call to Switzerland. Please."

"Listen, Henry. Bishop has gone. That was all that mattered to me. I should be elated but I`m not. That`s another story. But no more phone calls."

For Henry, the death of Bishop was just a step on the road to a US invasion of Grenada and Mariowitz`s ritual humiliation. Henry had two more shots in his locker. Only Lou could fire one of them.

"Just one more phone call. And then that will be it. Finished. No more. Never."

"And us? You and me?"

She wanted him to agree that their relationship would also be over. He stared blankly at her. Why didn`t she understand? Everything seemed so simple to him.

"Then there will be time for you to learn to love me."

Lou opened her mouth but gave up on replying. She just wanted to get rid of him.

"OK. The last call. But then you leave me alone. Yes?"

He nodded but she could see that his thoughts were elsewhere, no doubt constructing the final message she would send to the CIA.

She walked back up the beach with Henry, listening to his instructions, and then stepped into the phone box on the outskirts of the town. He waited outside and smiled as she stepped out.

"OK," she said firmly. "That is it. The end. Now I am going home. And don`t you dare follow me, Henry. Or I will slap your face again."

She put her handbag firmly on her arm and marched off.

Henry watched her go. He thought that when angry she was even more attractive.

Lou didn`t go straight home. She went to Dr Roy`s consulting room. Just to see if he was there.

She found him asleep in his chair, his feet on the table. He seemed embarrassed but then grinned and walked over to kiss her. She held out her cheek. He kissed it and tried not to look hurt. Lou perched on the edge of the couch and he thought that was a good sign but she made no move to get onto it. So he pulled the hardback chair round and faced her.

"You are a lucky lady, Lou. You`ve got Henry waiting for you outside your office every evening. And you`ve got lil' ol' Winston waiting for you here." He could see that she wasn`t smiling so he tried another tack. "It`s lovely to see you."

She replied formally.

"Thank you. I`ve come here because I want to talk to you about Henry."

Dr Roy leaned forward seriously but his eyes were smiling.

"That is why I am here. To talk to and about the mentally insane."

Lou twitched her lips dismissively and crossed her legs in what Dr Roy considered to be a most provocative manner.

"He`s not that bad."

"He might not be bad but he is most certainly mad."

"You are hardly impartial."

Dr Roy decided not to raise to Lou`s suggestion that he was jealous of Henry. He was jealous of no-one.

"So how can I help?"

"I`m not sending any more information to the CIA. I`ve told Henry that. I`ve sent my last piece of intelligence to the CIA. I`m not being a part of an invasion that will cause more bloodshed. Bishop`s gone. That`s all I wanted. And I`m telling Henry that our relationship is over."

Dr Roy put his hands behind his back and walked up and down the room staring at the dirty carpet that had come with the office.

"Whether you end your relationship with Henry is no concern of mine." He felt the need to say that because he was determined that Lou should not think him jealous. He looked at her and thought he detected a hint of a smile on her otherwise impassive face. “However, at the level of a friend, which is what I like to think I am…” He stopped again and looked up at Lou. She nodded in agreement and he sighed heavily. “I think that to end your relationship with him would be good for you. It is intrinsically an unhealthy relationship…”

Lou intervened.

“I want to be fair to Henry. He can be very sweet. Sometimes I have insights of great sensitivity in him. I have got to know him…” She paused and their eyes met. She spoke quickly. “I have got to know him very well. He can be kind and endearing and sometimes he looks just like a small boy. Lost and in need of protection.”

Dr Roy thought that it sounded very much as if Lou was getting broody. He found he had that effect on some women though in Lou`s case he wondered whether it really was Henry who was making her broody. He had always scooted when the subject of babies was raised by the women in his life.

“The essence of this issue,” Dr Roy continued, trying to sound as impressive as possible, “is not whether the relationship should be ended but the means by which it should be brought to its conclusion.”

“I`m just going to tell him.”

He shook his head.

“No. You must not end the relationship just like that…”

He saw Lou`s eyes flash angrily and felt genuine concern for her. She uncrossed her legs and stood up.

“I`ve just slapped the man`s face, Winston. I think I know how to handle him.”

Dr Lou looked very interested.

“Really! What did he…?”

Lou ignored him. Dr Roy walked to the table and picked up a pencil, playing with it as he talked.

“Henry has an acute obsessive personality. He won`t walk through a door unless his right leg goes first.

Haven't you noticed that, Lou?. He won`t step on cracks in the street. And there`s all the business with coins and soap that you told me about. Not to mention other personal obsessions, like his compulsive habit of looking at his watch. He is also a stalker. Even before you were…" He stopped and took a deep breath. "….lovers." He looked at her. "If that is what you were? Or are?" She turned and stared at the blinds, leaving him only her profile to look at. "Well whatever - he regards himself as your true love and protector. That image he has of himself will now be hugely magnified. He is very clever, a very intelligent man. But a man who probably does not recognise his inability to take pressure. In short, he is what his English friends would call nutty. As a fruit cake. I warn you – you will be in danger if you break off your relationship just like that."

He snapped the pencil in two.

Lou turned back to him. He thought she looked at her haughtiest.

"I can manage him."

"Lou, I`m really serious. Believe me. That man probably even counts the cracks he walks over. Ask him. Go on. Test him, then. Tell him that you have secret little rituals that calm you – like counting – and see what he says. Go on. Just try. He`ll tell you that he does the same. I`d bet on it."

She perched on the couch again.

"His obsession is trying to engineer an American invasion. He`s obsessed with revenge for what his Foreign Office did to him. No, I`m sorry. But I`ve had enough. I`m going to chuck him. And I`m not doing it for you. I`m doing it for me. And Grenada."

She stood up and walked to the door, turned back and gave him a small kiss on the forehead.

"But thanks for caring."

"There is another way. A better way. A safer way."

Lou stepped back from the door.

"What?"

"We disarm him."

She was puzzled.

"Disarm? How? What do you mean?"

"He`s very close to the edge of madness. We could just tip him over the edge. Into madness." He threw his arms open. "End of problem. Then he can go in the Crazy House."

She turned on her heel and walked back to the door.

"I`ve caused enough damage already." She shook her head and looked at him hard.

"Y`know – sometimes I think you`re the madman. And as it happens, I am rather fond of Henry."

Dr Roy nodded.

"Well, that`s fair enough."

She put her hand on the handle and he spoke again.

"Oh, just one other thing." She turned round. "As you had already made up your mind what to do with Henry, why did you come here?"

As she slammed the door she said one word.

"Bastard!"

Dr Roy put his hands on the edge of his desk, leant over and laughed soundlessly.

Chapter 36

In Kiddies` Wear, Rose put the `Closed` sign over the door and shouted her good bye to Jean at the counter. Jean walked onto the shop floor and began tidying the racks and sorting drawers. Outside in the street, Rose saw a silver saloon car slide to a halt and the face of Jack Reardon behind the wheel. Rose grinned. She knew that Jean was pregnant but had not asked who the father was. After pushing Jean to smarten herself and the shop, Rose was sufficiently streetwise to know when to stop. She walked on.

Bent over the three-to-four-year old's rail where something that looked like smeared ice cream had ruined a blue coat, Jean heard the rapping on the door and looked up. She saw the silhouette of Jack Reardon and shouted.

"It`s not locked!"

Jack didn`t hear so she walked over and pulled the door open with a smile. As soon as he was in, she clicked the lock shut. Jack was leaning on the counter as she headed back towards him. He smiled and went to kiss her. She pulled back sharply.

"No thank you, Jack. I don`t think Mrs Reardon would like that."

"Ah!" He looked towards Jean, now busy tidying the five-six rack. "So you know."

"Yes, Jack. Mrs Reardon was in here. With the children. Lovely little mites, aren`t they?"

"I thought…Well, I thought that you knew."

Jean paused from putting cardigans back in a drawer.

"That's clear, Jack."

"I`m sorry."

"Sorry for me or sorry for Mrs Reardon?"

"Well, both of you, I suppose."

Jean looked over a rail and smiled.

"That`s good. I think Mrs Reardon and I deserve equal treatment, don`t you?"

He pulled himself off the counter and plunged his hands into his trouser pockets.

"Look, I`m really sorry Jean. I thought…"

Jean was moving at a furious pace round the shop but suddenly stopped.

"I have some news for you."

She made him wait.

"Er, yes?"

"I`m pregnant."

She spoke in a matter of fact tone and then resumed her tidying.

Jack leant back on the counter again. His jaw went slack. His eyes became vacant. Jean heard him kick something. She assumed it was the large leather briefcase he had put down on the floor by the counter.

"You can`t be!"

Still she didn`t look up.

"I can assure you that I am."

"You lied!"

There was the outrage of a wronged man in his voice. It was a voice that accused her of tricking him into making her pregnant.

Finally she stood up and faced him.

"No, Jack. I didn`t lie. I honestly believed I couldn`t have children. The specialists, well, the specialists indicated I couldn`t. But there again, Henry had just one of his tests and then never had time to go back to the hospital. Always something more important at the Foreign Office." She sighed and smiled. "So it seems that the problem was at his end, not mine. So to speak."

Jack propelled himself from the counter for the second time, now with a glint of optimism on his face.

"Do you want to have it?"

Jean turned her back on him and resumed the final part of her tidying – the six-seven racks.

"Curiously, I don`t regard what is happening inside me as `it`. But yes, I want the baby. *It`s* what I`ve always wanted. Since I married Henry. Now sit down, Jack. I`m clearing up and you`re making the place look untidy."

He went behind the counter and perched on a stool.

Jean looked up at him over the rack.

"In fact, I think you should know that you may have done more than produce one child. Apart of course from your lovely two with Mrs Reardon." She saw that he was swaying slightly on the stool. "It could be twins. I was at the hospital this morning. Of course, it`s very early but…"

"I don`t believe you." Jack slipped from the stool and walked slowly towards her. "This has got to be a joke. Not twins!"

Jean put her hands on her hips.

"I can assure you that I`m not joking! I am one of twins. My grandmother had twins. My great-grandmother…"

With his hand, he reached back for the counter and once more welcomed its firm support. In less than five minutes, his progeny had doubled from two to four. His mind began racing through the financial implications. His thoughts kept coming back to Jenny. She was a trained accountant. It would be hard to deceive her. He began calculating whether he could launder through his company any monthly alimony payments to Jean. His thoughts were interrupted by Jean`s insistent calling.

"Jack! Are you listening? I`ve had the benefit, unlike you, of time to think about this." Clearly, her words were not penetrating his skull. She sighed and wondered whether she had been too hard on him. He looked crushed and was clearly pale. She decided on another tack. "Jack, before we forget - you said you were bringing the final papers?" He was looking at her but understanding nothing. She tried again. "Remember – this morning? I phoned and left a message for you to bring the papers?"

He nodded. The morning seemed a long way past. Two babies past. He pulled his briefcase onto the counter and flicked the catches open.

"I`d forgotten. Not surprising, really." He took out a wad of papers and spread them out on the counter. "You only have to sign here, here and here."

She picked up a pen from the counter and signed rapidly where his finger stopped along the line of papers. She stood back.

"So that`s all settled then. Let`s make sure I`ve got this right. Financially speaking, this shop has gone bust because I`ve put all the debt into the new one I`ve opened in Dulwich?" He nodded. "And the bank will call in the debts by slapping an attachment order on Henry`s pension because he had taken out a mortgage on our house to pay for this shop?"

"That`s it. Overnight Henry`s pension shrivels. For the foreseeable future. And in the meantime, well, you`ve made a lot of money at his expense. Oh, you`ll need to send him copies of those papers. As you have the others. I suppose you`ve still not heard…?"

She shrugged.

"Not a word. He could be dead for all I know." She motioned to Jack to sit on a stool and settled herself down beside him. She reached under the counter for a half full bottle of wine and two glasses and poured as she chattered. "So let me tell you my plan. I want to open another shop. And possibly one after that. I seem to have become successful at running shops." She giggled girlishly. "Even one that on paper has apparently just gone bust!" She put her arm through his and leaned towards him.

"Tell me, do you think I`m a hard bitch the way I`ve skinned Henry like this? All with your inspiration and help, of course" Jack swallowed. He wondered whether to make an informal offer of maintenance now. He didn`t want anything that Jenny could find out about. His brain began to click as he calculated at what point to start his bidding. Meanwhile, Jean was burbling on but he wasn`t listening. He did the final annual calculation, multiplied it by 18 years and doubled because it sounded as if he was going to be supporting twins. He gasped at the total figure. "Jack? Jack? You`re not listening, are you?" He groaned inwardly. Her voice had a nag to it. Just like his wife`s. And then he heard her repeating, again and again. "And that`s all I want from you. Nothing more. Not a penny."

He blinked.

"Say that again?"

"You`ve been a great help." She giggled again. "I mean, sorting out how to fleece Henry. But that`s all I want from you. Nothing more. Not a penny."

Jack gaped.

"Nothing?"

"I am very happy with what I have and even happier with what I am going to have. Now you may kiss me." She pointed to her cheek. "Just there." He gave her a peck and sat back. "Oh, but I will expect you to waive your accountancy fees from now on. Is that fair?"

He felt like a condemned man stepping back from the gallows.

"Very reasonable, Jean. Very reasonable indeed."

They raised their glasses and clinked them together.

Chapter 37

Marcus Mariowitz had been in the office since 5.30 am. He knew how those guys felt during the Cuba missiles crisis. At his desk, he pounded at the keyboard so fast that he barely had time to look up at the clock on the wall. There wasn`t even time to eat the banana on his desk. Banana yellow was just the shade he had chosen for the walls in the apartment he shared with Dolores and their two boys aged six and four. Not that he had time to see the lounge these days. He was lucky to keep his eyes open in the bedroom for more than a few seconds before he was asleep.

He could feel someone at his side as he pounded the keys. There did not waste time looking up. It had to be Ann-Marie.

"Marcus, can I help you?"

He nodded and watched out of the corner of his eye as she peeled the banana. She was a helluva secretary. And clearly an aficionado of bananas.

As Marcus lunged to take his first bite, the phone rang. He paused momentarily. Ann-Marie had picked up the telephone while continuing to feed the banana in her boss`s mouth. This lady was a professional.

"I`ll put you over," she whispered in a voice that sounded like the wind blowing gently over a dry desert. She handed the receiver to him.

It was the red receiver.

Dolores was hysterical.

"What is that woman....I thought you told me that this phone is for ME...ME you hear? I don`t have to listen to her voice.I`ve taken about as much as..."

Marcus`s mouth was full of banana. He handed the receiver back to Ann-Marie and nodded to the telephone cradle.

"I`m sorry Mrs Mariowitz but your husband is so tied up I`m having to feed him his banana."

She smiled at him as she replaced the receiver gently on the cradle, then lifted it off and lay it on the desk. He approved her action, but thought that in the circustances, Ann-Marie`s choice of words to Dolores was unfortunate. He kept typing and chewing.

He was writing the report that would make or break his career. Ahead of him that morning lay a meeting at the Defense Department, where all the other major Departments would be represented. State Department, National Security Council...It was a meeting so big and so important that it stopped just short of requiring the President to take the chair.

The flow of information from a telephone box in Grenada, via Switzerland to the CIA computer and Marcus`s terminal was now awaited daily by every Washington Department up to and including the White House.

What Washington saw was a tiny Caribbean island just off its shores that was making them nervous. It wasn`t just that it was run by Commies. Or that the Commies kept falling out with each other, but that each succeeding Commie was more left-leaning than his predecessor and was allowing more and more Soviet military hardware onto the island. The Soviets must be wetting themselves laughing.

To make matters worse, the island`s medical school was full of American nationals.

Mariowitz`s intelligence assessment would decide whether the United States moved to the highest state of readiness. The Defense Department was ready with a plan to fly into Grenada United States Air Force transporters to airlift the Americans from the island, whenever needed.

It was now 9am. The red phone was still off its hook and Ann-Marie, perched on the edge of his desk, was feeding him his third banana of the day. The black phone rang. Ann-Marie held the receiver to the side of Marcus`s head as he continued to pound the keys.

"It`s Hurlingham," she whispered.

"Hi Dick!"

Marcus was now on first name terms with Hurlingham.

"How`s it going?"

"Fine. Fine."

"I`ll stop by your room at 10 to pick you up. Your paper has got to be right first time, Marcus. We haven`t any time left for second drafts."

"Sure thing."

Five minutes later, Marcus stood up and stretched and let Ann-Marie sit in his chair to set out his final words neatly on the pages. He loved the way she could make each page look sort of cute and pretty before the document was circulated.

Ann-Marie left the room to circulate the document round the Agency. Marcus replaced the red phone and dialled home on the black one.

"Look Dolores, don`t do this to me. I`m in a crisis. No, she was feeding me the banana. No, she doesn`t do it regular. It was the first time. For Chrissake, it`s the nearest I get to having breakfast!" He slammed down the phone. The red phone rang. "Well tell your shrink! See if I care!"

Hurlingham shimmied into Marcus`s office, his dark blue suit complemented by the palest of blue shirts and a white tie. The Agency favoured white shirts for its staff but Hurlingham liked to strike a slightly defiant note. In his hand he held a copy of Marcus`s document. He held it aloft.

"Very good, Marcus. Very good." He raised his eyes skywards to the top of the building where the Director and Deputies dwelt. "Even the gods smiled on your analysis." He paused for thought, wondering if he had been too generous. "Still, with the sort of sources you`ve got on Grenada, it`s hardly difficult to write a report like that." He nodded to Marcus`s computer. "Any decent news from our guys in the field?"

Grenada was currently undergoing a mild tourist boom. That very morning a short paper written by Jackie in the tourism section was on its way to Lou`s in-tray outlining an astonishing influx of single, male Americans. All were CIA agents who had chosen Grenada as a last minute holiday destination. Lou found the economic statistic all the more surprising because, as Jackie had initially predicted, tourism in general had slumped since the army coup which had replaced Bishop with Coard.

Marcus pulled a face like he had a bad smell under his nose and gave it to Hurlingham straight.

"Those guys are a waste of money. Just tell us what we already know." He tapped the side of his nose. "There`s nothing like an agent on the inside."

In fact only last week Marcus had developed that very point at a CIA seminar which he had been invited to address. The Director himself had put his head round the door for five minutes to listen in.

It was Ann-Marie who put her head round the door now.

"Your office says your car is waiting downstairs, Mr Hurlingham."

Marcus gathered his papers.

"I`ll just go to the john," said Hurlingham. "Catch you at the ground floor."

As he walked past his desk, Marcus couldn`t resist checking to see if Beautiful Lady had signed in. It was a good few days since he had heard from Beautiful Lady and he was getting a teensy bit worried. With a new Prime Minister and government in Grenada, you never knew what was happening to an agent on the inside. He punched the last key and the screen changed. And there was Beautiful Lady. The message was short but so is a stick of dynamite.

Marcus gasped and raced for the lift.

Hurlingham was waiting downstairs where the limousines stacked up. He was tapping his watch.

"Time! Time! Departments of State must not be kept waiting!"

Hurlingham was talking crap and Marcus knew it. He and Hurlingham were only at the meeting as back-up to the Chiefs. Their role was to sit and gaze in awe at the big chiefs up on the rostrum.

In the john, Hurlingham had decided that the journey to the Defense Department should be used as a tutorial for his protégé. He wanted to impart his experience to the junior man. He leaned back in the stretch limo and expounded.

Marcus tried to interrupt. His news couldn`t wait. But Hurlingham was looking out of the window as he recalled previous Defense Department meetings he had attended. Vietnam took up a lot of the time. Hurlingham had operated on the ground in Vietnam and then back with the CIA in Washington.

Marcus looked at the car phone and knew that Hurlingham would want to use it – if only Hurlingham would give Marcus a moment to interrupt him. Finally, as Hurlingham stretched his legs out still further and elaborated on the Viet Cong, he noticed that a shoe lace was undone.

As he paused and bent down to tie the lace, Marcus spoke.

"The Grenadan Prime Minister is going to take our students hostage to stop us invading."

"Good God man!" Hurlingham sat up, holding a

broken end of his shoe lace. "Now look what you`ve made me do!"

Marcus thought that Hurlingham was reaching for the car telephone. Instead he pushed the button that opened the glass window between the passengers and driver.

"Can we stop off somewhere for shoelaces?"

The driver shook his head.

"No way. No time."

The window slid back and Hurlingham turned to Marcus.

"This is dreadful."

Marcus wasn`t sure if Hurlingham was referring to hostage threat or his shoe lace. Hurlingham held his right foot up and wiggled it. The black shoe flopped around.

The limousine pulled into the Defense Department and Marcus followed his limping boss through the security checks and into the lift. In the corridor, a mutual friend from the Defense Department walked quickly past, slapping Hurlingham on the back.

"Howdee Hopalong!"

In the conference room, the Chiefs had yet to take their places at the top table as Hurlingham and Marcus walked the length of the room to sit down. Someone from the National Security Council stopped Hurlingham and asked if he had missed in the john and pissed in his shoe.

When the top table began to fill up, Hurlingham limped over and whispered in the ear of the CIA Chief. Then everyone on the top table whispered in everyone else`s ear. Hurlingham limped back.

"Well Marcus, you are in the shit for holding out with that important piece of information. I can tell you…"

He stopped for the announcement from the top table.

The meeting was being postponed until the evening so that an alternative plan could be worked into a state of immediate readiness. A plan to invade Grenada and forestall the taking of American hostages.

Back in his office, Marcus put his head on his keyboard and fell asleep. When the red phone rang, his mind scarcely skimmed into consciousness as he lifted the receiver from the hook and returned his head to the keyboard. At the other end of the line, all Dolores could hear was heavy breathing.

Chapter 38

Henry felt that his apartment, initially in his fantasies the location for wooing Lou, had become a small torture chamber.

That cockroach worried him. Flattened it might have been but just as there is never just one mouse or one rabbit, so he knew that there is never one cockroach.

Some nights he woke suddenly, reached out with one hand for a heavy book and with the other for the light switch. Often he thought he heard a cockroach scuttling into a dark corner.

He became ever more fastidious with hygiene. He bought bottles of disinfectant, cans of polish, dusters and a new mop to replace the one with the crumbling head in the cupboard in the kitchen.

He cleaned the place rigorously each day but not at the expense of his exercise regime. The jogging and the counting of everything he came across (including seabirds on the beach) continued as usual. Floors were swabbed, the kitchen working top and paintwork were wiped down daily and sand and dust was removed from all surfaces.

When the whole apartment stank so much of disinfectant that he thought no cockroach could survive, the termites appeared.

He was just about to put down the biography of Lord Randolph Churchill and turn off the light when he saw the thin, straight line of termites coming down the wall above his head.

He leapt out of bed in time to haul it into the middle of the room. The termites continued their march down into the floor and the bed stayed out in the centre of the bedroom all night He had read that termites eat books. So in the lounge the sideboard was pulled into the centre of the room, where it stayed, his books perched precariously without a wall to lean upon.

Noise kept him awake at night, too. The fractious Germans in the apartment above him had been replaced by equally loud Americans. Why did couples on holiday spend all their time shouting at each other?

He had identified the early morning typist as an insomniac, insensitive and spotty young Canadian trying to write his first novel. Henry knew he was insensitive because he refused to take his hint about the nocturnal typewriting keeping everyone in the small apartment block awake.

It worried Henry that he could no longer concentrate on anything for long periods of time. No longer could he bury himself in a biography of a European statesman. It occurred to him that he never finished the Robespierre biography. Other biographies that he had started and abandoned had been returned to the sideboard weeks ago.

Every morning he turned on his radio and listened to the BBC World Service but there seemed no indication that an invasion of the island was a serious possibility. Henry could not understand why. He knew that the bogus intelligence that Lou had sent should be sufficient to spur the Americans into action.

What worried him most – and added most to the pressure he felt himself to be under – was the way Lou`s attitude towards him had changed since the execution of Bishop. She had become more distant and at a sub-conscious level he picked up disturbing signals. Her body language was now entirely defensive. She avoided eye contact, no longer put out an affectionate hand, seemed to look through him instead of at him and glanced down the street as if she wanted to be elsewhere. Superficially, she was still friendly when she stopped by to chat to the increasingly sad figure at the café table. In the town, he knew he was becoming a bit of a joke. The café owner even shooed other tourists away from the table with the green umbrella when it was time for Henry to arrive.

Lou remembered Dr Roy`s warning and reduced her contacts with him. But she was careful not to cut him. For all her bravado with Dr Roy, she didn`t doubt his psychiatric analysis of Henry. Always she stopped for a chat as she left the Government building. But she stopped walking with him along the beach or joining him for an evening meal. Just once she stopped for a drink and that was to test Dr Roy`s theory that he counted everything.

"You know Henry…" She sighed and shook her head a little. "Sometimes I worry about myself."

He looked concerned.

"What? Why?"

"Well, sometimes I think that it`s all because I work with figures in the economics section. You know, I leave work and find myself counting everything. The steps I take when I walk back home. The numbers I come across. That sort of thing."

"I shouldn`t worry. It`s quite normal." He smiled. "I do it all the time, too. It`s quite nice really, that both of us should share…"

She smiled back but it was a reflex.

He still followed her around St George`s but so discreetly and at such long distance that he quickly lost her. He no longer cared so much where she was going when he trailed her. It was being close to her that occupied his thoughts and gave him comfort.

He noticed that Lou stopped turning to check whether he was following her. What he did not know was that she no longer had a lie in her life to hide from him.

Dr Roy continued to stop by at his consulting room late of an afternoon and kidded himself that he was working on his books. But Lou did not show up. He would wander on to the courtyard bar, alone.

Henry`s spirits rose briefly when he heard on his radio that some of the other Caribbean islands were even calling for an invasion to restore political stability to the region. But nothing came of it.

One evening, after Lou had stopped by at the café table with time barely for a wave and a peck on his cheek, he decided to fire at the CIA the last shot in his locker. It was the one piece of bogus intelligence that he could lob into Mariowitz`s lap without Lou`s help. Its impact would be so huge that no-one in Washington could ignore it. Just to think of it made Henry laugh and call for another drink. Except that this evening, for a change, he didn`t order Carib beer. He called for a rum punch. And then another.

After he lost count of the number of rum punches he had drunk, he stood up, swaying slightly, to go to the beach. There was an old, disused canvas hut at the far end that was the key to his final piece of bogus intelligence. He set off to dismantle it. Then he remembered. He had always planned to use Lou`s jeep to bring the canvas back to his apartment. He had even thought – before Bishop`s death and Lou`s change of attitude – that she might drive him there and act as look out while he took the hut to pieces.

So he set out for Lou`s apartment.

He knocked at the door just as Lou stepped out of the shower and pulled her short white dressing gown round her. Her first thought was that it might be Dr Roy. The second thought was that his nerve had cracked and he was prepared to re-establish their affair on her terms. In fact, that night as so often since Lou had left, Dr Roy was in the bar in the hotel courtyard watching a skeleton dance for the ever-dwindling tourists.

She opened the door just enough to peer out into the darkened street. The sight of Henry made her instrinctively draw her breath in fright.

"I`m sorry…"

She began to shut the door but not before Henry put his foot in the gap.

"I need to talk." She could smell the rum on his breath as he leant on the door, forcing it wide enough to lurch in. In the narrow white-painted hall, he looked at Lou, her hair wet, her eyes angry and the skimpy gown tight around her body. He thought she was beautiful beyond description.

"So….lov…lov…lovely. Lovely Lou. Oh, Lou."

"What are you doing here, Henry? What the Hell do you mean by this? You promised to leave me alone."

"Lou, I need your jeep. That's it. Jeep. Or you can drive me if you like."

He slurred his words. He was clearly in no state to drive her jeep in his drunken condition. And she had no intention of going out in the dark with him. She folded her arms.

"Why?"

"For the invasion. Last piece of the jigsaw…"

Lou lost her temper and forgot Dr Roy`s warning.

"Henry, get out. Can`t you understand? I am not interested any more in an invasion. Sometimes I wish to God that I hadn`t done anything – hadn`t sent any of your ridiculous messages. It cost lives, Henry. Lives! So just get out. Get out and I don`t want to see you again. You annoy me. You make me unhappy. I want to get on with my life. Without you. Go home to London. I could never, ever love you." She paused. Henry`s face seemed to have gone blank. "Henry, do you understand me?"

They were standing facing each other across the tiny hallway. He stretched out his hands and put them round her neck. As she felt his grip tighten, she couldn`t scream. Only gurgle. Then he began to shake her. He was strong. Very strong. She put her hands around his and tried to unlock them. To stop her kicking and punching, he pressed himself against her. She struggled but it was like trying to fight a statue.

It was the way Lou smelt – all fresh from the shower and without her perfume – that made Henry lessen his grip on her throat. He couldn`t understand why she did not smell of the sultry, spicy perfume that he instinctively associated with her. Lou saw a small frown cross his impassive face and the pressure on her throat eased. He shook his head as if to clear the muddle inside and his eyes widened as he spoke.

"Your perfume. I`ll buy you more perfume."

Lou put her hands up to pull his fingers from her neck.

"I …um… that would be kind."

She tried to edge away but he was still standing over her.

"You do love me. Don`t you?"

She nodded. She now knew she was dealing with a maniac. She would have to say anything to get him out of her home.

"If you go home now," she said, "I`ll visit you."

His eyes sparkled.

"When?"

"Tomorrow."

"Where?"

"At the café."

He shook his head. He was in control of her. He felt power and he was going to use it.

"No! My apartment."

She agreed. At the door, he turned back and held out his hand. She was too scared even to look puzzled.

"What?"

"The keys. To the jeep. Please."

She told him to stay where he was. She found her handbag in the kitchen and pulled out her keys.

"There," she said, thrusting them into his open palm. "Now, please go."

He nodded and moved to kiss her. She turned her cheek but he put his hand on the side of her face and pushed until she moved her head back to face him.

He kissed her on the lips and she dared not resist. At the door he turned and she feared he was coming back. She gripped the wall behind her, scratching the distemper with her red nails.

"After tonight," he said, "an invasion will be inevitable."

He opened the door and she shut it quickly behind him, pulling over the bolt and weeping with relief. She was still crying an hour later when Dr Roy opened his front door and saw the redness on her neck. He took her into the living room, sat her on the sofa and held her until she finally looked up and dried her eyes.

"Do you want a drink?"

She shook her head.

"You were right about Henry."

"That gives me no satisfaction." He had noticed that she hadn`t used her key to get into the apartment and felt the need to reassure her. "You could have used your key you know. And I have been waiting at the consulting room for you to call." As soon as he mentioned how he had waited, he regretted it. She was making him weaker, driving him towards submission.

"I`ve missed you, too, Winston. Especially about an hour ago."

He felt better when he heard that. Perhaps Lou would want to stay over. Maybe they could get things back as they were before. He pushed down the neck of the red top she had put on with her slacks and examined the red marks on her skin. He shook his head.

"You don`t have to tell me. You told him you were ending…Heck, what was it between the two of you? An affair or what?" Lou said nothing. So far as Lou was concerned, Dr Roy could continue to wonder. "Anyway, you told him that whatever it was isn`t any more. And then you had to retract it?"

"Oh yes. And fast. For a moment, I thought he was going to kill me. I didn`t think I would live to retract it."

"What did he say exactly?"

Lou was deliberately vague.

"Oh, lots of personal stuff. About his feelings for me. And he made me give him the keys to my jeep. I could hardly say No."

Dr Roy told her she had to make a decision.

"Do you want to end your relationship my way? It will get him off your hands for good. But you`ll have to do exactly as I say."

Lou turned and looked away. This sounded like more of his control freakery. Soon he would be telling her that she could trust him.

"Winston, I`m not sure…"

He leaned forward.

"Lou. You can trust me."

She gave a great hoot and doubled up with cynical laughter. She laughed until her sides ached and tears ran down her cheeks. She knew that it was in part the release of the night`s tension. Dr Roy sat by her on the sofa and put his arm round her.

"It`s just a little hysteria. Quite under-standable."

That sent her into a new round of soundless mirth. He went for a glass of water, made her drink some and repeated his question.

"So will you do what I say?"

She nodded. She had no choice. Once again, she knew she was under his control. His total control. Again, he was beginning to run their relationship the way he wanted. She wiped the corners of her eyes with her handkerchief.

"OK what do I have to do?"

He ignored her.

"Did you ever ask him about counting rituals?"

She nodded.

"I told him I counted everything. He said he does, too. He said it`s quite normal."

Dr Roy looked thoughtful for a moment.

"OK. Now, we need to get you and Henry together. I know that sounds difficult but…"

"I told him I would go to his apartment tomorrow. It was the only way I could get rid of him."

Dr Roy said that was very good.

"You don`t need to worry about him. He`ll be all right so long as you don`t cross him. Just follow my instructions to the letter and then say you`ve got to leave for an hour or so but you`ll meet him for lunch at *my* apartment. Tell him to be here at 1pm. Tell him anything to get him here. Tell him that the three of us need to talk about the invasion. He couldn`t bring himself to miss that."

Lou said she would feel safer sleeping at Dr Roy`s apartment that night.

"Sure thing."

Lou patted a cushion on the sofa.

"I`ll sleep here."

She noticed that he couldn`t bring himself to look at her.

"I`ll just get a drink for myself," he said as he walked to the kitchen. "And you go in the bedroom. I`ll sleep on the couch."

When he came back into the living room, she was in the bedroom and the door was shut.

Dr Roy found it hard to sleep that night. Not just because his feet were hanging over the end of the sofa but because he was angry. What did that girl think she was playing at? First the emotional blackmail in her letter. Now she wouldn`t even share his bed when she needed a bit of comfort. And all because he refused to use the love word. Heck! If he gave in on that, next stop he`d be marrying her.

While he turned uncomfortably on the sofa, Henry parked the jeep along the Grand Anse beach as close as he could to the old beach hut. In the moonlight, he began taking it to pieces, turning round to check whether he was being watched. As he tugged at a large piece of the canvas, he muttered to himself each time he pulled.

"Bitch! Bitch! Bitch!"

As the first piece of canvas fell free, he rolled it up and began tugging at other pieces, rolling each up as it came free. With the rolls under his arms, he carried them back to the jeep. In the kitchen of his apartment, he slashed at the canvas with a kitchen knife. Outside in the lobby, the American tourists returning to their apartment after a late night out stopped briefly and sniffed the smell of fresh paint. Long after the tourists were in their bed, Henry drove off again in the jeep. He did not return until just before dawn.

Chapter 39

Marcus Mariowitz did not know whether to be worried or angry. Beautiful Lady hadn`t filed any intelligence for days. Should he be worried lest something dreadful had befallen his key agent in the aftermath of Grenada`s bloody coup? Or should he get mad? Hurlingham kept demanding more information on what was happening on the island. Marcus could only provide standard garbage filed by CIA agents who had recently flown in.

He took a kick and the bin flew over the room. It landed on the bomb blast curtains. Ann-Marie put her pretty head round the door.

"Is there anything I can do, Marcus?"

He looked at her face and knew why sometimes it was good to get angry in the office. Ann-Marie was so caring. She always wanted to help. He settled into his chair and smiled up at her and shrugged. Being angry made him feel happy when she was around.

Ann-Marie disappeared and returned quickly with a banana. She had taken to stopping off at a supermarket to buy a bunch on her way to work. She peeled one. Marcus thought he had never seen a banana peeled so sexily. She dangled the white flesh in front of him until his head snapped forward and he bit off a chunk.

Hurlingham put his head round the door just as Marcus was about to take his second bite. He shut the door quickly. Relationships other than strictly professional were frowned on by the Agency because of the risks of blackmail. He decided to ignore what he had seen because Marcus was so important. Upon Mariowitz's inside information depended a lot: Item 1: Operation Urgent Fury, the code name given by the Pentagon to the plan to invade Grenada. Item 2: The rescue of the American students on the island before they could be taken hostage and Item 3: Restoring order.

Halfway down the corridor, Hurlingham turned back. OK, Marcus was important but for days he hadn`t come up with a reliable new intelligence update on what was going on. He again walked into Marcus`s room without knocking. Marcus was at his computer. Ann-Marie had gone.

Hurlingham marched over to the bin and picked out the evidence. Between pinched fingers, he held aloft the banana skin.

"Marcus, I know what is going on between you and your secretary."

Marcus sat up.

"Hey! All she does is feed me bana..."

Hurlingham was having none of it and, still grasping the skin, waved his protest aside.

"I`m sorry, Marcus. I`ve seen you. And it`s disgusting. It would be bad enough outside the office. But in here!" He tossed the skin back in the bin and wiped his fingers on a handkerchief. "More than that, this is no time to be playing suggestive games with your secretary. Operation Urgent Fury needs an update on what the Hell is going on in Grenada! You`ve told us that our American students will be taken hostage in the event of an invasion. I have to tell you, Marcus, that the President takes that very seriously." Marcus stood up and to attention, looking at the Stars and Stripes flag in the corner of his office, as Hurlingham continued. "We know that Soviet missiles have been secretly brought onto the island." Hurlingham shook his head sadly. "I cannot overestimate the seriousness with which the President views that news." Hurlingham noticed that Marcus was standing to attention and felt it would be dishonourable to the flag not to do the same. With his thumbs down the side of his trousers, he went on. "And finally, Marcus, we know that the Soviets have plans to turn the new runway they are building into a military airport. The seriousness with which the President views that is such that..." Hurlingham wanted to shake his head to emphasise the enormity of the President`s seriousness but felt that he could not do so while standing to attention. "The big problem, Marcus. The big problem for the President. And the even bigger problem for you..." Hurlingham began to shout. "IS THAT THERE IS NO DAMNED SATELLITE EVIDENCE TO SUPPORT ANY OF THIS INTELLIGENCE!"

Ann-Marie opened the door and saw the two men standing to attention in front of the Stars and Stripes. She felt that she had no choice. She pulled herself upright, put her heels together and addressed the men in military style.

"Mr Hurlingham! Sir! You are wanted urgently on the phone!"

She turned and marched back to her desk.

Hurlingham grabbed the black phone and shouted to Ann-Marie to put the call through. Marcus sighed. He saw Hurlingham`s face brighten as he listened intently,

"We`re on our way up to your room!"

Hurlingham slapped Marcus on the back and opened the door for him.

"I knew you had it in you! I always trusted your judgement!"

There was a crowd waiting to get into the lift so Hurlingham ran up the one flight of stairs. Marcus puffed behind him and followed him into the satellite analysis room. A crowd of photographic interpreters were huddled around a large picture on one of the many desks. Hurlingham and Marcus pushed through and there, on the grossly magnified picture of the new airport site, was a red circle round the new discovery.

"Wasn`t there yesterday," said a voice tapping a stick at the spot inside the red circle.

"Sure couldn`t miss it today."

Marcus whispered as he peered at the picture.

"Jeez!"

Hurlingham squinted.

"It`s a Goddamn missile silo!" He turned to Marcus. "Those missiles are nukes!"

From that moment, Marcus became a bystander. Even Hurlingham was a bystander. Suddently, all the action transferred to the White House. While the drama unfolded, Marcus joined Hurlingham in his room and both men paced back and forth. Down below, in Marcus`s room, the red phone rang repeatedly. Ann-Marie felt that she couldn`t just let it ring like that even though it was Marcus`s personal line. So each time it rang, she broke off from painting her nails to breathe something reassuring down the line to Dolores.

"Don`t you worry, honey. I`ll see he gets your message. And don`t worry! I`ll look after him."

In Hurlingham`s office, the phone rang late in the evening. He was given a briefing on the events in the White House. President Reagan had joined his Cabinet in the planning room, looking grave as he took his seat at the head of the long, rectangular table.

When the President sat down, so did everyone else in the room. He looked down at the briefing paper in front of him and started at the top. Was that really the date? It was even later in October than he had thought. He moved his finger down the paper to the heading. GRENADA. Ah yes, he remembered now. Damned island was full of Commies who had been killing each other. Well, that was fine by him. So what was the meeting about? He reached out for his jar of jelly beans and cursed. The jelly beans were on his desk in the Oval Office. Why couldn`t he have jelly beans in here as well? He looked around the table at all the faces, some in uniform. They looked pretty damned serious. Probably not a good idea to ask about the jelly beans.

His finger was moving quickly down the page now. Ah yes! This was an emergency. That was why everyone looked so serious. He put on his serious face and looked up.

"Gentleman, we meet in emergency session."

He looked slowly round the room. Should have checked first that there were no ladies present rather than just reading out what was written down.

Out of the edge of his eye, he could see the Stars and Stripes in the corner of the room. He liked that. It reminded him of who he was. He moved his finger down the page.

"Let`s hear the latest on Grenada."

He pronounced the word "Grenayda". It sounded better that way.

A figure in a suit leant forward down the table. Nice suit. Wonder where he had it made? Try to remember to ask him. On the side of the sheet of paper the President wrote carefully SUIT. The figure waited for him to finish writing before he began to speak. That was nice of him. Polite guy. Wonder who he is? By the side of SUIT he put a question mark.

"We have the latest satellite pictures from Grenada, Mr President."

Great! Love pictures. Used to be in pictures myself once. But why did this guy pronounce the name of that island "Grenahda"? He tried to write "pronounci-ation" on his piece of paper but gave up. Anyway, a huge screen on the far end of the wall was coming to life. How did they do that? It looked to be an airport but not yet finished. Hadn`t he seen a picture like this before? The man in the good suit was talking. Best to sit back and listen.

"As our intelligence reports show, the Soviets have plans to develop the new airport so that it can take Soviet transports and become a full-scale military centre. The analysis of the satellite pictures shows that the work is proceeding at speed with the help of Cubans. But we have a further development." The screen filled with a huge magnification of one, tiny part of the airport. In the centre was a large, red ring. The President leant forward to get a better look. The heads round the table looked at him. His face was grim. He looked down at his briefing paper and moved his finger down. Nope. Nothing here about flying saucers. But the ring was red. Had the Commies got a flying saucer? The man in the nice suit continued. He was good, this guy. Clear, distinguished voice. Face seemed familiar, too. "CIA and other analysis shows this development to be a missile silo. A silo capable of launching a Soviet nuclear missile. As you can see, the land in this area is also in a state of preparation – we believe for further silos."

All the faces round the table turned to look at the President. He looked down at his paper. Nope. That wasn`t the bit. He could remember saying something a few moments back about this being an emergency session. Ah yes, there it was. Oh boy! That`s a nice line. Who the heck writes this stuff?

"I don`t need to elaborate on the obvious. What we are talking about is our backyard. That silo is so close that the Defense Department cannot guarantee to bring down a missile fired at the United States."

He looked up. Everyone seemed to be staring at him again. Wasn`t that enough? Surely there wasn`t more? He moved his finger down. Well, I`ll be jiggered. It sure was a busy morning.

"Well, this is when it all comes down to the President. Are we ready Mr Defense Secretary to go with the invasion plans I've authorised?"

At the table, another, older man in a civilian suit leaned forward.

"Yes, Mr President."

Well, that was reassuring. Always good to be ready to go with plans. But who the heck was that? Surely that couldn`t have been the Defence Secretary. Where was his uniform? Either it wasn`t the Defense Secretary or he needed a uniform. The President looked closely at him. Face seems somehow familiar. So it was a uniform he was missing. Carefully, at the bottom of the piece of paper he wrote UNIFORM. Well, he`d be danged if they weren`t all looking at him again. His finger moved down the page. He felt the page between his fingers. Yup, just the one page. Soon be over.

"Then we invade. Thank you gentlemen."

Yup, he was sure about that. They were all gentlemen. He`d checked that himself before. So we were invading. Didn`t do that very often. Still, it had to be done. Was it time for lunch? Or had he had lunch? Maybe he`d just settle for a jelly bean or two back at the Oval Office.

As he stood up, there was a great scraping of chairs as everyone followed him.

At the door, the President saw the younger man in the nice suit. The man who couldn`t say Grenada properly. He clapped him on the shoulder.

"I say Grenayda. You say Grenahda."

From the back of the crowd the President heard a voice singing the third line of the stanza.

"Let`s call the whole thing off."

The President laughed.

"Too late now!"

The man who had sung out the punchline pushed through to stand at his side. The President smiled and slapped him on the back. He liked this man with the good singing voice. He was the guy who was always trying to settle things the peaceful way. A man who didn`t like wars. Now the guy was speaking to him.

"Er, Mr President. D`you think we ought to tell the Brits? Y`know – the Queen. She`s Grenada`s head of state. And there`s Mrs Thatcher, the British Prime Minister."

The President nodded. Yup – nice ladies. He liked

them a lot. Were they sisters? He could never remember. More importantly, where was that piece of paper? He slapped his pockets. Couldn`t do anything without a piece of paper. Nope – no paper. He looked up.

"Aw shucks! They`ll understand."

He strolled off. What was it those ladies would understand? Heck, he`d forgotten already.

What the heck were they all going on about?

Chapter 40

Lou arrived at Henry`s apartment in the late morning and saw her jeep parked along the road. It appeared to be packed in the back. She peered through the window. The jeep was full of pieces of rotting canvas.

At Henry`s door, she felt frightened and her hand shook as she knocked. She tried to remember what Dr Roy had told her - to reassure Henry about their relationship. Then he would be no problem. As she waited for him to answer the door, she felt nauseous.

He opened the door and she quickly leant forward to offer cheek. He smiled and kissed it, smelling her perfume and feeling reassured. She dropped her head and spoke quickly.

"I`m sorry about last night."

He stood back and waved her in. The lounge was covered in fragments of canvas.

Lou sniffed the unusual mix of disinfectant and fresh paint. On the sideboard she saw a spray can of silver paint.

"I was clearing up," he said. "Terrible mess. Didn`t get back until the early hours."

He was going round the floor on all fours picking up the scraps of canvas. She said she would make coffee. When she came back with the tray, he was still on the floor picking tiny pieces of thread off the small rug.

"Haven`t you got a vacuum cleaner?" He looked up and shook his head. "Well, why not try a brush?"

"Ah!" He came back from the kitchen with a stiff brush and removed the final pieces from the rug. "I`ll wash the floor later."

She saw the keys to her jeep on the cabinet and picked them up.

"Finished with them?"

"I haven`t cleared out the canvas."

"Do you need the jeep again?" He shook his head. "Then I`ll get rid of the stuff in the back." She just wanted her jeep back. She sat on the sofa with her coffee and became brisk. "Before I forget, Winston wants to know if you can join him at his apartment at 1 o`clock. He wants to talk about the American invasion. Something he`s heard. Or something like that. I`ve said I`ll be there."

Henry became agitated.

"What`s he heard about the invasion?"

"Henry, I don`t know! That`s what Winston is going to tell us. Now can you join us or not?"

He nodded vigorously.

"Oh yes. Yes."

"Well that`s good. Just don`t forget. One o`clock at Winston`s place. Now, about last night. I said I`m sorry. I know how you feel, Henry. I really do." She put her cup on the arm of the sofa and stood up. "It`s not that I`m a woman who doesn`t have – well, a woman`s needs. And I am very fond of you. You know that." She moved towards him and briefly touched his arm. "But I said that I need time."

"Time?" His voice rose in an angry question. "But yesterday you tried to end our relationship."

She kept smiling to try to reassure him.

"Exactly! That`s how I react to pressure. Why can`t we take it nice and easy? After all, it`s little more than five months, just 159 days, since you arrived here." She touched his arm again. "I know – I counted them."

Henry`s brow wrinkled briefly.

"A hundred and fifty seven, actually."

She held his arm for a moment.

"It`s wonderful that we have discovered that we both share a need to count everything." She drew away from him a little. Dr Lou`s forecast of how Henry would react had been correct so far but she was worried about antagonising him. "But it *is* 159 days."

She watched anxiously as Henry recoiled slightly.

"No!"

She smiled and squeezed him army quickly.

"Now, Henry – just stay calm. I was top of the class at maths." He stood frowning and she kissed him quickly on the cheek. "If we are going to get really close in this relationship, you must accept that I am right on these matters."

Henry seemed unable to accept what she had said and stepped towards her.

"No!"

Lou spoke quickly.

"Now, I need the bathroom."

She didn`t like the way he was reacting and quickly picked up her handbag from the sofa. She tried to smile reassuringly as she walked into the bedroom. She heard him muttering to himself.

"There are 30 days in June and 30 in September and 31 in July and 31 inAugust and…"

He heard the sound of running water in the bathroom, then Lou`s shouts.

"Shit! Oh, Henry. I'm so sorry! I`ve just used your soap! And your towel!"

He ran through the bedroom and towards the bathroom. Lou saw him coming as she left the bathroom and stepped smartly aside as he rushed to the basin.

"I can`t stop any longer. I need to get through some work at my apartment. I`ll meet you at Winston`s place for lunch at 1 o`clock. OK?"

She deliberately swung her handbag at the piles of

stacked coins and row of parallel pens and pencils on the bedside table. As they fell noisily to the floor, she ran from the room and to the front door, where she paused and shouted.

"Damn! Sorry about the mess, Henry. Must dash."

He stepped from the bathroom and stared at the coins, pens and pencils on the floor. He sank onto the edge of the bed and hugged his knees, moaning.

Lou stood by the front door and called again.

"Catch you at Winston`s at 1 o`clock. Oh – and I just know it`s 159 days! I`m never wrong about that sort of thing."

He heard the front door slam and rose from his bed moaning softly. "Oh, Lou! Lou!" He bent down slowly to replace his possessions in their precise order on the bedside cabinet. Later, he put into the rubbish bin the bar of soap Lou had used and put the towel in the laundry basket. After pouring disinfectant into a bucket of water, he mopped down the floors, counting each movement of the brush.

He left his apartment in good time to be at Dr Lou`s for his lunch appointment. He was dressed in shorts, white shirt and sandals. Like his flat, he smelled strongly of disinfectant. He still felt badly shaken and stood in the lobby looking at the dry sand that had blown into the corners under the door. He wondered whether he had time to clear up the mess when a postman walked up the steps to the apartment block. This was a new postman, appointed following the Govenrment review of St George`s failing postal service.

He was tall and lanky with a lopsided smile. Henry looked blankly at him. Not to be put off, the postman made a declaration that he hoped would put into the past the postal service`s recent reputation for unreliability.

"Hello! I`m your new, efficient post man!" He looked at the strip of paper in the tiny metal rack by Henry`s front door, then at the mail in his hand. The two names matched. He beamed again. "Are you Mr Henry Turville?"

"Yes."

The postman thrust the envelope into his hand and then a large box wrapped in brown paper.

"Well then, that`s for you! You have a nice day. Don`t forget - I`m your new post man. Service with a smile!"

He walked up the stairs to deliver to the next floor as Henry stood, not knowing whether first to open the envelope or the box. He returned to the apartment to think about it and then became even more anxious for fear of being late for his appointment.

He knew that the box must contain his extra strong mints. By ritual, he should keep the box to open last because it would contain good news. The envelope was thick, heavy and in Jean`s handwriting. It seemed threatening. After much pacing up and down, he opted to open the box first. He was desperate for a soothing mint. Just holding the box reminded him of how much he relied on them. He pulled off the brown paper, lifted the lid of the old chocolate box and found that his sister had packed the mints as neatly as he expected. He removed two packets and put the box carefully in a sideboard drawer. Feeling the strength of the mint as it dissolved in his mouth, he put both packets in the back pocket of his shorts and opened the envelope. He turned the pages of written documents quickly, wiped his hand across his forehead and moaned.

"The bank!"

He slammed the apartment door behind him and ran all the way to the centre of the town, waving the letter and muttering.

"I`m ruined! Ruined!"

His distraught appearance and distracted manner caused little surprise among the townsfolk that morning. Increasingly he was becoming known as Mr Jig-a-Jig, the eccentric Englishman who, when not running everywhere talking to himself, sat at a café table trying to win a smile from the town`s most beautiful young woman.

As Henry ran towards the bank, Dr Roy was settling down with Lou in the double bed in his apartment. However, appearances were very deceptive. For after Lou climbed reluctantly into the bed, she sat up with her arms folded over her bra. Lying on his side, Dr Roy stroked her hair but without the usual satisfactory results. She refused to purr.

"And you can stop that!" she snapped as she pulled his hand from her hair. "I`m not even considering letting you touch me again until this business with Henry is over. And even then, don`t get your hopes up Winston Roy!"

He looked at his wrist watch.

"Well Lou, you know I`d rather this was the real thing. But let`s put on a good show for old Henry."

He pulled Lou astride him.

She looked fiercely down at him.

"You keep your hands off my pants Winston Roy!" She began to move up and down on him. "This had better work, Winston." She stopped and giggled. "I feel so silly doing this!"

Dr Roy loooked up at her.

"Shall I take over?"

She resumed her humping motion.

"Not on your sweet life!"

Henry was standing at the counter in the bank impatiently popping mints into his mouth. A kindly, middle-aged woman cashier was trying to be helpful but she couldn`t make the figures in front of her look better than they were. Behind her, a clock ticked as the cashier tried again to make Henry understand.

"I`m telling you Mister Turville, that`s all there is. There ain`t no more money in your account. That`s all that`s come in this month!"

Henry banged the wooden counter with both fists.

"But it`s my money! Where`s my money?"

His voice became more plaintive as the cashier scribbled on a slip of paper.

"There. I`ve written the balance down for you."

She pushed the slip across the counter. Henry waved it aside as his widening eyes alighted on the clock. The time was 12.57 pm. The cashier stood back in alarm as her customer screamed.

"Arghhhh! I`ll be late!"

As he crashed through the doors and ran full pelt down the street, the skies over St George`s opened in a storm that was spectacular even by the island`s standards. While islanders fled for cover, the mad Englishman ran on, a drenched, white blur through rain so heavy it looked like fog. He moaned at every crack of stone that he stepped on.

"Arghh! Arghh!"

In Dr Roy`s apartment, Lou was rising and falling on Dr Roy, who ostentatiously yawned and then suddenly stared hard at her before speaking.

"Hey! You aren`t enjoying this, are you? You know, imagination can be a mighty powerful force."

Lou giggled and collapsed on him as he turned his head and again inspected his wrist watch.

"Henry`s late. Have you ever known Henry be late for anything?"

Lou was now lying at his side smiling at him. It was difficult to remain angry or serious with Dr Roy when he was being funny.

She shook her head.

"Henry is *never* late."

Dr Roy asked her if she knew what Henry`s problem was. She shook her head again.

"That man is forever looking at the time."

"He`s even got a clock in his bathroom."

Dr Roy whistled.

"Never! He must time his tooth brushing. Even, perhaps...Well, it blows the mind just imagining it." Lou pulled herself over Dr Roy again and smiled down at him. “Do you know the first thing I would do if Henry was my patient?”

“What?”

“I`d make him give me that wrist watch. And then I`d stamp on it and say – Henry Turville, you gotta realise that you aren’t in London. Or New York. Or Washington. This is little old Grenada where time doesn`t matter!”

Lou`s smile became a frown.

“And would that be professional? Stamping on his watch?”

“Heck, no. But it`d make me feel a damned sight better!”

She collapsed on him in helpless laughter.

“Winston, sometimes you are irresistible!”

Dr Roy turned his head sharply.

“Shush! That`s Henry.”

Lou rose over him again and began humping furiously.

The rain was still lashing Henry as he slopped on the steps leading to Dr Roy`s apartment. He stood on the first step, pulled the sodden papers from his back pocket, replaced them, pulled them out again and made as if to read. He remembered the time, looked at his watch, gasped and pushed the papers back into his pocket. All the time he was muttering.

“The cow! I`m ruined! And I`m late. Never late…Worth less than half what I was! No! Two thirds gone! What the hell is happening?”

He put his thumb on the bell on the door, which stood slightly ajar. The pressure sent the door crashing back against the inside wall of the hall. Down the short passageway he could see into the bedroom. He saw her back and long black hair. It was Lou. Having sex with Dr Roy.

Henry stood motionless, then swallowed the mint in his mouth whole and sagged against the door jamb calling her name.

“No! Lou!” He staggered down the hallway, his

sodden shoes squelching on the wooden floor. “Everything – gone.”

He stood at the bedroom door and Lou slowed her humping. Dr Roy raised his head slightly from the pillow and his eyes met Henry`s. Henry blurted out the words.

“You said you were gay!”

Dr Roy lifted himself a little more from the bed and peered round Lou`s hunched body.

“Hey! A man can try to be persuaded, can`t he?”

Lou couldn`t see Henry but she could hear him. The sound was unmistakeable. He was hyperventilating. Then there was a great squelching noise as he rushed towards the bed, picked up the bedside lamp and let out a great roar.

When Lou saw the table lamp in Henry`s grasp, she screamed and threw herself off Dr Roy. To protect himself, Dr Roy raised a hand and dodged enough for the lamp to miss and come down harmlessly on the pillow. Henry lurched forward, his hands outstretched for Dr Roy`s throat. Dr Roy kicked out with his feet and Henry fell back against Lou`s empty wardrobe. Each man crouched, ready for the other`s move. Dr Roy was dressed only in his shirt and pants and Henry dripped puddles on the rug. Finally, Dr Roy hurled himself forward and the two men grappled, each trying to force the other to the ground.

As Dr Roy felt Henry`s strength overwhelming him, he called to Lou.

“Help me! Do something!”

Under the sheets, Lou pulled up her legs and gripped them with her encircled arms, ignoring both of them. She was fed up with men seeking to control her. Why couldn`t Henry go away and Winston get on with loving her? She wanted to be treated like other women. Dr Roy looked imploringly at her and shouted again for help. Lou was so consumed with her anger that she unthinkingly uttered the thought in her mind at that moment.

“None of my friends seem to have these problems.”

It seemed such an extraordinary remark to make to a man struggling for his life, that Dr Roy`s concentration slipped and Henry pushed him to the ground, snarling.

"I don`t need a woman`s help."

Dr Roy`s last memory was of the table lamp coming at him again. This time the glass lamp splintered on his skull and he sprawled motionless on the soggy rug.

Without a glance at Lou, Henry slopped out of the room and down the corridor, oblivious to everything around him save for the gaps in the stone tiles. He stepped round or over the gaps, straight-legged and detatched from the rest of the world. Outside, the rain still flooded down. Huddled in doorways, the islanders watched the eccentric Englishman run back through the town.

Lou peered over the side of the bed at the still figure.

"God, he`s killed him!"

Then she noticed a tiny rise and fall of his chest. She kneeled on the bed and reached up to the windowsill to grab a dying pot plant from its saucer. She poured the dirty liquid onto Dr Roy`s face. He opened his eyes and looked slowly round the room as Lou knelt over him.

"Well, Mr Psychiatrist. That worked well, didn`t it? Why do I listen to anything you say?"

He rose groggily from the floor, first holding the side of the bed and then Lou`s arm. He waved aside her criticisms.

"No, no. You don`t understand. The psychiatric analysis was fine. It was the joke. I shouldn`t have made the gay joke."

"It was in bad taste."

He sank back to the floor, holding his head.

"Sure, but not that bad!"

Chapter 41

Dr Roy lay on the couch in his consulting room. His black medical bag lay open on his desk as Lou applied ointment to the bump and scratches on his forehead. He was protesting.

"I didn`t need you to do this!"

She picked up the scissors and cut off a square of plaster.

"If you`re as lousy a medical doctor as you are a psychiatrist, then you definitely need me to do this."

He grimaced.

"Hey! That hurts!"

She leant over him and smiled sweetly.

"It`s meant to. It`s called revenge."

Dr Roy crossed his arms on the couch.

"Well, Henry's safely tucked up in the Crazy House. I`d say that was a success."

She gently patted the plaster down on his forehead.

"I`d have thought a psychiatrist would count it a success getting someone out of that place, not putting someone in it. And anyway, I wish you wouldn`t call it the Crazy House."

"It`s what everyone calls it."

"It`s not the correct term. It`s the mental institution."

She stood back from the couch. Dr Roy sat up and asked her if she had ever been there.

"Well, no."

"Then take my word. It`s the Crazy House."

The Crazy House was in Fort Matthew, another of the island`s ancient colonial forts. It had been built by the French then taken over by the British.

With his fingers, Dr Roy gently felt the growing bump on his forehead. He sat up and held out his hand to Lou. She passed him the medical bag and from a bottle he shook three tablets into the palm of his hand.

"Henry will be quite happy inside."

At Dr Roy`s suggestion, the local police had picked up Henry and the other doctors at the Crazy House had agreed that he was a danger to himself and the community.

Even as Dr Roy replaced the bottle in his medical bag and shut it, Henry was counting the floor tiles in his new home. There were 400 and they were so tiny that the only way to avoid the cracks was to walk on tip toe. When he wasn`t on tiptoe, he was lying on his bed. Either way, he was happy. His brain had given up, at least for the moment. Where once his mind heaved and bubbled, now the surface was as empty and serene as the smile on his face. His only nagging anxiety was that he was down to his reserve tube of mints.

In the consulting room, Dr Roy lay down on the couch again while he waited for the tablets to get to work on his headache. Lou asked if they really were safe from Henry.

"You don`t get out of the Crazy House easily. Believe me."

She put the medical bag back in the cupbard and asked Dr Roy if, while he was at the mental institution, he had heard any news of an invasion.

"Shucks, no. There ain`t no news. It`s all gossip. Didn`t you say Henry had a view on that?"

"He says it`s inevitable now."

"Yeah, but look who`s talking. I wouldn`t believe what anyone in the Crazy House told me."

Lou pulled up the hardback chair and put it at the

head of the couch.

"Two men and neither of them ever give a damn what an invasion would mean for me." He made to get up but she shouted at him. "Lie down on the couch Winston!" He sank back, protesting.

"Hey – you`re the one who goes on the couch!"

She put on her sweet voice and leaned forward again. He could see her cleavage and that reminded him of the way she had straddled him in his bed that morning. It still seemed a tremendous waste of effort. All that time pretending. He decided that the tablets must be working because he was starting to feel relaxed. Lou was talking sweetly to him.

"You`re on the couch because I`m thinking of your health, dearest. I`m not expecting you to take off your trousers." She pecked him on the nose. "And I don't *want* you to, either."

"I just don`t know what`s come over you!"

"Oh yes you do, darling. But for now we have more serious things to talk about. Winston, do you know what invasion means for me? It means that more American soldiers than even Henry could count are going to crawl over the island. And when they realise that what I`ve told the CIA comes off the back of a cereal packet, they`re all going to start looking for one lady. Me!"

Dr Roy sat up.

"Yeah! And the guy who was responsible for all this – old Henry – will be banged up in the safest place on the whole island. Who`s going to look for him there – let alone take any notice of what he says?"

Lou pushed him back onto the couch and picked up the clipboard. He tried to sit up again but she hollered at him.

"You just stay there!"

He settled back as she strolled to the blinds and pretended to look out.

"Dr Roy, do you love me?"

He stared at the ceiling.

"I knew that the love word was behind everything that`s gone wrong between us. It`s behind why you walked out. It`s behind why you don`t want to sleep with me any more. It`s behind why…well, why the way you are these days. That`s the trouble with the love word. Believe me baby, if we both stay away from that word, we can get on real fine."

She tapped the clipboard with a painted finger nail.

"You`re on the couch, Winston. You answer the question. Yes. Or No. Do you love me?"

He paused, agonised and answered finally and reluctantly.

"You know the rules, Lou. We don`t talk of love. Love is an abstract concept. Unprovable."

She threw the clipboard to the floor.

"Winston, when I last got off that couch and walked out through that door and you called me back, I thought for just one moment that you were going to say that you loved me."

Dr Roy made no reply. But he recalled that for a moment *he* had thought he was going to say he loved her. He had rescued himself just in time.

"Look honey…"

"No honeying please, Winston. Do you love me? Yes or No?"

"Well, I`ll answer but first *you* define the concept."

She bent down, picked up the clipboard and mimicked him.

"You know the rules, Dr Roy." She suddenly spoke fiercely. "Questions by the patient are not permitted! I`ve got the clipboard tonight!" She stood silently and looked at Dr Roy. He had shut his eyes, pretending to be asleep. She felt herself go limp with physical and mental exhaustion, walked slowly across the room and slumped behind his desk. She put down the clipboard.

"OK. Game`s over, Winston. What do we do about the Americans? And me?"

He sat up

"Well, I`ve been thinking about that. If the Americans come, they`re bound to seal the harbour and everything in it. Including my boat. But we can phone the Levitts up the coast. Now. Tell them we want to moor my boat up there. I`ll take it up there. While I do that, you do some packing. Get a few suitcases together and then drive up to the Levitts in the jeep. We put the cases on the boat." He got off the couch and paced the room. "Then we`ll drive back here and get all the cash together that we can. And jewellery. Anything small we can sell. Then, if we hear that Uncle Sam is on his way, we drive back to the boat and head for Tobago. I`ve got friends there who`ll put us up. We just wait for good old Uncle Sam to kick out your man Coard and his cronies and install a good free-enterprise government. Then, when the dust has settled, we`ll come back and pick up where we left off. How about that?" He stood waiting for her to reply.

"Do you know what I`m thinking?"

He scratched his head.

"As a psychiatrist, I should be able to make a good guess. But you`ll have to tell me."

She stared hard at him.

"I`m thinking – what if you just get in your boat and go straight to Tobago without me? You see Winston, I know what`s been going on in your mind all these weeks. You pushed me into the arms of Henry Turville because you wanted Bishop out of the way. And then you kept pushing me there because you wanted an invasion to get rid of Coard. You`d do anything to use me so long as you could get a free hand again to run your drugs!"

Dr Roy came close to shouting.

"That`s not fair! You wanted Bishop out!"

Lou nodded.

"Sure! But you kept me going with Henry to try to get an invasion so that Coard would go, too!"

He shrugged.

"Once started, it wasn`t something that could be stopped. It had to run its course. But if you`re saying that you can`t trust me, well that`s as bad as saying I don`t care. And I do. You can trust me to take you safely to Tobago."

Lou stood up wearily from the desk.

"I have no choice."

Chapter 42

In the moonlight, hand in hand, Lou and Dr Roy walked along the beach where, less than five months earlier, they had walked with Henry. Lou held her shoes and handbag in her free hand and she spoke less than lovingly to him..

"You were a total shit that night, going off and leaving me with him."

Dr Roy did not like the turn of the conversation. He had been on the point of suggesting that she go back to his apartment with him. It was now past midnight. Lou had driven to the Levitts, dropped the luggage in his waiting boat and then returned with him. He tugged at her hand.

"OK Lou, I`ll tell you the truth. If I had that bit of my life again, I wouldn`t do it that way. So I suppose I`m saying I`m sorry. Not easy for Winston Roy to do."

They walked on again and she squeezed his hand.

"Well, thank you, kind sir. But then again, there are quite a few things that Winston Roy finds it hard to say."

"Trust. Caring. They`re what matters." He decided to leave the sex bit out. He did not want to push his luck. "And, you see, you can trust me. Can`t you? The boat is at the Levitts. And I`m not in Tobago. I`m here. With you."

She smiled and nodded and tried to explain her feelings.

"I suppose these last few weeks…it`s all too much.

I`ve become so cynical. I now know what it is to think old."

Dr Roy leant over to kiss her bare neck. She liked that.

Just as his lips touched her flesh, a flash lit up the hill on which St George`s stood. A huge, thumping noise made them start and clutch each other. Another, giant flash of light momentarily illuminated everything. They stood transfixed as a distant drone filled the sky. It was the noise of approaching aircraft and helicopters.

Dr Roy spoke first.

"Oh shit!"

His hopes of a night in bed with Lou had gone up in fire and smoke.

Lou shrugged her shoulders.

"I guess our next stop`s Tobago."

Back in London in a richly furnished bedroom, a telephone rang with the shrill insistence that only comes with a call in the middle of the night. From the double bed, rose the hand of Sir Geoffrey Waltonbury. Beside him, a woman stirred. She was in her late thirties and she was not Sir Geoffrey`s wife, who was sleeping undisturbed more than a hundred miles away in a county town. Sir Geoffrey`s aimless grasp eventually found the bedside lamp, which he switched on, revealing his blue and white striped pyjamas. Beside him, his mistress examined the traces of her mascara that had come off on the pillow. She wished Geoffrey wouldn`t do that – rushing her into bed before she had time even to take off her make up. The wandering hand moved on, located the telephone receiver and drew it down to Sir Geoffrey`s hairy ear.

"Yes?" He listened for a few moments. "The two-faced idiots! Thank you." He sat up, replaced the receiver and remained leaning on the headboard.

Through her pillow, the voice of his mistress reached him.

"Is everything all right?"

Sir Geoffrey thought that it was pretty darned obvious that everything was not all right. A Foreign Office Minister did not get woken half way through the night to be told that everything was all right. However, as he was in bed with his mistress and not his wife, he said none of this.

"No, it damned well isn`t. Bloody Yanks have just invaded Grenada."

The woman`s head raised itself a few centimetres from the pillow.

"Isn't that ours?"

"Part of the Commonwealth! Her Majesty is Head of State! And the bloody Yanks go ahead and do this after I cut our aid to the island to please them! Not so much as a word by way of asking if they could!"

Sir Geoffrey`s friends said that his mistress had a sharper political brain than his. His enemies said that almost any mistress he chose would have that benefit. She got to the point.

"And what if the Americans had asked for permission?"

Sir Geoffrey spluttered.

"We would have refused. Of course."

"Well, there`s your answer. Now put the light off."

In Lou`s jeep, the headlights cut a path through the darkness, illuminating the banana and spice trees as the road wove through the small plantations. It had taken the couple only a few minutes to collect their money and valuables and secure their apartments as best they could before climb-ing back into Lou`s jeep.

Lou had changed into shorts and now she sat, her shoes on the floor and her feet on the dashboard as she gripped her knees and listened to Dr Roy.

"This could be a bit of a holiday," he said. "A few weeks, that`s all it should take before we can come back. A couple of months at most. The Americans won`t want to hang around here. Wham! Bang! Thank you mam! That`s old Uncle Sam when his dander is up."

Lou felt bright, almost positive. The waiting was over and the adrenalin was flowing.

"I reckon my cash will hold out for a couple of months," she said. "But will I be able to get to my bank account from Tobago? Will the Americans freeze the account? And how long will your friends be prepared to put up with us? And how long will the money last if my account is frozen? And what will we do if…?"

"Hey!…"

Dr Roy got no further. The jeep was about a mile from the Levitts`s house but an American jeep was in the way, pulled across the road. Dr Roy hit the brakes. He could see three soldiers and they were all pointing rifles at him.

One sauntered up and Dr Roy was surprised how angry he felt at this foreigner coming to tell him what to do on his own island. The soldier motioned with his rifle for Dr Roy to wind down the window and spoke with a thick, Southern drawl.

"You folks just get out now, nice and slow." Dr Roy climbed from the jeep and put up his hands. He hadn`t been asked to put them up but it seemed the sensible thing to do. Lou saw his hands go up and for a moment thought he looked rather silly. Then the soldier motioned with his rifle to her to get out. "Nice and slow, ma`am," said the soldier. She heard one of the other soldiers speaking. "Oh yes mam! That`s real nice." She flounced forward and stood with her hands on her hips.

"What do you mean, stopping us like this?"

The soldier just smiled and motioned up with his rifle. She put her hands up and stood next to Dr Roy.

"Well," said the solider, "now where you-all going this time of night?"

Dr Roy lowered his hands to speak but put them up when the soldier stood back and moved his rifle menacingly.

"To friends. Just down the road."

Overhead there was a loud noise. It could have been

an aircraft. Or a helicopter. The other soldier intervened and shouted through the noise.

"They're lying. On a night like this, no-one with good intentions is out making social calls. Let`s take `em in."

As Lou and Dr Roy were pushed into the back of the military jeep, their hands cuffed behind their backs, another flash lit up the sky over St George`s. They heard the thump a second later.

A soldier climbed into the driving seat and turned to them.

"Are you two Commies?"

Dr Roy and Lou shook their heads.

"Heck no!" said Dr Roy.

"`Cos if you are," said the soldier, "the folks we`re taking you to will kick the living shit out of youse." The soldier let out the clutch and Lou and Dr Roy lurched back as a second flash lit up the sky over St George`s.

The first military strike on Fort Matthew threw Henry out of his bed and onto the tiles. He picked himself up and peered at the floor. It was too dark to tell where the cracks were in the tiles. He bent down and traced the outline with his fingers before, doubled over, he tip-toed back to bed.

In Henry`s mind – or what now passed for a mind – there was a vague realisation that the invasion had begun. But the exultation that he should have experienced was missing. So was much else missing from his mind. He was no longer thinking. It was more a case of occasional and unrelated thoughts taking a leisurely stroll through his head. The overload that his mind had suffered when he found Lou in bed with Dr Roy had blown a mental fuse. That Lou was prepared to go to bed with a gay man rather than him was just too much. Especially coming on top of his discovery that Jean had somehow removed two thirds of his monthly pension from his bank account.

The second military strike on the Crazy House blew down one of the walls in Henry`s cell. In the process, a large quantity of ancient stonework fell on him, sending him into the blissful unconsciousness that his brain yearned for and the drugs that the doctors had pumped into him had failed to deliver. When he finally awoke and struggled out from the pile of stones, originally laid by the French more than two hundred years before, he felt brighter. It was a general feeling of wellbeing that pervaded his body. His brain was still taking a rest.

The first shards of daylight were lighting the hole in the wall as Henry stepped out. Other figures shambled round, some fighting each other and one in what Henry took to be a straitjacket. Henry took a stroll. The air smelled fresh after the stale body odours of the old fort. Strains of music beckoned from a distance. And then a familiar, English voice. It was the BBC World Service. He walked on and, through the gap where a wall once stood, he saw a desk covered in debris. On it was a small, rectangular portable radio that had been black but was now grey with dust. He leaned in and borrowed it. As the light of the day hardened, he pressed the radio to his ear and, still dressed in shorts, short sleeved shirt and sandals, ambled through the town. Occasionaly, he stopped to bellow with laughter at the World Service news bulletins. Two American soldiers in a jeep picked him up and, because of his clothing, mistook him for someone sane. He was quite happy to walk with the soldiers to their jeep but when they cuffed his hands behind his back and tossed the radio into the gutter, he sat in the back and cried. His weeping became uncontrollable when he remembered his final, reserve packet of mints. It was buried under the rubble.

Chapter 43

Out at sea, the US battle fleet headed by Admiral Joseph Metcalf the Third, under orders from President Reagan, was about to head towards Grenada. The mission was Operation Urgent Fury.

In Marcus`s office, Hurlingham stood over the desk of the Agency's most prized employee and jumped from one foot to another. Hurlingham, waiting for Marcus to end his conversation on his red phone, was regretting ever fighting to have it installed.

Marcus held the phone away from his ear while he tried to mouth to his boss that he wouldn`t be a moment. Hurlingham mouthed to Marcus to get a move on.

On the other end of the phone, Dolores was saying that she and Marcus needed to sit down as a couple and have a talk to "clear the air, reach some decisions…make some space…" It was important that they sat down together, she explained, because her therapist had told her so. Marcus felt that all this was a poor return for the amount of money he had spent on the therapist.

Hurlingham listened aghast as Marcus prepared to replace the red receiver.

"Yes darling, I promise. I`m coming home now. Absolute promise. We`ll talk. Yes. Absolute promise. Love you honey."

When Marcus looked up, Hurlingham told him that a car was waiting outside the building to take him to the helicopter that would take him to the battle fleet that was going to Grenada.

"But I`ve just told Dolores I`m going home for an early night."

Hurlingham pushed him out of the door.

"Admiral Joseph Metcalf the Third needs you more. Don`t worry about your wife. I`ll sort it out with her."

In the lift, Hurlingham again assured Marcus that he would talk to his wife.

"Promise?" said Marcus.

"Scout`s honour."

After pushing him into the stretch limo and giving him the thumbs up, Hurlingham strolled through Marcus`s office and into the smaller one occupied by Ann-Marie.

"Hi. Do me a favour. Get onto Marcus`s wife and tell her he`s going off for a few days. Can`t say where."

He smiled politely and shut the door.

Ann-Marie smiled too as she picked up the phone but it wasn`t a polite one.

At Marcus`s apartment, Dolores` mother was walking through the front door after flying up from Alabama to help her daughter try to save her marriage. Her mother had just poured herself a cup of coffee and sat down when the phone rang. Dolores moved to the small table to answer it.

"Hullo…"

The voice on the telephone oozed with sex and sensuality.

Dolores mouthed silently to her mother.

"It`s the bitch!"

The voice continued breathlessly.

"Marcus can`t get home to you tonight. He`s otherwise engaged. He`s got an *enormous* challenge ahead of him and we wanted you to know how sorry he is. If it goes as planned, he could be kinda tied up for quite a while."

Dolores threw herself onto the white sofa next to her

mother and sobbed hysterically into a cushion. Her mother tried to comfort her, then saw the receiver hanging over the side of the table bobbing gently on its cord. She walked over and picked it up.

"This is Dolores` mother. Just what is going on?"

Ann-Marie smiled unseen and became brisk and businesslike.

"The President of the United States has personally ordered Marcus on a Very Important mission. It's urgent. I`ve been told that Marcus`s last words before he went off to war were that he wanted his wife to keep phoning and get through so that he could explain."

Dolores's mother, committed to trying to save the marriage, dialled the CIA, the Pentagon, the State Department and the White House. With one hand on her daughter`s shoulder and the other dialling and re-dialling the CIA, the mother kept up a reassuring patter.

"Marcus is doing this for the President, darling. And Marcus does want you to speak to him. He can explain everything."

"That`s not the impression I got from his bitch secretary!"

Her mother wondered whether Dolores was getting a little paranoid. Ann-Marie had sounded quite normal to her.

After many hours, a telephone operator at the Pentagon, who was tired and about to go home, flicked a switch the wrong way and inadvertently started the call on a labyrinthine progress through America`s defence system. Eventually, a telephone buzzed in the command room of Admiral Joseph Metcalf the Third as he led his nine naval ships towards Grenada.

"Call for Mariowitz!"

The shout went up just as Marcus was about to board one of the 26 helicopters on the amphibious assault ship Guam. He had been tasked by Hurlingham to take charge of the CIA operation on the island. The helicopter was stuffed full of American soldiers laden with weapons and ready to shoot their way through Grenada to rescue a thousand American students who they guessed were, even at that moment, being taken hostage by Grenada`s Commie bastards.

The marine running towards the helicopter had taken up the cry.

"Call for Mariowitz! Call for Mariowitz!"

The marine stuck his head through the helicopter doorway.

"You Mariowitz?"

"Yup."

"Sir. It`s a call for you."

"Who wants me?"

"Your wife."

A collective derisive groan went up from the soldiers. Marcus turned and looked at the faces lined up, blacked with camouflage paint and ready to kill. He had no choice.

"Tell her to go suck!"

The marine looked very surprised.

"Sir, do you really want me to say that?"

Marcus had no choice.

"Yup!"

He climbed back aboard the helicopter.

"Now let`s get the Hell to war!"

The soldiers nodded admiringly.

Within a day, the American Army had taken control of the island`s airport and had pushed into the hinterland. Marcus had established his CIA base within the growing US base established only a few miles from where Dr Roy`s launch still bobbed by the jetty.

Inside a military tent, Marcus was soon in an uncomfortable conversation with a General. To the General`s surprise, the American special forces had not only found the American students safe and well but there was no sign of any attempt by the Grenadan army – or anyone else - to take them hostage.

"Well, that`s good news," said Marcus.

A young soldier put his head round a door.

"Mr Mariowitz…Sir! Urgent call."

The General frowned, then nodded permission to Mariowitz to take the call. Marcus turned to the soldier.

"Who is it?"

"Your mother-in-law, sir."

The General looked surprised.

Marcus picked up the phone but couldn`t get a word in. He never could with his mother-in-law.

"Sixteen hours it`s taken me to get you, Marcus. But it`s your phone bill so who cares? Dolores has left you. Gone back to Alabama with the children. And with her therapist. Now good bye."

Marcus was in a black mood when he turned round, found the General gone and two dishevelled civilians, their hands cuffed behind their backs, staring at him. One was clearly a local man. The other was a woman in her early twenties, coffee-coloured skin and quite a looker. A young soldier patted Lou`s backside with his rifle butt.

"Sir, she said her name was Louise Dread. We went through her handbag. Her real name seems to be Louise Hope."

Marcus put his hands on his hips and nodded to the man.

"And him?"

The soldier gave him a prod and Dr Roy stepped forward.

"A doctor, sir. Says he`s a psychiatrist."

Marcus looked irritably at the soldier.

"So? What`s the problem. Have you checked the names?"

"I don`t understand it, sir. Local records show that Lou Hope works for the local government. But our computer claims recognition of Miss Hope. It won`t give details. Just throws up some sort of code, sir."

Marcus took his hands off his hips and stepped forward. "Oh really!" He walked right up to her so that she could smell that he hadn`t washed in days. "Well, we know what that means, don`t we?"

He turned to the solider.

"Get me the code."

"Yes sir!"

Marcus was walking round Lou, looking her up and down and generally trying to make her feel uneasy when a corporal pushed through the flap in the tent. The corporal held what looked like a roll of material under his arm. He threw it on the ground.

"We thought you should see this, sir."

The corporal kicked back the roll of canvas cloth so that it opened on the floor. It was circular, six feet across and painted silver.

Mariowitz didn`t understand and threw out his hands in incomprehension.

"So? So? Is this some game?"

The corporal stepped closer.

"No sir. It`s the…er…silo sir. The underground missile silo. It was this canvas fixed over a hole for a new cesspit on a building site. Where the new airport is being built."

Marcus knelt down on both knees in front of the canvas. He appeared to be praying. In fact he was praying but his prayer wasn`t answered. Finally, when God told him that it wasn`t a joke and neither was he asleep, he stood up.

"Holy shit!" He pointed to the canvas. "You mean that`s what we told the President was a silo? What the CIA told the President...?"

The corporal shuffled his feet.

"I guess so, sir!"

Marcus was feeling despair so deep that it couldn`t get worse. Then he looked up to see the tent flap being pulled aside and Henry Turville pushed in by a sergeant. Henry`s eyes were vacant and he kept trying to take his own route as the sergeant roughly pulled him along. All the time, Henry counted.

"One hundred and twelve, one hundred and thirteen..."

Marcus gaped and signalled to the sergeant to let the cuffed prisoner go. Henry walked straight-legged round the tent, still counting, before looking up at Marcus. A faint look of recognition dawned on his face.

"I know...Yes! It`s Mariowitz!" He saw the canvas circle on the ground and beamed. "And you`ve found the silo! Excellent! Excellent! Well done, Mark!" He threw his arms out expansively. "You wanted another Cuban missile crisis! You`ve *got* another Cuban missile crisis!"

With that, Henry slipped back into a reverie and wandered round the tent counting softly. The sergeant yanked him back and told him to listen to what Mr Mariowitz had to say.

"Turville – you are a...."

He was cut off by the soldier returning and handing him a slip of paper.

"The code number you wanted, sir."

Marcus looked at the slip and his face crumbled into despair.

"Beautiful Lady!" He turned to Lou. "Bitch! You bitch!" Then he span round to the sergeant and nodded towards Henry still counting and smiling happily. "Where d`ya find this jerk?"

"Sir, he had wandered out of what`s left of the island`s mental asylum. Holding a radio to his head sir and shrieking."

Marcus looked puzzled.

"Mental asylum? Whaddya mean – what`s *left* of the mental asylum?"

The sergeant looked down in embarrassment.

"Er, well sir. The asylum is in an old fort, sir. Or rather, it was an old fort, sir. It`s not much at all now. The air force hit it, sir. You see, the air force thought it was Fort Frederick, where the enemy army is headquartered. But they hit Fort Matthew, the asylum, by mistake."

Marcus kicked the piece of canvas.

"Holy shit! We hit a mental asylum? Goddam airforce!" He looked puzzled. "Anyway, what the hell are these damned Commies doing locking up lunatics in a fort?" He rubbed his forehead. He hadn`t been to sleep for more than two days and on the Guam there hadn`t been a banana to beg or borrow. "And how many forts are there here for Chrissake? No wonder we got confused."

Lou spoke for the first time.

"In fact there are a number of forts on Grenada – left over from imperialism. French imperialism. British imperialism…And now we appear to be suffering from American imperialism."

Marcus turned on her and snarled.

"And you shut up! When I want a history lesson, I`ll ask for it."

Henry began to laugh, at first quietly but quickly rising to hysteria. Unable to move his arms, he kept nodding his head as if still listening to the radio. He stomped a foot to stop himself shrieking. "Mark, old man! You Americans are bloody wonder-ful! On the radio. Listen. Wonderful joke. Queen is Head of State in Grenada. Got that? Britain and America are longest, biggest allies. Got that? And you invade Grenada without even mentioning it to the Queen! Let alone our Prime Minister!" He buckled with laughter. "Old Geoffrey Waltonbury will be *furious"*

Marcus turned to Dr Roy.

"Are you his psychiatrist?"

The psychiatrist rolled his head and shrugged his shoulders.

"Well, I had him put away."

"Why?"

Momentarily, Dr Roy was struck speechless.

"Well, business was slack. So I thought – Hey, let`s stick someone in the bin!"

Marcus put his face up against Dr Roy`s

"A funny man." He stepped back and looked from face to face of the three prisoners. "So you were all in this together, were you?"

Henry nodded. Dr Roy shook his head. Lou made no movement.

Marcus bellowed.

"God help us! You can`t even nod in tune!"

He put his face close up against Lou`s.

"And you`re the one that sent us all that bullshit?"

Lou put on her sweet, innocent act.

"What do you mean? I sent occasional bits on what I saw. A Cuban here. A Soviet there. An East European somewhere else."

Marcus growled.

"Yeah! Until old Turville comes along!" He kicked the canvas again. "Old Turville comes along and helps you set up the scam doesn`t he?" He swung round and stepped up to Henry. "So what`s your problem? Henry - old chap! Got the hots for the broad?" Henry was again in a reverie, somewhere far away. This time Marcus turned to Dr Roy. "And what about you and the broad?" Dr Roy shrugged. "What d`you two do? Work together? Screw together? Or what?"

Unobserved, Henry had emerged from his reverie and his eyes were swinging wildly round the tent. As Marcus glared at Dr Roy and repeated his questions, Henry piped up.

"He said he was gay!"

Marcus looked slightly embarrassed and stepped back, shrugging to Dr Roy as if he didn`t care about his sexuality.

"Really? Sorry. No offence meant." Marcus paced backwards and forwards between Lou and Dr Roy, glowering at each in turn. "So you two ain`t friends?"

Dr Roy spoke up for Lou and himself.

"Look, Grenada`s a small place but..." He turned to Lou and nodded at her. "Look, she`s so nearly white she`s almost a honky. While me..." Dr Roy held his head back and opened his eyes wide so that the whites stuck out against his black face. "I`m black trash."

Marcus nodded in agreement.

"Sure. Sure. That makes sense."

He took a deep breath and addressed the soldiers.

"Well, that`s it for now. Stick `em in a cage. But in separate cages. We don`t want `em talking to each other. Not that there`s much chance they could get their act together if we left `em together all night."

As the soldiers took one prisoner each, he barked again.

"And remember, you guys – you forget what you`ve heard. OK? You ain`t been here tonight. Understood?"

They spoke in unison.

"Yes sir!"

Chapter 44

For all three of the prisoners in their cages, it was their second night without proper sleep. Henry seemed not to need sleep. As the cages were on grass, he had nothing to count but the holes in the wire walls that encased him. As there were thousands of irregular holes in the mesh, he could never count every one but found endless satisfaction in trying. Lou and Dr Roy were uncomfortable, unhappy and unable to sleep. They tried to shout to each other and woke the soldier who was guarding them. He suggested, impolitely, that they shut up. Dr Roy said he wouldn`t shut up but soon piped down when the soldier said the alternative was for him to go and shoot his girlfriend. Lou kept shouting for Dr Lou until she heard a shot. The soldier wandered up and said that next time he wouldn`t miss. Now could be get to sleep? After that, all three stayed quiet for the rest of the night.

It was almost dawn when soldiers unlocked the cages and led the trio to the front of the tent in which Marcus had interrogated them. From the light leaking from the tents and other smaller ones nearby, each could see how dirty and dishevelled the others looked. Dr Roy and Henry had stubble. Lou hadn`t washed for so long that she was worried that she was beginning to smell bad.

This time, the soldiers hadn`t put the cuffs back on the prisoners but two gum-chewing armed soldiers stood guard over them. Dr Roy tried to chat.

"How`s the invasion going then?"

"Cut the crap!"

The soldier spat out his gum and stuffed a fresh slice in his mouth.

Marcus pulled the tent flap aside and stepped out onto the grass. The soldiers stiffened as he addressed the trio.

"Now look, you creeps. You`re never going to know just how lucky you are. If it was me, I`d shoot the lot of you." He glowered at Henry. "And I`d make no exception for your insanity, Turville! In fact it would encourage me! But it`s been decided, way above me, that while we clear up the Commie mess on this God-damned

island, you can carry on with your lives. We`ll talk to you all again sometime later. In the meantime, you have to give your word not to talk of these events to anyone. OK?"

Lou and Dr Roy nodded vigorously.

"Oh yes. Yes. Yes."

Henry was in one of his vacant moods. Marcus stepped up close to him.

"I`ll take that as a Yes, Turville."

Marcus went back into the tent and came out with Lou`s handbag and the keys to her jeep. She seized them happily. He handed Dr Roy his wallet. Henry held out his hand. He wanted something, too. Hopefully a packet of mints. Mariowitz just motioned to the trio to follow him round the side of the tent. There, in the first glow of dawn, stood Lou`s jeep, parked on the grass two hundred yards away.

He looked hard at the three in turn.

"You`re all free to go."

As he walked back to the tent, he growled at the soldiers.

"Watch them from here and make sure they scram."

Dr Roy glanced at the soldiers. They were standing easy, just keeping an eye on the trio. He pulled Lou to one side and whispered.

"This stinks. They`re going to kill us. The jeep! If it`s not booby trapped then we`ll be ambushed."

She looked towards her jeep and put a hand to her mouth. She couldn`t remember when she last ate but she felt sick. Dr Roy gave Henry a nudge.

"Henry – what do you think?"

Henry stared back vacantly.

Dr Roy snapped his fingers in front of Henry`s face. He did not blink.

"Why, oh why," Dr Roy asked the dawn, "do I bother?" He thought Lou looked a strange colour but it could have been the early morning light. "Hey, Lou, if you were that American ape, would you let us go? OK, I`m a lousy psychiatrist but even I can work that one out." He could now see that Lou`s face was green and she was gagging. She wanted to say something but was afraid to open her mouth. Dr Roy felt that they couldn`t wait any longer. "Let`s make a run for it. We might get over that ridge before we are shot." He pointed towards what looked like a spice plantation in the distance.

Lou made a sudden rush to the side of the tent but Dr Roy grabbed her arm and pulled her back. "When you`ve stopped throwing up, start running. I`ll follow." He let her go. She just looked at him and then pointed at Henry before lurching away. Dr Roy saw that the soldiers didn`t seem interested that Lou was out of their sight. That seemed to be a good omen for their planned escape. To be safe, he shouted to the soldiers.

"My friend – she is ill."

One soldier shrugged while the other spoke.

"So call a doctor, bud."

Dr Roy debated leaving Henry behind, then made a snap decision. Lou would never forgive him for running out on Henry. He whispered in Henry`s ear.

"We`ve got to go. Can you hear me? Run?"

Henry grinned mindlessly and whispered.

"Radio. Radio. Bloody funny."

Dr Roy looked hard at him.

"You`re off the wall, Henry. An English fruit cake."

Henry nodded in delight. Oh yes, he liked fruit cake.

When the wretching noises stopped, Lou staggered from the side of the tent. Dr Roy grabbed her arm and pulled her roughly to start running to the cover of the plantation. His other hand grabbed Henry. At first, Henry wouldn`t move and then when his feet eventually engaged, his progress was painfully slow. Hauling him behind him, Dr Roy could feel panic rising. Then Henry began jogging. And counting. Soon he raced ahead unassisted and Dr Roy found it hard to keep up.

Behind the trio, the soldiers turned and looked at one another before shouting.

"Hey! Your jeep! Whadda `bout the jeep?"

Inside the tent, Marcus was in conference with the General. Marcus was now trying to explain away the canvas circle that was supposed to be a silo as well as the American students who had been under no threat. He was just wondering which damned soldier had split on him to the General when he heard the shouts. He raced through the tent flap without stopping to pull it aside. He summed up the situation in a glance and issued his instructions.

"Shoot them for Chrissake!"

One of the soldiers was insolent.

"You told 'em to use the jeep!"

Marcus felt like having him put on a charge except there wasn`t time. He leapt up and down in frustration.

"I`ve changed my mind! Just shoot them! For Chrissake shoot them! That`s an order!"

The second soldier was even more mutinous. That was the trouble, thought Marcus. If you let one soldier get away with lip, they were all at it.

"You can't do that. One is a woman, another is a mental patient."

Marcus gave up trying to reason and snatched the rifle from the second soldier.

"Well at least shoot the damned psychiatrist!"

"Sir! They`re all unarmed civilians!"

Marcus blazed away with the automatic rifle but by now the trio had slipped into the plantation.

As they raced on through the nutmeg trees, bullets sliced through the branches high above them. When the firing stopped, Dr Roy slowed and gasped to the others.

"OK, I think we might have made it."

They stumbled on until the spice plantation gave way to banana trees. Somewhere ahead of them lay the coast and Dr Roy`s boat. Behind them, the sky was momentarily lit by an explosion. The trio stopped and felt the last traces of the blast through the trees as the leaves rustled angrily.

Dr Roy took Lou`s arm.

"That`ll be your jeep."

She stood transfixed, then thought she might be sick again. The feeling passed.

Outside the tent, Marcus and the soldiers ducked as pieces of Lou`s car showered around them. Marcus hurled the rifle to the ground and ran towards the tent, shouting.

"Put out an alert! Find them!"

The General pulled aside the tent flap and surveyed the nearby smoking hole in the clearing. He stood silently, his fingers tucked in his belt. As Marcus hurtled past the General leisurely removed a hand and grabbed Marcus`s shoulder.

"Not so fast. When you have a moment, Mr Mariowitz, perhaps you could explain this hole in the ground? And the silo. And the hostages. Or rather, the absence of a silo and the absence of hostages..."

Marcus wasn`t listening. He was racing to the communications room.

Lou, Dr Roy and Henry half-walked, half ran through plantations and across tracks until the coast came into view. Below them lay a small cove and on the edge of the beach a house.

Dr Roy gasped. Not just at the view in the growing light.

"The Levitts!"

Beyond the Levitt's house, jutting out into the calm sea, was the rickety wooden jetty against which was tied Dr Roy`s launch. The sight gave Dr Roy and Lou new impetus and energy. They raced on, slowing only once to wade through a deep and muddy stream created by an overnight cloudburst. Henry jogged, unaware of where he was going but happy to follow them. When the trio reached the jetty, Dr Roy whispered to Lou.

"What about if we leave Henry here? He`s a liability. What the heck are we expected to do with him in Tobago?"

Lou didn`t answer.

Dr Roy ran down the small steps and jumped into launch. He looked up the beach to the edge of the final plantation through which they had escaped. A US army jeep was coming down a track. He fired up the engine and began untying the rope securing the launch. He gestured to Lou to hurry up. But she was standing on the jetty staring down at him. Henry, gormless and waiting for someone to tell him what to do, stood at her side. Dr Roy signalled urgently for Lou to step down to the boat. She remained on the jetty.

"Hurry up, Lou. For Chrissakes, what are you waiting for?"

"I`m not coming with you unless I know what our relationship is."

He looked up.

"Holy Dr Freud! Lou! The Yanks are coming for us!"

She stood her ground.

"What is it to be, Winston?"

He dropped the rope a beaten man.

"Is this all about the damned love word?"

"That`s not the way I would describe it."

She clearly wasn`t going to move. He glanced back up the hill. The jeep looked to be stuck in the swollen stream and soldiers were jumping out into the water. Dr Roy sighed. It was a sigh of great weariness that seemed to him to sum up the lot of man in a world of women.

"OK Lou. You win. I love you. Do you hear that?" He bellowed at the top of his voice. "I LOVE YOU! Now will you please come down here before you get shot?"

She didn`t move and put her hand on Henry`s shoulder. He was lightly jogging on the spot. She knew she couldn`t leave him. Marcus would shoot him. Yet he was as harmless as a baby now. Dr Roy, still standing with the rope ready to cast off, heard her voice.

"And what about Henry?"

He thought this was going too far.

"Sorry Lou. It`s you I love. Not Henry."

"Winston! I mean can Henry come with us and will you help him? Give him therapy?"

Dr Roy thought of his happy hours drinking in the bar in the hotel courtyard.

"Heck, can`t we leave him to La-jab-less? I mean, he deserves to be left. Doesn`t he? Oh shit! C`mon then. Bring him down."

Henry was last down into the boat. Just as Lou untied the rope, Marcus gave up trying to shift the jeep from the stream. He ordered the soldiers to join him in opening fire on the launch.

As the bullets started flying, Dr Roy took the launch up to full speed so fast that Lou and Henry had to grab the rail to stop falling backwards into the water. When a bullet pockmarked the sea, Lou pushed Henry onto his back on the deck and lay down beside him, looking up at a cloudless sky. Dr Roy had a horrible premonition that he would be shot in the back and also got down on the deck on his back, reaching up with one hand to keep the wheel steady and the course straight for the headland.

Back on the island, Marcus threw down his rifle and looked around him. Exhausted through lack of sleep and tension, he hadn`t realised he was in a banana plantation.

For a second, he looked up and thought he was in heaven. Thoughts of the General back at base and Hurlingham flying out to the island momentarily disappeared as he raised his eyes upwards to a bunch of bananas. He blazed with his automatic at the top of the bunch. It fell heavily and Mariowitz plucked the biggest banana of his life. The launch was out of range but the soldiers continued firing at their wake. Marcus was oblivious to the gunfire as he slowly peeled the fruit and took his first bite. Ahhhh. With his free hand he called base on his radio. He tried to make himself heard above the gun fire as he shouted his orders to headquarters. As the launch disappeared from view and the gunfire ceased, the plantation fell silent. Marcus shouted his appeal for help to the battle fleet`s command room.

Dr Roy stood up and whistled with relief when the shooting stopped. The launch was at the tip of the headland and he turned the wheel to head it out to open sea. Henry jumped up from the deck and began racing around shouting orders to imaginary figures and saluting.

"Stand by to cast off! Make way for the Captain! Prepare to repel borders!"

Dr Roy shouted to Lou, There`s still time to tip him over the side."

Lou put her hand on his arm.

"I thought that with all the free time you`ll have in Tobago you could help him."

Dr Roy pulled a face.

"Well, I suppose his hyperactivity is a good sign. I might be able to do something for him."

She squeezed his hand.

"Good."

The boat was now veering towards the headland and Dr Roy expected to face the open sea. Instead, he shielded his eyes with his hand to try to make out what was blocking his way. It was the US battle fleet at anchor.

Dr Roy stood open-mouthed at the wheel.

"Holy Dr Freud! We`ll never get past that lot."

He picked up his binoculars and scanned the ships. Figures ran up and down the decks waving their arms. From a deck, an officer peered through his binoculars. For a few seconds, both men stared at each other.

Close by the launch, the water was suddenly thrown up by a shell. Then a second shell threw up a spout of water. Henry ran up and down excitedly shouting and counting.

Another shell threw up water.

"Three!"

Then another.

"Four"

Henry elbowed Dr Roy from the wheel and began throwing the launch violently from side to side as he counted more shells. Lou spoke calmly to Dr Roy.

"Get Henry`s head down and try to restrain him. I`ll take over here."

Dr Roy led Henry by the arm to the back of the launch and forced him down. Lou swerved the launch from side to side and then the shells began to fall farther and farther behind the launch`s wake as it cut swiftly through the Caribbean.

Henry turned to Dr Roy as he settled beside him and wimpered.

"Mints."

Dr Roy nodded.

"I know how you feel, Henry old chap. None of us has eaten for days."

Henry looked back to the horizon. Somewhere over there lay the tubes carefully packed by his sister into the old chocolate box. He became desperate.

"Mints! Mints!"

"Not long now, Henry. Minced fish. Minced lamb. Whatever you want. Lots of it, soon. When we get to Tobago."

Henry snorted with contempt. He had always known this psychiatrist was a fool. He glared and shouted.

"No, mints! Mints!"

This was going to be an even harder case than Dr Roy had imagined. He called to Lou.

"You OK in charge? I'm having problems back here with Henry."

Lou answered with a smile. Turning back to face the clear blue sea ahead, she spoke into the wind.

"I should have taken charge a long, long time ago."

Printed in Great Britain
by Amazon